infuriating

infuriating

AN
ELITE PROTECTION SERVICES
NOVEL

ONLEY JAMES

INFURIATING

Elite Protection Services Book 4

Copyright © 2020 Onley James
WWW.ONLEYJAMES.COM

All rights reserved. No part of this publication may be reproduced, stored in a retrieval system, or transmitted, in any form or by any means (electronic, mechanical, photocopying, recording, or otherwise), without the prior written permission of the publisher.

This book is a work of fiction and does not represent any individual living or dead. Names, characters, places, and incidents either are products of the author's imagination or are used fictitiously.

ISBN: 979-8-6705-3718-6

TRIGGER WARNING

This book contains brief portrayals of childhood emotional abuse as well as discussions of past child sexual trauma and one scene of on-page physical violence to a main character at the hands of somebody other than the main character.

prologue

DAYTON

"WHAT DO YOU MEAN YOU DON'T GET IT? SOUND IT OUT."

Dayton stared at the letters until they swam, his brow wrinkled and his bottom lip trapped between his teeth. She always acted like it was so simple. Maybe it was. Maybe he really was just stupid. "Cuh-T-uh."

"Cuh-T-uh?" she mocked. "That sound like any word you ever heard of, Dayton? Use your fucking brain. If you even have one. C-A-T. Cat. Cat. How fucking hard is that?"

Day's heart shriveled in his chest, and he bit down on his tongue until he tasted blood. If he cried it would only get worse. She got real mean when he cried. *"Men don't cry,"* she'd said. Babies cried. Was he a baby? "Sowwy," he managed, wincing.

His head shot forward as his grandma's hand connected with the back of his head. "Sah-REE. Not sowwy. Christ. What am I gonna do with you? You're as stupid as your fucking mama was, but unlike her, you can't make a living shaking your ass for money, so you better figure it out."

At least she got away. Day hoped she did anyway. Nobody deserved to be trapped in this stupid, gross house with its icky stained walls and dirty floors and poop everywhere from Grandma's two yappy dogs that bit his ankles and snapped at his face. He hated it there. He didn't know why he even had to be there. He had to have a dad somewhere, right? Sarah had a dad. Xander had a dad. Joel had two moms, but they were nice. Why hadn't his mom at least left Day with him?

Day stared down at his homework, relief flooding his system as he heard the screen door open and shut, his grandma muttering under her breath as she walked away. She was going next door to Jack's place. She'd be there for a long time. Sometimes, she stayed all night. Day hated being by himself but he loved when she stayed away. He couldn't use the stove yet, but he had taught himself to use the microwave. But he didn't have to do that today.

Today was fried chicken day.

Day grabbed his book and flew out the door, running the four houses down to Sarah's house. He skipped knocking on the door. Sarah wouldn't be there. She was in the fort. Sarah's dad was the coolest. He built her a fort at the top of the big tree in her backyard. Sarah's mama also owned a restaurant in town, and they always had the best food at home.

Day let himself into the backyard, tucking his workbook into his jeans before climbing up the steps nailed to the big tree in the backyard, tapping out their secret knock before flinging open the door. Sarah lay in the corner, putting together a puzzle, her feet swaying as she worked, her black hair plaited along her shoulders in two braids. The tubes that helped her breathe stuck into her nostrils, a small green tank beside her. Sarah was the smartest person Day knew. She was a year older than him but she was two years ahead in school. She looked up as Day came in and slammed the door a little too hard.

One look at Day's face and she forgot her puzzle. She sat crisscross applesauce in her overalls and a pink t-shirt that matched her favorite pink sequined Skechers. She handed him a plastic container, and Day's stomach growled. He attacked the fried chicken and mac and cheese with his fingers, ignoring the fork that sat just to his left. Fried chicken day at the restaurant was Day's favorite, so Sarah's mama always made extra just for him.

While Day shoveled food into his mouth, Sarah took his notebook and carefully finished his homework, doing her best to make their handwriting match. Sarah thought of everything. Day knew it was cheating and that it was wrong, but the last time the teacher had called Day's grandma, she'd beat him with a switch from the tree out back. The teacher said he had a learning problem. That things were mixed up in his brain and that there were programs to help. His grandma had beat him for embarrassing her. He always embarrassed her. It was bad enough he talked funny, now he couldn't read. She'd called him the R word. The one the teacher said they weren't allowed to say.

When his homework was done and his belly was full, they lay on the floor of Sarah's fort, staring up past the branches of the tree to the sky above, watching the clouds roll by as the sun set. Sarah's feet pointed one way and Day's the other, their heads slotted together so they could both see.

"When I finally get my new lungs, I'm going to fly away to California and be a movie star," Sarah said with a sigh. She always said that. She was going to be a big star and be on the tv.

Day couldn't imagine wanting that kind of attention. People staring at him, listening to him talk, making fun of him. "Not me. The idea of a bunch of people sta-staring at me sounds kinda awful."

He tried to avoid words with Rs and THs. They always made the w sound. His teacher said those were his 'problem letters.' He didn't know what that meant other than that was when the other kids started laughing. His teacher tried to make them stop but she wasn't with him at recess. Sarah said she thought maybe his eyes and his tongue didn't talk to each other. His grandma said all letters were his problem, that he was just born dumb…like his mama. That was why he still couldn't read.

"Nah, acting is neat. You get to be anybody you want, and you get to wear costumes and makeup and jewelry," Sarah gushed, ignoring his slowed speech.

Wearing makeup and jewelry sounded fun, but Day would never do that again. He might be dumb, but he wasn't *that* dumb. His grandma had flipped out when she'd seen Day and Sarah playing dress up, said dressing up was for girls and sissy boys. She always liked to use that word. Sissy. She called him that every time he cried, anytime he showed any sign of pain.

But Sarah always looked pretty in her fancy clothes and her mama's big earrings and her scarlet lipstick, even if she sometimes put it on outside the lines. Day's grandma said makeup was for sluts. He didn't know what a slut was, but it had to be bad because his grandma spit it at him like she did the R word. Day liked the way girl clothes felt. They were soft and silky, and Sarah's sneakers had sequins. Day didn't understand how a fabric could be made just for a girl or just for a boy but he didn't argue with his grandma.

"I don't want to be he-ar wif-without you," Day said, blushing as the words didn't come out right once again.

As far as Day could see, anywhere was better than Challis, Idaho.

"You'll come with me. I'll need people."

"Why?" Day asked.

Sarah shrugged. "I don't know. Movie stars and famous people have people that just do things for them. You could be the person who just does things for me and then we can be friends forever."

Sarah started to cough, not a regular cough but one of those coughs that triggered spasms in her lungs. There was nothing to do but wait it out. When it finally died down, she looked pale, with purple crescent moons under her eyes. Sarah had something she called CF. It scarred up her lungs. It was why she needed new ones. But there was a list for new lungs so she had to wait her turn. It seemed weird that there was a list of people who needed new parts. But Sarah didn't really seem bothered by it. She just sort of acted like it was normal.

Day wished somebody would give him a new brain or maybe a new tongue, then maybe his grandma would stop hating him. Sometimes, he didn't think he wanted her to stop hating him. If she loved him then maybe that meant he was like her. He didn't want to be like her. He hated her back. Sarah said it wasn't nice to hate people, and he guessed that was true, but he was scared of his grandma. He hated going home. Shouldn't it be okay to hate somebody who made you scared? Who hit you and was mean to you all the time?

"Promise me you'll come with me to California when I get my new lungs," Sarah said, holding up her pinky.

Anywhere was better than Idaho. He hooked his pinky with hers. "Okay. As soon as you get new lungs."

one

DAYTON

"HAVE YOU MISSED DADDY?"

Dayton tilted his head to the side, giving the man on the other side of the screen a secret smile, the one they all thought was just for them. "Of course, I have. I was starting to think you'd ghosted me."

Jay laughed. That wasn't his real name. That was the thing about this business. Nobody used their real names. Day was almost positive Jay was some kind of attorney given that he was always in a fancy office when they talked and there were rows of hardback law books behind him. Like most of Day's clients, Jay was married, most likely to a woman who didn't understand him. That was always their excuse. It sucked for their wives, but Day had to make a living, so he tried to put all of that aside. That was what they paid him for. His time and his attention.

Day was a liar, too. On the internet, he was Danny from Florida who was just camming to make it through college. Total bullshit. Day hadn't even made it past the seventh grade, and his shitty LA apartment probably cost three times as much as a shitty Florida apartment. But it was still better than where he started, so if he had to smile and bat his lashes and convince some balding fifty-something-year-old guy with a paunch hanging over his belt that he was the only guy Day truly cared about, then that's what he'd do. He'd made Sarah a promise. Even if this had never been what she'd had in mind.

"I would never disappear on you, beautiful. I've just been working on a really big case."

Jay lived in Los Angeles, just like Day, but he certainly would never tell him that.

"That's what you all say, and then poof, you disappear. But that's alright, another's always waiting in the wings to take your place." Day crossed his legs, leaning back for Jay to get a good look at his white silk corset set, complete with lace panties and thigh highs. He crossed his legs, running his nails over the top of

infuriating

the hose, teasing a finger under the elastic.

"Damn, you look so sexy. Model it for me."

Jay had a fetish for lingerie, one Dayton was happy to indulge since he knew for a fact he looked damn good in satin and lace. Besides, Jay had sent Day a lot of money to buy this outfit. Not that Day had spent it all on this bit of frippery. It paid to live in the fashion district.

Day stood, stepping away from the camera so Jay could see the effort he'd put in for their call. He had on sparkly silver ankle boots and enough makeup on to make a drag queen jealous. He put his hands on his hips and sashayed across his room like he was walking the Paris runways, making sure Jay got a good look at the thong underwear that highlighted the perfect curves of his ass.

When he made it back to the computer screen, Jay had slouched down in his chair, his computer no longer on the desk but balanced on his knees so Day could see that Jay was most definitely enjoying all of his efforts. "Oh. Looks like somebody's liking what he sees."

Jay had his dick in hand, but he wasn't furiously working it like some of Day's cam clients did. Jay paid for the boyfriend experience—or rather, the Daddy experience. He wanted Day all to himself three times a week, and he was willing to shell out Day's monthly allowance to get it. For what Jay paid, Day would call him St. Francis of Assissi if that's what got him off. What the fuck did Day care? He was just a performer.

Some part of Day did wish he could have a real Daddy, not a guy who handed out money just to hear Day call him by the honorific, but a real Daddy. One who cared about Day. One who didn't care about his flaws and was kind and encouraging when he needed it but was stern and punishing when warranted.

Los Angeles had a huge kink culture, but with Day's disability, he wasn't really sub material. He'd tried a few times to search for a Daddy, but all he'd found were posers who just wanted an excuse to take out their aggression on another person, and Day didn't have a humiliation kink. He spent enough of his life feeling humiliated, he didn't need to hear it from a person who was supposed to love and care for him as much as they were supposed to train and discipline him.

"Get on the bed, baby."

Day did as he was told, trying his best to keep his head in the game and not let his mind wander. "How do you want me, Sir?"

"You know what I want."

Day sighed inwardly. For somebody who claimed his wife wasn't kinky enough, Jay's requests were always the same. Day turned away from the camera, popping up on his knees, canting his hips back, head and shoulders to the mattress.

"Open your legs. Wider. Fuck yeah, that's it." Day's eyes caught on a chip in his silver polish. Fuck, he really needed a manicure. "You like that, baby?"

Day rolled his eyes, grateful the camera couldn't see his face. "Mmm, yes, Daddy."

Day waited for Jay to tell him to lower his panties and start jerking off, but instead, he made a startled noise, a sort of half cry-half shout that had Day spinning around. Even from the strange angle of Jay's laptop, Day could see crimson blooming from the older man's collar, overwhelming the snowy starched white fabric faster than Day could even comprehend what was happening.

Jay made a horrific gurgling sound, and then his laptop tumbled backwards. Day sat frozen on the edge of the bed, hand to his mouth for a solid minute. Hands trembling, he crept closer to his monitor.

"Jay?" he whispered. There was no response. Day felt like his whole body was electrified, a metallic taste coating his tongue. "Jay?" he tried again, his voice one step above his last attempt.

A shadow swept across the camera's lens, and then a figure stood above, peering down at the laptop. It felt like he was looking directly into Day's soul. Day wanted to disconnect before the man saw him, but it was already too late. Day sat in a well-lit room. He was probably visible from Mars, unlike the man shrouded in darkness, with only Jay's amber desk lamp for light. Before Day could think to do anything, a booted heel came towards his face, causing Day to yelp and jump away even though he wasn't the victim of the man's assault. Jay's laptop was.

Day sat there at his desk for far longer than he should, but his limbs felt like they were encased in cement. Jay was dead. Somebody had killed him. Right? Nobody could survive that kind of blood loss. Had the killer seen Day? Did it matter? Day hadn't really seen him. But did the killer know that? Could he find Day if he wanted to? Day bounced on his heels. What the fuck was he supposed to do? Report a murder of somebody named Jay in Los Angeles? What if that wasn't even his real name?

"Fuck! Fuck. Fuck. Fuck."

Day picked up his cell phone and dialed 911, his teeth gnawing through the polish on his already chipped thumbnail. "911. What's your emergency?"

"I think I just saw a man get murdered."

There was a pause. "You think…you saw a man get murdered?" the woman asked, her tone edging on boredom.

infuriating

"Yeah. I was on a video call with a…friend, and I think somebody slit his throat."

"What's this friend's name?"

"Uh, Jay."

"Jay what, sir?"

"I-I don't know."

"You don't know your friend's last name?"

Day sighed. "Look, I'm a cam model. I talk to men for a living. I only know he was an attorney named Jay, and he lives somewhere here in Los Angeles."

"Sir, please hold the line."

Day did as she asked, grimacing at the feel of nail polish flakes on his tongue even though he had no intention of stopping.

"Sir? Please give me your name and address. I'm sending officers to your home to get more information."

Day didn't have any more information to give, but he rattled off his name and address anyway. As soon as he disconnected, he set about changing his clothes, ditching his satin and silk for threadbare black athletic shorts and a red cropped hoodie. He scraped off his makeup and tossed the makeup wipes into the trash just as his phone dinged.

It was a notification.

DannysDaddy666 has sent you money.

It wasn't unusual to get notifications like that. Day was auctioning off his virginity to whichever of his patrons donated the most this year as long as they met his minimum bid of ten thousand dollars. A price that Day had assured himself none of them would be willing to give just to be his first non-silicone dick. Day usually received anywhere from one hundred to five hundred dollars from most of his clients once or twice a week. At least, the ones he considered his private patrons. But there was one who never wanted to be seen on camera. He only wanted to watch. DannysDaddy666. Day hated the name as much as he hated the black screen that accompanied their playtime. The man even disguised his voice. It made Day leery, but as long as his money cleared, Day was willing to tolerate his weird stipulations.

Day signed into his CashApp and frowned. Six thousand dollars? Nobody had ever sent him an amount that high. Not even Jay and he paid Day fifteen hundred a month. He had anyway. Day felt like a dick for missing the money more than the man, but Jay's money paid half of his rent and Jay had no interest in ever meeting face to face. He'd been the perfect client.

Day clicked on the note section, and his blood ran cold.

infuriating

Soon it will just be you and me. Love, Daddy.

Day shivered. Talk about bad timing.

He tossed his phone on the bed just as there was a knock on the door. "Police, open up."

two

JACKSON

"THANKS FOR AGREEING TO SEE ME TODAY. I KNOW you were supposed to be heading back to Miami."

Jackson Avery leaned back in his chair, giving a tight smile to the old man seated on the other side of his desk. It had been years since he'd seen Detective James Sadwell—or Jimmy as he was known to his friends. Jackson hadn't actually agreed to meet with him. Lincoln Hudson's secretary had booked the appointment after Jimmy had told her that he and Jackson were old friends. They were not. Jackson didn't feel the need to point that out though since Jimmy hadn't arrived alone.

infuriating

"What do you need, Jimmy?" Jackson asked, refusing to use his title of Detective.

Jimmy rubbed the back of his neck, his tongue darting out to moisten deeply chapped lips. "So, I got a bit of a situation, and I was hoping you might be able to help me out."

Time hadn't been good to Jimmy. Jackson vaguely remembered the man coming to his house for barbeques, smoking stogies with his father, drinking far too much beer. He had seemed old back then, but now, he was horribly thin, his yellowing teeth pointing this way and that. His checkered pants and stained golf shirt clearly had seen better days. Unless the LAPD had gotten very lax with their dress code, Jimmy wasn't there on official business.

Jackson glanced out the glass wall of his office to where a young man with platinum hair and skin the color of cream sat at an empty desk taking selfies from every angle as he made faces at the camera. He reminded Jackson vaguely of Wyatt, though the boy seemed rougher somehow, like maybe he'd lived a harder life than Wyatt.

Jackson forced his gaze back to Jimmy. "Does this situation have anything to do with the supermodel out there?"

Jimmy's gaze flicked back to the boy, and he rolled

his eyes when he saw the boy snapping away with his phone. "Yeah. Yeah it does. So, this kid, his name is Dayton Daniels. He witnessed a murder, and I need somebody to watch over him until we can apprehend the suspect."

Jackson arched a brow. "Isn't that your job?"

The old man scoffed like Jackson was being deliberately obtuse. "Come on, Jackie. You know Wit Sec doesn't include protecting a potential witness when there's nobody in custody."

Jackson did know that, but he didn't know what made this case so unique that this guy—Dayton— needed protection from someone who hadn't even been caught. It didn't really make much sense unless the suspect somehow knew Dayton was a witness. Still, there was something off about Jimmy's assessment.

"How close are you to catching the guy?" Jackson asked. Jimmy's gaze slid away, which was an answer in and of itself. "Are you asking me to have one of my guys watch your witness for an indeterminate amount of time while you guys try to run down a murderer? My guys make mid six figures a year. You think I owe you a six figure favor?"

"I don't think I can put a price tag on what I did for your family, Jackie. Think of the heartache I spared your mother. The financial ruin."

infuriating

"Nobody asked you to do any of that, but that's neither here nor there. You need to start telling me why this kid is such a high priority target."

"I don't know that he is. Normally, I'd just add extra patrols and tell the kid to be careful about what he posts on social media, but as you can see, he doesn't listen for shit."

The 'kid' in question was now recording a video, animatedly talking about something Jack couldn't hear. He found himself sidetracked, watching the boy's full candy pink lips as he swept his hands from one side to the other as he talked.

Jackson couldn't tear his gaze away from the boy's face. "I'm still not following."

"Look, I'm gonna level with you, but this has got to stay in the vault."

Jackson forced himself to give Jimmy his sole attention, nodding so he knew he'd heard him.

"He's the sole witness to the murder of Assistant District Attorney, Bradley Jansen."

Jackson had heard of the case. It was big news. But there'd been no mention of a witness. "Sounds like that would be worthy of a few extra patrols. How exactly did this boy end up witnessing Jansen's death? And why haven't we heard a peep about him? They said Jansen had his throat slit in his office after hours.

Was this kid a client?"

"No," Jimmy said, rubbing a hand over his face. "Jansen was the client…if you get my drift?"

Jackson glanced over at Dayton once more. "You saying the kid's a pro? Jansen's gay?"

"The kid's not a hooker, but he was in the middle of a…performance when the killer ambushed Jansen."

Jackson really wished Jimmy would get to the point. The man had been a cop for decades. Why was it so hard to just spit out the story? "The killer left a witness behind?"

Jimmy shifted uncomfortably. "Dayton was performing for him on camera. A private show. He's a camboy."

Jackson frowned. "A what?"

"A virtual hooker. A cyber prostitute. Whatever you want to call it. The client tells him what to do and he does it."

"Sex worker," Jackson corrected, unsure why the mislabeling annoyed him.

Jimmy frowned. "What?"

"We don't call them prostitutes. They prefer the term sex workers," Jackson explained.

Jimmy sneered. "Call him whatever you want. The kid is infuriating. He refuses to stop seeing clients. He refuses to stay off social media. He's auctioning off his virginity to the highest bidder for fuck's sake. Not that I believe for one second that kid's a virgin. You should see the toy box he travels with. It's not right."

Jackson examined the young man closer this time. He wasn't alone anymore. Wyatt now peered over the boy's shoulder, waving and talking to whatever audience might be on the other side of the lens. Wyatt was a YouTuber with a huge following and was the husband of Jackson's LA branch manager, Linc. Linc, who would have a fucking stroke if Wyatt somehow ended up on a porn channel, or worse, on a murderer's radar. Not that Wyatt wasn't perfectly capable of endangering himself. Sometimes, Jackson was sure Wyatt and his crew of misfits were there just to keep him in business.

Jackson sighed. "I can't ask my guys to forgo a paycheck for an indefinite amount of time. Where are you on this case? Any ideas about who specifically might have had it out for the ADA? I imagine the list is insanely long. I can't babysit the kid forever."

"I need your help, Jackie. I'm calling in my favor."

Jackson clasped his hands on his desk, forcing himself to remain calm. He wasn't one to anger quickly. "Three months. Tops. If you don't have this figured out by then, he goes back to being your problem. That's the best I can do."

"That's fair." Jimmy looked around the office, eyes landing on Linc, who was currently running a meeting in the conference room. "You're going to need somebody who can handle him. The kid looks sweet and innocent, but he's a real bitch."

Jackson shook his head. "I'll do it."

Jimmy did a double take. "Wait. You? You don't even live here. I mean, I guess I could try to clear it for him to leave the state, but…"

Jackson waved a hand, dismissing the man's words. "I have a house here. I can run things from this coast as easily as I can the other. Besides, my mom will be thrilled I'm still here so she can harass me about not giving her any grandchildren."

All tension seemed to leave the detective. "Don't your sisters have, like, three kids each?" Jimmy asked with a laugh.

"Della has three. Mariah has four. Ruby has three. Somehow, that doesn't take away from the fact that I've provided her with none. She keeps pointing out that I'm not getting any younger, ignoring the fact that my lifestyle doesn't really provide the ideal environment for children or that I'm very much single."

"What happened to that little blonde actress you used to hang out with?"

"Charlie? She was dating Linc's sister. We're just

infuriating

friends. She's...not my type."

Jimmy nodded. "Give my love to your mother and sisters. I'll have the kid's things delivered to your place if you text me the address. Again, I really appreciate you doing this for me. I miss your pops every day. He was one of the good ones."

Bullshit. Jackson didn't comment any further. Jimmy rose and shook his hand. The movement seemed to capture both boys' attention, and Dayton seemed to notice Jackson for the first time. His eyes widened and he said something to Wyatt, who laughed, his look growing alarmingly conspiratorial.

Jimmy walked to the door. "Dayton. Come here, please."

Dayton rose from the chair in one regal move. He wore tight jeans that clung to long shapely legs and a baby blanket pink sweater that fell off one pale shoulder. Every move he made, from the way he walked to the way he held his hands fascinated Jackson. It was like the boy was a puppeteer with strings dangling from each elegant finger.

Dayton slid past Jimmy in the doorway, giving Jackson what he could only describe as a hungry look, a slow smirk crossing his pretty face. "Hey, Daddy," the boy murmured, his voice just dripping with sex.

Jimmy's face flushed. "Dayton!"

Dayton shrugged his bare shoulder, batting dark lashes at the old man. "What? What'd I do now, Father Flanagan? Not everything I say is a scandal. Take a pill before your heart gives out."

Jimmy looked like he wanted to strangle the boy. "Look, Jackson's agreed to take you on as a client until we apprehend the man who murdered ADA Jansen. You could at least show him some respect."

Jackson watched as the first crack in the boy's armor appeared. His smirk slowly melted away as his brows drew together in confusion. "What? What does that even mean? I don't want to be anybody's client."

Jimmy scowled. "You're going to stay with Jackson, and he's going to keep you safe until we find our suspect."

Dayton jerked his head back and forth. "No. No way. I have a business to run. I can't be sharing a space with some cop while I'm performing. It's bad for business." Once more, Dayton looked Jackson up and down like he was a piece of meat. "Unless, of course, you want to join me on camera. I bet my fans would love to see us together. All that perfect dark skin pressed up against my peaches and cream complexion."

"Dayton!"

Dayton rolled his eyes. "Ugh, fine. But I'm not going to stop working. I have a really good following, and

infuriating

maintaining that following takes constant content creation."

"You'll have your own room. It's none of my business what you do as long as it stays in that room," Jackson said, feeling the need to suddenly adjust himself, grateful the desk blocked his semi-rigid cock. The thought of Dayton touching himself on camera was a tantalizing enough prospect, but the thought of Jackson having access to all of him, doing anything he pleased while the world watched… That was far too alluring for three o'clock on a Friday afternoon. He forced himself to keep his face blank.

Jimmy also frowned at Jack. "Uh, are you sure he should be…uh…working? What if the killer traces his IP address or something?"

"There's nothing in my apartment that's not encrypted. I built each of my apartments to be my own private Fort Knox. He'll be fine. You asked me to do this. Don't question my methods."

Jimmy gave Dayton one final look. "I'll guess I'll leave you to it then."

three

DAYTON

THE MAN ON THE OPPOSITE SIDE OF THE DESK WAS beautiful, Day hadn't been lying about that. He was also insanely intimidating. Even from across four feet of mahogany, the man seemed to take up all the space between them. He was large—wide-receiver huge—with warm umber skin that stretched across biceps bulging from beneath a black v-neck t-shirt, leading to muscular forearms and strong hands. He had a close cropped fade, bushy brows, lashes that highlighted whiskey-colored eyes, and a thick beard that only seemed to enhance the perfect pout of his lips. The man made Day both scared and horny.

infuriating

With Jimmy gone, all of Day's bravado dissolved. Jimmy had called the man Jackson. Jackson didn't appear to be as easily excitable as Jimmy. In fact, he had a stillness about him that set Day's teeth on edge. He crossed his legs, flicking at some invisible spot on his nail, afraid to make eye contact with the larger man.

"You okay? You want some water or anything?" Jackson asked.

Day brushed his hair from his eyes, giving Jackson a haughty look. "No, thank you," he said, voice sounding prim. "I'm fine."

Jackson grunted, opening up the MacBook in front of him. His fingers were surprisingly nimble on the small keyboard, which sent Day's mind drifting to what other things Jackson might do with those hands.

"Full name?"

"What?" Day blurted.

Jackson arched a brow. "Your full name. Can I have it?"

"Dayton Lee Daniels," Day mumbled. He hated how hick his name sounded.

"Birthday?" Jackson asked, his deep voice stirring something in Day's belly.

"December twenty-first, nineteen ninety-seven."

"Address?"

Day hesitated before rattling off the address of his

shabby efficiency apartment off of Wilcox. Jackson apparently had multiple apartments that he called home, one of which he'd be sharing with Day. Part of him thought the whole thing was stupid, while another was just the tiniest bit relieved that he wouldn't panic every time he so much as heard a neighbor coming home at night.

Day jumped when the printer whirred to life. *Pull it together, crazy.* Jackson reached beneath his desk and pulled three pages from the printer and passed them across to Day. They were still warm to the touch. "What's this?" Day asked.

"Just a standard contract. I've removed the compensation part since this is being done pro-bono, but I still need it for the files. Just look it over and sign the line on the third page."

"Okay," Day managed, trying to quell the sudden panic arching through his blood like lightning. He glanced down at the page, hands shaking as he pretended to peruse the contract, uncertain if he seemed to be reading too fast or too slow. Most of the words and sentences were as jumbled as hieroglyphics. He understood some words simply by sight, but most made little sense to him.

"You're so stupid, Dayton."

He shook the voice away, slowly looking through

infuriating

each page before finally signing on the bottom line with a mad squiggle that looked like it was done by a child. When he finished, he handed the pages back, tilting his chin up to look Jackson in the eyes. He refused to be ashamed. He might not be able to read, but he got by just fine.

"You might be the first person who ever read this contract," Jackson said with a deep rumble of a laugh. "Most people just sign their lives away."

"My life is mine, but for you, Daddy, the rest is definitely negotiable," Day said with a wink.

Jackson stood, coming around to lean on the desk beside Day's chair. "You can call me Jackson," he said, a slight warning to his tone.

Day sat forward, pressing his elbow to the chair arm so he could prop his chin on his hand. "You're no fun." He pouted.

Jackson shoved his hands in the pockets of his track pants, bending at the waist so he was hovering close enough for Day to feel his breath. "I'm lots of fun, Hollywood. But a word of warning. Don't call me Daddy unless you mean it."

Day was positive his heart stopped, his dick hardening in his much too tight jeans. Before he could think of a comeback, Jackson was gone, walking to the copier, presumably to give Day a copy of their contract. What if Day did mean it? *Fuck.*

Day couldn't think about that. He couldn't think about anything but working. He needed to keep up his hustle if he eventually wanted to make enough money to get out of this industry and out of that town. He'd made a promise to Sarah, but this wasn't what she would have wanted for him, and he just wasn't talented enough to be famous for anything other than his body. Sarah had been the talent. Day had always been the sidekick. He'd give anything to be able to be Sarah's sidekick once more.

Sadness overwhelmed him. He clicked his phone on, checking how many likes and comments he'd gotten on his Instagram story. He smiled when he noted that Wyatt had tagged himself and shared it to his Twitter. That was guaranteed to bring more people to his social media and his OnlyFans accounts.

Day spent the next several minutes losing himself to scrolling, not sure what else to do. Jackson had disappeared into the big conference room with all the other beefy looking security guys. Even Wyatt was in the room, sitting on a chair in the corner, legs criss crossed, as he tapped away on his phone. Day wondered if he was texting the big guy running the meeting because every few seconds the man would look at his phone and then give Wyatt a dirty look,

infuriating

which only seemed to amuse Wyatt.

Day longed for a relationship like that. He couldn't imagine what it would feel like to be with somebody who loved him no matter what. Not some sappy greeting card love with hearts and rainbows and flowery speeches about unconditional love, but the ride-or-die love you have through cancer and missing limbs and fifty pounds of stress eating or finding out you didn't qualify for a lung transplant... That kind of love. But Day didn't think that kind of love was real. It was just some gimmick used to sell Hallmark movies. Real relationships came with all kinds of conditions, and Day didn't think he'd ever find somebody willing to overlook his many, many flaws.

"You ready to go, Hollywood?"

Day dropped his phone as Jackson's voice boomed from behind his shoulder. "Uh, yeah. Sure."

Day turned to find Jackson wearing aviator sunglasses and holding a pair of keys with the Mercedes emblem on them. Day kept a death grip on his phone as he followed Jackson to the elevators, feeling like the entire office watched them both depart. Maybe it was just because Jackson was the boss. Day snuck another look at him where he leaned against the back panel of the elevator, ankles crossed as he stared straight ahead. Well, at least, Day thought he did. It was hard to tell with his dark lenses.

As they exited the elevator, Jackson's hand settled at the small of Day's back, warmth seeping through the layers of denim, making goosebumps rise along his skin. He led Day to a brand new Mercedes sedan, opening the passenger door for Day. "Thank you," he mumbled.

Jackson closed the door before walking around to slide gracefully into the driver's seat. "Seatbelt."

Day followed Jackson's command without thought. The engine purred as Jackson turned on the car with the touch of a button. A woman's voice spilled from the speakers, and it took Day a moment to realize it was a book on tape. The woman had a crisp, melodic tone to her speech, reminding him a bit of Mary Poppins. Jackson went to turn it down, but Day reached out and gripped his wrist. Jackson stared at Day's hand, and he quickly removed it. "Sorry," he muttered. "I… You can listen if you want to. I-I like it."

Jackson examined his face for what seemed like an hour before he gave a single nod. "Alright. I'll start it over. We have a long drive ahead."

Day gave him a smirk. "It's LA. All drives are long."

"You're not wrong."

"I rarely am," Day said in a singsong voice, flushing when he earned another smile from Jackson. He had

infuriating

perfect teeth. He had perfect everything if Day was being honest.

"So, we need to discuss some ground rules."

Day's smirk disappeared, and he cut his eyes to Jackson. "Excuse me?"

"No strangers in my house. You can still perform your nightly shows, but you perform alone."

Day bristled at his tone. "As opposed to the thousands of men I usually let parade in and out of my bed?" he asked, tone snippy.

Jackson raised his hand in a placating gesture. "I didn't say all that. Jimmy said you were auctioning off your virginity. I don't know when you were planning on picking a winner, but it won't be while you're on my watch."

"Look at you, guarding my purity," Day said, deadpan. "And they say chivalry is dead."

Day stared out the window, skin hot, fuming. He didn't know why it annoyed him that Jackson knew he was a virgin…at least in the most technical of terms.

"It's a good gimmick."

Day tossed another look at Jackson. "What is?"

"The whole virginity thing. I could see guys standing in line for the chance to be your first."

"Thanks?"

"Is it real, though?"

"Is what real?" Day asked, genuinely confused and already wishing this conversation would end.

"Are you really a virgin? And, if so, are you really going to have sex with some random guy?"

Day coughed in surprise. "Have I ever had a dick in my ass? Is that what you're asking me after having known me twenty minutes?"

"You have very delicate sensibilities for a guy who makes his living in sex work," Jackson said, tone still conversational. "You obviously don't have to answer. I'm just genuinely trying to understand."

"It's not like I've never fooled around with a guy before. But I've never lost my virginity in the technical sense. As for fucking some random guy… I don't know why everybody puts such a huge value on virginity, like it somehow changes you as a person to take a dick. But if some guy is willing to meet my ridiculously high price tag, sure. I'll fuck him and broadcast it on my OnlyFans."

Day waved his hand as if the whole conversation bored him, but, mostly, he just felt stupid. Something about the calm and rational tone of Jackson's questions made Day feel childish and immature.

"Good for you," Jackson said, sounding sincere. "Just not while you're on my watch, okay? I need to be able to vet anybody who comes near you just in

infuriating

case the killer knows who you are."

Jackson's words made Day's heartbeat skip. He tried not to think of what he saw that night. He felt bad for Jay. That's what he called Jansen. It was the only way he'd ever referred to himself. The whole thing had happened so fast it had taken Day a solid minute to understand what he was looking at. He'd never even seen the killer's face, so Day didn't know why anybody thought he was in danger.

"I do just fine with my solo performances," Day said, once more staring out the window.

"I'm sure you do," Jackson murmured, his deep voice setting off goosebumps across Day's flesh. "Hey, you hungry?"

Jackson's question once more caught Day off guard. "Starving."

Jackson grinned. "Good. Me too. I know just the place."

four

JACKSON

AS JACKSON PULLED INTO A PARKING SPACE IN FRONT of the Gourmet Market, Day's face took on a disgruntled expression that made him laugh.

"What are we doing here?"

"Shopping. You said you were hungry." Jackson walked around to the passenger side, opening Day's door and offering his hand. Once more, he looked on with confusion. "You have gone grocery shopping before, right?" Jackson asked.

"No, my staff usually does all my shopping for me," Day said, tone breezy, before giving Jackson a pissy look even as he accepted his hand. "Of course, I've

infuriating

gone grocery shopping before. I live in a one bedroom efficiency in the middle of the hood."

Jackson chuckled. "You'd never know it, with that attitude and your wardrobe, Your Majesty."

Day narrowed his eyes at Jackson, like he wasn't sure if he was making fun of him or not. Jackson wasn't entirely sure, either. He found he liked picking on Day. There was something about the boy's haughty demeanor that intrigued Jackson. As much as he liked his super sexy prickly exterior, he couldn't help but think it was hiding something more. He wanted to pick at the layers of varnish Day had painted over himself to see what hid underneath.

"You know what they say, dress for the job you want," Day said as he sashayed through the doors.

Jackson grabbed a basket. "And you're dressing for the job of…trophy wife?"

Day slid his gaze upward, once more fluttering long lashes at Jackson, who noticed for the first time how bright blue Day's eyes were, the clear crystal blue of a swimming pool or the waters of the Caribbean. "I don't know, Daddy. Are you looking for a trophy wife?" he drawled.

Jackson leaned in close so as not to offend the elderly lady perusing the apples. "Not really, but if you keep calling me Daddy, we're gonna be skipping straight to the honeymoon."

"Don't threaten me with a good time," Day purred, biting his plump lower lip and giving Jackson a saucy look.

"Not a threat, just a warning."

Jackson could swear Day blushed, but then the boy sighed. "My fans would just love you."

Ah, yes. Day's fans. The audience that watched him get off every night. The audience that wanted to watch Day auction off his virginity to the highest bidder. "Sorry, gorgeous, but I work strictly off camera, and I don't do virgins."

Day's mouth fell open, and Jackson realized what he'd just said. Still, he refused to take it back. Day was a shark, and if Jackson backtracked, he'd definitely smell blood in the water. Besides, as much as Jackson hated to admit it, he liked the way Day's lips curled around the word Daddy. He didn't see the harm in playing along. He hadn't flirted with anybody in a very long time. Not for lack of trying on the part of others, but Jackson had been busy creating an empire and dealing with the women in his life, all of whom were related to him.

"That's really too bad. If we were ever together, I'd want to be able to watch it over and over," he murmured, leaning into Jackson's space, bumping their shoulders together. "We'd look so hot together, don't you think?" He started to walk away before he turned back to face Jackson, voice carrying in the vegetable section. "You'd be shocked at the things I can do and still be considered a virgin."

With that, Day took off towards the prepared foods section, leaving Jackson and the little old lady gaping after him. The woman smirked at Jackson before replacing an apple in its bin and wandering away with her cart.

Jackson had wandered into this game of sexual chicken, and for the first time ever, he wasn't sure he'd win. Day might not be everything he seemed, but he was just stubborn enough to push the envelope if it meant he could win this battle of wills. Jackson wasn't sure he wanted to win. He'd never felt such an instant attraction to another human being before, and his good sense seemed to have taken the day off because, even as his brain reminded him Day was a client, pro-bono or not, his dick was telling him that they were both adults and could do what they liked. It was Jackson's company, after all.

Jackson walked over to where Day was scrutinizing the prepared food under the heat lamps, like he was a judge on *Top Chef*. Jackson peered at the food from over Day's head, liking how the younger man fit just under his chin. "See something you like?" Jackson murmured.

Instead of the witty comeback Jackson expected, Day shrugged. "It's sort of criminal to charge that much money for fried yuca, don't you think? I mean, it's just a bougie fake potato. Who wants fake potatoes?"

It occurred to Jackson then that Day assumed he'd have to pay for his own food, which made sense. Usually the client picked up at least their own portion of the tab and, more often than not, the security staff's as well. "Well, only the bougiest of fake potatoes will do for my trophy wife."

Jackson meant it to be a joke but the way Day's startled gaze shot to his sent a shock of acknowledgement straight to his dick. Jesus, this kid was trouble.

"I'm not really hungry," Day said, his stomach growling loud enough for Jackson to know he lied.

"Well, this lunch is my treat, and if you say no, you're gonna hurt my feelings. So, get yourself some fancy fake potatoes or overpriced green juice or a vegan donut that cost the price of ten non-vegan donuts. Whatever you want."

Day's teeth worried his bottom lip for a long minute as he examined the food before shaking his head. "You pick. There are too many choices," he said, sounding far less confident than he had all day.

Jackson wasn't sure what had triggered this sudden

infuriating

change in attitude, but he was determined to change it back, not at all sure why he cared. "Anything you won't eat?"

Day made a face. "No mushrooms and no olives."

Jackson nodded. "Fine. I'll get the food. But you get the dessert." He pointed Day towards the bakery.

"Anything you won't eat?" Day asked, mirroring Jackson's question.

"I hate cherries," Jackson said.

Day looked scandalized, but then mischievous. "That's too bad," he said, hips swaying as he sauntered away.

Jackson shook his head before going about the task of filling up containers with all manner of food from marinated kale to chicken fingers. If he thought Day might want it, in the basket it went. By the time he met Day at the bakery, his purchase was already bagged, leaving Jackson to wonder what he'd chosen, but he let Day keep his secret. They grabbed juices from the cold case and got in line.

Two customers were in front of them, a younger blonde woman in a flowy floral dress with a toddler in the cart and a baby on her hip and a middle-aged woman with a severe haircut and a scowl on her face. Day immediately set about watching the scowling woman, like she might steal something. It didn't take long before they realized the source of the middle-aged woman's rage. The young mother's card kept declining.

The middle-aged woman sighed heavily, rolling her eyes and shifting her weight from one foot to the other. The girl flushed, looking down at her purchases. "I'm really sorry. I don't know what's wrong with this stupid card," she said. "Maybe if I put this back?" She handed over the generic cold medication, and once more, the cashier tried the card. When it declined again, the girl's eyes filled with tears, and the cashier gave a nervous look to the line forming behind her.

The woman sighed once more then sneered. "If you can't afford to shop here, maybe you should try the Save-A-Lot downtown with the other poor people."

The girl sucked in a breath, tears spilling over. Before Jackson could defuse the situation, Day fixed the lady with a look Jackson hoped to never be on the other side of.

"I'm sorry? Where are you going in such a hurry, Karen? Is there some kind of grumpy California cunts meeting you're late for? I see you're wearing yoga pants, but given that the size of your ass is even bigger than your sour attitude, I doubt you're on your way to the gym. So, why don't you calm your tits and stop huffing and puffing before somebody thinks you're having an asthma attack and shoves a paper bag over

infuriating

your head and accidentally smothers you with it."

The woman turned on Day with murder in her eyes. "Why don't you mind your business and put on some boy clothes?"

Jackson's eyes went wide, and he put a hand on Day's shoulder, but he shook it off, cocking his head and his hip in a stance that made both Jackson and the cashier slightly nervous.

"You know what they say, all clothes are boy clothes if you just stop being a little bitch about it. You should try it, or maybe you could just try pulling the stick out of your ass and shove it up your—"

Jackson slapped his hand over Day's mouth, pulling him back against him. Jackson thought Day might actually chew through his hand as his mouth was still moving, his words muffled.

"I'm reporting you to the manager."

Whatever Day said behind Jackson's hand came with two middle fingers aimed directly at the woman. Jackson couldn't stop his laugh as the lady hurried towards the counter at the far end of the store. "Easy, killer. You've made your point. She's gone." He dropped his hand from Day's lips.

"Fucking twat," Day muttered before realizing the cashier and the woman both stared at him with wide eyes. "Sorry," Day tacked on almost as an afterthought, not sounding sorry at all.

Jackson pulled his AmEx card free and handed it to the cashier. "I've got her purchases."

The girl shook her head vehemently, adjusting the baby on her hip. "No. I'll just come back later. My husband is just being a jerk. He does this sometimes. He turns off the card to teach me a les…" She trailed off. "Sorry, you don't care about any of this."

Jackson nodded to the cashier who rang up the girl's purchases and then theirs, ignoring her protests before handing back the card and the receipt. Before the girl left, Jackson handed her his business card. "I do care. If you need help, call the number on the card. It's my cell phone. I always have it on me."

She gawked at him for a minute before nodding and hurrying from the store with her purchases. Jackson took the bags, but Day took his bakery bag back, like he was guarding it from Jackson as if it was a surprise. Day was mercurial to say the least and Jackson couldn't get enough.

"Come on, crazy. Let's get you out of here before you get arrested for beating up an old lady," Jackson said.

"Wow, you're, like, a knight in shining armor," Day said with a smirk as they walked through the parking lot.

"Yeah, and you're like a rabid poodle," Jackson said,

infuriating

nodding towards his car.

"A rabid poodle?"

"Yeah, all frills and bows on the outside, but snarling and vicious deep down."

"Sorry, but I refuse to be somebody I'm not."

"Did I ask you to?" Jackson asked, enjoying how easy it was to rile Day up.

"You just called me a rabid poodle."

Jackson grinned. "Yeah, but I'm a dog person."

five

DAYTON

DAY STAYED SILENT MOST OF THE WAY TO JACKSON'S place. He had no idea why he'd agreed to this farce of a security detail because he'd wanted to jump Jackson the moment he'd seen him and let him do things to him he'd never even considered letting anybody else do. The worst part? It seemed like Jackson was definitely down to fuck. Or whatever might be fuck adjacent. At least, until after he sold his virginity. All these wannabe Daddies all thought they had a shot at being the one who fucked him for the first time, as if being the first one to stick their dick in him was some kind of fucking prize. But Day was the one who'd

infuriating

made it a prize.

Day slid his gaze to Jackson, who looked so relaxed as he drove, his one hand draped over the wheel and the other draped over the center console. Day found himself wondering what it would feel like to just ride in the car, hands clasped together like a couple. Jackson seemed so calm. Day's outburst hadn't raised so much as an eyebrow from him, and he'd even said he'd liked it. Day had never been part of a real couple. He didn't really think love was a real thing, at least, not for somebody like him. There was too much wrong with him.

It sucked, too. Day had never met anybody like Jackson. He exuded this calm that made Day want to curl up against him, like a cat finding a warm spot in the sun. Jackson had this innate confidence. He was tall and large and sexy, and he unapologetically took up space. Day bet he'd never been embarrassed a single day in his life.

He sighed. He wasn't sure if he wanted to fuck Jackson or be Jackson.

Jackson looked over, catching Day staring at him like an idiot. He could already feel his cheeks pinking when Jackson flashed those perfect white teeth in a wicked smile, his eyes hidden behind his Cartier sunglasses. Nope. No. Day was sure. He wanted to fuck Jackson. But worse than that, he wanted to call Jackson Daddy, wanted to snuggle on the couch with him, wanted to know each other's coffee orders.

Day didn't even return Jackson's smile, just snapped his gaze to stare out the window, his heart beating out of his chest as he did his best to hold back the panic attack trying to claw its way up his throat. What the fuck was wrong with him? The whole Daddy thing was a gimmick. A way for Day to work his baby face and pouty lips for the older guys who didn't know a thing about actual BDSM. Not that Day really did, either. Not in reality. He'd looked on fetish sites, like Fetlife, once, but had panicked when he'd seen how many guys had aggressively messaged him to tell him in detail to sit, stay, or obey as if they had a right, making him feel less like a sub and more like a dog.

Jackson definitely looked like a man who was used to being in charge, not because he wanted to be but because people seemed to naturally turn to him for guidance. Maybe it was his military training. Day couldn't miss the Special Forces tattoo on his forearm. But just because somebody liked being in charge didn't mean they wanted to Dom a stranger. Although, when Day had baited him with Daddy, Jackson had responded in kind. So…maybe?

What the fuck was wrong with him? He'd known

infuriating

the man less than a day. This was why Day stayed home. Why he rarely went out or tried to date. He was permanently broken in every way. Too much work for little reward. A dark shadow fell over his mood, chasing away the butterflies Jackson had put in his belly.

Jackson pulled into a parking garage in front of a sky-high building made of chrome, glass, and steel, parking in a spot marked 25. He then walked around to Day's side and opened the door, once more extending a hand to help him up. Part of Day wanted to refuse and be the bitch he'd always been. Better to pull the tape off quickly, let Jackson know that he talked a good game but was, deep down, a big bag of crazy. When Day hesitated, Jackson gently took his hand and tugged him from the seat before grabbing the bags and leading him to the elevator. Day immediately felt uncomfortable in the mirrored box, meeting Jackson's curious gaze as the floor numbers ticked off above the doors.

Jackson placed his hand at the small of Day's back again, guiding him to the last apartment at the end of the hall, pressing numbers on a keypad before using a key to turn what sounded like a heavy tumbler. Jackson pushed the door open and stood aside to let Day in. He stopped short just inside, scanning the enormous apartment. It was ultra-modern with glass windows that spanned two stories, a living room filled with mid-century modern furnishings, a large kitchen with dark wood cabinets and fancy appliances, and a floating staircase that led to a second story with three doors. Day could only assume those led to the bedrooms.

"Jimmy dropped off your things. I had the valet set them in your room. We're in for the rest of the day if you want to get more comfortable. I can find something for us to watch and put the food out?"

Day looked down at what he was wearing. Did Jackson not like what he was wearing? Was he trying to subtly tell him this was a Netflix and chill thing? Day was not fit to be among normal humans. It occurred to him then that maybe this would be the perfect way to let Jackson know that everything he saw was just a costume. No…armor. It wasn't that he didn't like wearing feminine clothing or makeup, but it was also a lot of work. He didn't always look that way. Maybe Jackson needed to see Day as he was on a normal day before he started the process of getting ready for camming.

"Oh. Yeah. Thanks. I'll be down in a few."

"Your room is the one on the right. You have your own bathroom."

Day didn't even speak, just bolted up the stairs like he was being chased. Jackson was right. His meager belongings were sitting in two bags on his king-size

infuriating

bed. The room was huge but sparse with an empty closet open against the far wall and a door he assumed led to the bathroom. He pulled a pair of black joggers free and a thread white t-shirt he'd had since middle school. It really showed off just how slim his frame was. Jackson could definitely do so much better. Once he'd put on his ratty attire, he went to the bathroom and removed his contacts, replacing them with his large black framed glasses. At the last minute, he added his knee length athletic socks and blue furry bunny slippers. There was no way Jackson would find him attractive in this attire, and part of Day died at the notion. He held his breath for a moment, puffing out his cheeks before letting the air leak out. It was no good wishing for things that weren't for somebody like him. This wasn't Day's first crush. It wouldn't be his last. With that final depressing thought, he skipped down the stairs, stopping short when he saw that Jackson had changed into basketball shorts and a tank-top with the sides cut.

He grinned when he saw Day's clothes. "Hell, yeah. That's what I'm talking about. See, already dressed to get messy and pig out."

Jackson gestured to the ottoman that sat surrounded by a large wraparound sofa. He'd set a ton of food out like a picnic, and on the tv, he'd paused a movie. Day approached the ottoman like it was a trap, that telltale feeling of panic sparking along his skin, telling him to run. Instead, he plopped himself down in the corner of the couch, surveying over a dozen containers of food before looking at Jackson with wide eyes. "How much food do you think I eat?"

"Shit. I'm here, too, ain't I?" Jackson asked, snagging a set of chopsticks from the middle of the spread and snatching a California roll.

Casual Jackson with his bare feet and tattered clothing seemed like a whole different Jackson, which left Day feeling dizzy and confused because it made him no less attractive. It was all too much to process. Day snagged a fork and picked at a few things before settling on a fancy pasta salad. Jackson pushed play on the remote as he stuffed another bit of food into his mouth. Some kind of cold ramen dish.

The opening music to *Moulin Rouge* started playing, and Day narrowed his eyes at Jackson. "Really? Was *Pretty Woman* not available? I'm not a hooker, you know."

Jackson snorted. "This is my favorite movie. Satine was not a hooker. She was an entertainer. A sex worker. And Baz Luhrman is a god, and Ewan McGregor is hot."

"You expect me to believe you like the movie *Moulin*

Rouge and that this isn't some subtle dig at what I do?"

Jackson gave him a look. It wasn't a mean look or even a stern look. It was this steady eye contact that shot goosebumps along his skin and sent a shot of heat to his dick. "If you think I have time in my busy life to pretend to like shit I don't just to low-key throw shade at your job, you haven't been paying attention. I don't say shit I don't mean. I'm an adult. I love this movie. If you don't like it, we can watch something else. Would you like to watch something else, Day?"

"No," Day managed, gaze falling away.

"You sure?" Jackson asked, voice gentle. "I should have considered you might find this a little… triggering, but you seemed like you really love what you do, so I thought it would be okay."

"I do love what I do." *For the most part.* "I just don't really know how to deal with people who don't instantly treat me like a circus sideshow or an easy hookup."

Jackson gave him an almost feral grin. "When you look like me, all hookups are easy. Now, shut up and let's watch this movie."

Jackson proceeded to eat his fill, while Day picked bits here and there, far too nervous to eat for some reason. Time ticked by, the blue sky fading to pinks and oranges then navy before finally settling on a star-filled, cloudless inky black. By the time the movie ended, they'd both settled in the same corner of the couch, not touching but close enough for Day to feel the heat of Jackson's body.

When the credits started to roll, Jackson looked over at Day, close enough for him to lean forward and seal their lips together if he truly wanted to. "Do you want to watch something else?"

"I should probably start getting ready to film," Day murmured, dipping his head closer as if he couldn't help himself.

Jackson reached out, his thumb tracing just below Day's bottom lip. "Anything I can help with?"

Day didn't think about it, just maneuvered himself into Jackson's lap in one graceful move, cupping his face in his hands. "You could film with me, be my Daddy for real tonight?"

"I don't have the kind of job where I can be seen on camera."

"I'm not going live tonight. I'm just filming for my OnlyFans. You could wear a mask. Hide your face. I'll even show you the video before I post it so you can see there's nothing anybody could use to identify you."

"I'm not going to deny there's something here between us, but I don't know if I want to share it with the entire world."

infuriating

"I'm flattered you think the entire world subscribes to my OnlyFans account, but, truthfully, it's only about five hundred people."

Jackson smiled. "Maybe when you're done filming your video, you can stop by my room and we could talk more about what this might be between us."

Day sighed, resigned. "I'll think about it," he said, forcing a blasé tone. "And if you change your mind, my door will be unlocked. Just come on in."

Jackson closed the distance between them, soft lips sliding over Day's in a kiss that stole his breath. "I'll think about it."

Day rose on shaky legs, doing his best to make a quick retreat. "You do that."

six

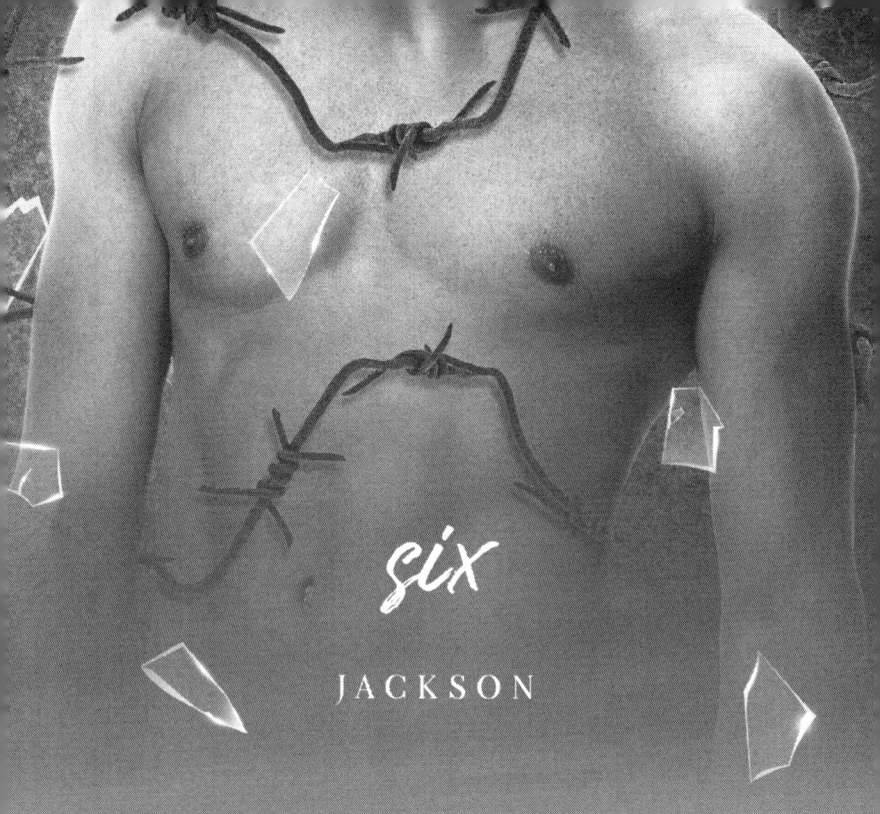

JACKSON

JACKSON SPENT THE NEXT HALF HOUR PUTTING AWAY the leftovers and actively not thinking about Day stripping down and getting ready to put his hands all over his tight little body for the enjoyment of strangers. The idea of it intrigued Jackson. Day intrigued Jackson. So ballsy, so brazen, so hot for Jackson he worried they might have set the couch on fire if Day had straddled his lap for one moment longer.

There was something about Day that triggered this weird gut instinct in Jackson that had always served him well. Jackson didn't believe in love at first sight or fairy tale romances, but he did believe there was

infuriating

such a thing as soulmates, and when you find that one person, you just know. He'd never tell a single soul that he had decided, while in line at the grocery store, that mouthy, brazen, beautiful Dayton Daniels was the one for him. He especially would never tell Dayton. Still, if Jackson was a betting man, he'd put money on Dayton being his person.

Jackson was a patient man. He'd waited a long time to meet somebody who stirred that feeling in him, the one his mom said she had for his father the day she first laid eyes on him. And now that Jackson had found it, he had no fucking idea what to do about it. Jackson was good at reading people. It was his fucking job, and it didn't take an expert to see that Dayton didn't just have walls around his heart, he had cement barricades a hundred miles high, surrounded by razor wire. For all his bravado and flirting, underneath, he was terrified and wounded. And, like any wounded animal, Jackson knew Day would attack to protect himself.

If Jackson wanted Day, he was going to have to work his way in. It would have to start with sex. It was the only place Day's walls were weak. He'd let his guard down the moment he called Jackson Daddy.

The way he'd said the word…sensual and seductive, but also hopeful. It was as if he didn't dare dream it was possible, but if he could make Jackson want to fuck him, maybe he could trust him enough to be whoever he was under all those layers.

Except, he wasn't wearing any layers right now. Jackson's cock hardened at the reminder. Just up those stairs, Day was laid out on the bed, his pale skin a stark contrast to the navy blue comforter on the bed. He'd invited Jackson inside. He'd asked Jackson to touch him on camera. Jackson turned the idea over in his head. Showing his face on camera in a porn movie would probably cause a great deal of issues for Elite, a company he'd built from nothing to more than six offices around the country, even with the men he hired and their tendency to marry his clients.

Jackson was walking up the stairs before he was even consciously aware of it. He wanted Day, with or without the audience. Day's door was cracked open just enough for a small sliver of the room to show. He could see cameras set up all around the bed at perfect angles. It was a surprisingly professional looking setup.

Jackson pushed the door open but stayed where he was, leaning his large frame against the door. Day's nervous gaze jumped to Jackson and then away, his tongue darting out over his full pink bottom lip in a show of nerves that quickly disappeared, replaced by a seductive smile.

Jackson didn't know where to look first. Day was

naked from the waist up, his skin shimmering like a rainbow whenever the lights hit it just right. His lips were glossy pink once more and his long lashes were tinted black, but other than that, he wore no other makeup. Without the baggy clothes he'd lounged in, Day's body was slight, lean and lanky, almost feminine. If anything, Day was delicate, all long limbs and elegant fingers.

"What do you think?" Day asked, slowly spinning in a circle.

Jackson accepted the invitation to look his fill, taking in the red lace garter belt that skimmed his trim waist, the satin underwear that barely covered Day's bulge in the front and left most of his pert, perfect bottom on display in the back, highlighted by red lace thigh-highs. "I think you're beautiful."

Despite his slow turn and request for the compliment, Day still seemed taken aback by this declarative statement, his gaze snapping to Jackson's as if to see the truth of his words in his expression.

"Thank you," he said, sounding a little breathless. Jackson pushed himself from the doorway, closing the distance between them, but Day held up a hand. "The cameras are hot. I can edit you out, but I didn't want you to think I was trying to trick you or something."

Jackson moved closer, capturing Day by the elbows

and tugging him in close enough for their size discrepancy to be obvious. Day's pupils dilated, and he chomped down on the corner of his lip, gazing up at Jackson through thick lashes.

"You wouldn't trick me," Jackson murmured, using his thumb to tug Day's lip from between his clamped teeth and rubbing the impressions left in their wake. "Brats get punished. You wouldn't want me to have to punish you our first time together on camera. Would you?"

Day's eyes went glassy and he nodded. "Yeah, probably."

"Is that how you speak to me?" Jackson asked, his hands dropping to give Day's ass a squeeze before he gave him a gentle swat.

"No, Daddy," Day whispered.

Jackson rubbed the spot where he'd spanked Day, but then he cupped his face. "Say it again."

Day swayed toward him. "No, Daddy."

"Good. I need something to cover my face."

Day stumbled back and walked to the dresser, pulling open the second drawer, sending all kinds of lace and fluff spilling out. He dug for a minute before turning back with two masks in his hands. One looked like something out of *Phantom of the Opera*, but the other was just a black hood that left his nose, mouth,

infuriating

and chin exposed. The *Phantom* mask wouldn't cover much, but the other looked like he was a professional wrestler. He took the hood and slipped it on.

This time, Day's hands came to rest on Jackson's cheeks, his shiny nails scratching gently over the older man's beard. "You're so hot, but you look a little like a thief," Day said before chewing on his lower lip once more.

"Oh yeah?" Jackson said.

Day could only nod. Jackson wrapped his arms around him, gripping handfuls of his ass as he lifted Day up. His arms and legs came around him, and, for the first time, Jackson could feel how turned on Day was. "I mean, yeah. A really kinky one. One I'd let steal my virginity…if I hadn't already promised it to my fans."

"Is it stealing if you let me have it?" Jackson murmured.

"Would you take it if I refused?" Day countered, sounding like he hoped Jackson would be willing to play rough. Rough was fine, but Jackson wasn't one for taking things by force. He preferred to ask nicely, then dole out punishments when they were necessary.

Jackson shook his head, his lips finding Day's in a kiss that lingered. He smelled like a flowery light perfume, and Jackson buried his nose behind Day's ear where the scent seemed strongest, inhaling deep, dragging Day's hips against Jackson's so Day could feel what he was doing to him. "Limits?" he growled against Day's ear.

Day didn't hesitate, his words coming out in a breathless rush. "No penetrative sex. No water sports. No blood play. No humiliation. All my results are negative, and my safe word is unicorn. You?"

Jackson chuckled. Day was…something else. Something completely different than anything Jackson had encountered before. "The same?"

Day stopped, leveling a serious look at Jackson. "Your safe word is unicorn, too? Weird."

This time, Jackson laughed outright, earning a scowl from Day. Jackson kissed his nose to placate him. "I don't have a safe word. I've never needed one. Nobody ever thought they could Dom me. I'm the Daddy. You're the brat."

Day rubbed his nose against Jackson's. "Fine with me, Daddy."

Jackson couldn't take the teasing anymore. He crashed their lips together, and Day opened up for him beautifully, tongue teasing over Jackson's as his fingernails played at the base of his skull. Jackson carried Day to the bed and sat with the boy in his lap. Day started writhing against him almost immediately,

infuriating

the flushed head of his hard cock peeking out from those barely there red silk panties.

"Fuck, I want you so bad," Day whispered. "God, I can already feel how hard you are."

Jackson swiped his thumb over the tip of Day's cock, gathering the fluid there and presenting it to Day. He stuck his tongue out, capturing Jackson's finger and sucking it into his mouth. Jackson pulled free, swiping his finger across Day's lower lip. "I've got something much better for you to do with that pornographic mouth of yours."

Day was nodding before the words were even out. "Anything, Daddy."

Jackson leaned back with his hands on the bed and looked down at his cock tenting his shorts. Day slipped from Jackson's lap, going to his knees before him, his hands reaching for the waistband. Jackson raised his hips and let Day work his shorts down, his cock springing free and slapping against the taut muscles of his belly. Day's nostrils flared at the sight of Jackson's erection, like it was a gift.

Day's nails dragged along Jackson's thighs before he looked up at him from beneath a dark fringe of lashes. "Can I, Daddy?"

Jackson didn't answer right away despite his compulsion to want to force Day to swallow him down. He just let him sit there on his knees, gazing up at him, plump lip in a slight pout, like there was a chance Jackson might say no. "Say, please."

"Please," Day whispered, his fingers spasming against Jackson's thighs. Jackson buried his fingers in Day's hair, bringing his face closer before stopping. "Please, what?"

"Please, can I suck you off, Daddy?" Day begged without hesitation.

"Sure, baby. Since you asked so nicely."

At this point, Jackson usually just closed his eyes and focused on the sensation, but he couldn't take his eyes off Day as he rose up on his knees, pushing Jackson back just enough to get some room. Jackson leaned back on his forearms, watching his cock disappear into the hot, wet suction of Day's full, glossy lips. Jackson growled low as Day bobbed his head twice before taking Jackson to the back of his throat and swallowing, his breath rustling the hair at the base of his cock. Christ.

Jackson expected Day to pull off but he just stayed there, his tongue teasing across the thick vein along his shaft until Jackson couldn't help but grip Day's head and flex his hips, fucking into Day's throat with tiny aborted thrusts that sent bursts of pleasure through his entire body. "Oh, fuck. That's it. Suck me. You look so good like this. So fucking pretty."

Day tapped Jackson's thigh, and he let him free. Day sat panting, tears and mascara running down his face as he ran his tongue up one side of Jackson's cock and down the other before pumping his cock and sucking on just the tip.

"Fuck, your tongue should come with a warning label."

Day gave him a smile, running his tongue along the base of Jackson's cock again as if to prove his point.

"You keep looking at me that way and I might forget that you're saving yourself."

Day's smile wavered, his pupils blowing wide, like the idea of Jackson fucking him was more than he could handle. If Day only knew how much he was testing Jackson's control. If he did, he'd be a lot more concerned for his precious virginity auction, because Jackson couldn't stop thinking about what it would feel like to throw Day on the bed and work him open, first with his tongue and then with his fingers, before fucking him nice and slow and deep, watching his face as he took every inch of him.

"My turn," Jackson snarled. "On the bed." Day rose in one graceful motion and sat on the bed. Jackson stood, dragging him to the edge of the bed by the ankle and flipping him over roughly until he was on his belly. Day looked back at Jackson just as he dragged Day's hips upward. Jackson didn't take Day's panties off, just pulled the string from between his cheeks to pet over his entrance. "Red is definitely your color.

Jackson leaned down, sinking his teeth into Day's ass cheek hard enough to get a startled cry out of him. When he didn't utter his safeword, Jackson bit him on the other cheek as well, liking the way his bite marks looked on Day's pale skin.

Day whimpered when Jackson splayed him open, teasing over Day's hole with the flat of his tongue. "You like that, baby?" Jackson asked, burying his face before Day could formulate an answer.

Jackson couldn't get enough of the taste of Day or the way he whined and moaned as Jackson licked and sucked at his entrance, pushing himself back on Jackson's tongue, begging him for more. "Please, Daddy. I need more. Please. I'm so hard. Can I touch myself? Please? Please?"

"No," Jackson said, giving Day one last lick before he went for the lube that Day had conveniently left on the side table. Jackson brought the whole bottle with him. "On your back."

Day rolled onto his back, bending his legs at the knees, watching Jackson with a look that was slightly more timid than when they'd started, noting the way

infuriating

Day's legs were already shaking. Jackson shed the rest of his clothing and climbed on the bed, above Day's head, facing his feet. Day lay there, like the perfect boy, just waiting for Jackson's orders, watching him with wide eyes. He looked so innocent like this, almost nervous. It made Jackson want to turn off the cameras and hold him, but he knew Day would never allow that. When Jackson lubed up the fingers on both hands, Day's gaze shot to his, the slightest fear bleeding through.

"Relax," Jackson crooned. "I'm not going to hurt you."

seven

DAYTON

JACKSON'S WORDS HAD DAY SHIVERING. HE HAD NO idea what Jackson intended to do to him, and it was shredding his nerves. He hadn't anticipated this level of nerves. It was just sex. Day tried to convince himself it was because he'd never had a partner on camera, but the truth was Day had stopped caring about recording the moment Jackson had kissed him. Kissing Jackson was like nothing Day had ever experienced before. The few guys Day had kissed had kissed him like it was just a precursor to other things. Jackson kissed him like he was branding him, like he was letting Day know he was Jackson's. He was just so big and strong, and when his arms went around Day, he felt safe.

Day shook away the stupid thought. It was just sex. Just touching. Day didn't do feelings. He just wanted Jackson's hands, his mouth, his tongue, and, oh, that fucking beard. The way it ran rough across Day's skin, leaving a burning trail in its wake. Jackson was so fucking hot, and Day regretted ever starting his virginity auction because he'd never wanted somebody inside him the way he wanted Jackson, and that was after five or so hours together. What was Day going to do when he was next to him day after day, knowing Jackson would take him if he asked? That he'd hold him down and fuck him into the mattress and be as rough or gentle as Day wanted? It twisted Day's insides and made his cock throb.

Jackson came up on his knees to rub his heavy, veiny cock across Day's spit-slicked lips before leaning forward and feeding it to him, nice and slow. Day sucked it down greedily as Jackson fucked his mouth in short rhythmic strokes. Day couldn't keep his hands to himself, running his fingers along Jackson's muscular thighs or the perfection of his ass, teasing his fingers across his balls, thumbing the spot just behind until Jackson did that half growl thing that made Day's toes curl.

Jackson pushed the scrap of red silk to Day's thighs

before taking his cock in his slick fist and teasing the fingers of his other hand into the crease of his ass, probing his entrance. Day whimpered, pulling off Jackson's cock to cant his hips, hoping Jackson would get the message. Day needed Jackson inside him. Day released a stuttering breath, trying to relax at the sudden blunt pressure of Jackson's thick finger. He tried not to grimace at the slow familiar burn, bearing down as Jackson probed his entrance, whining as he slipped inside.

"Jackson." Day couldn't help the slight tinge of panic in his voice. He wasn't scared, just overwhelmed, like he couldn't breathe.

Jackson placed a kiss on Day's lower belly, and the simple act choked Day up. He didn't want to think about why. He slid Jackson's cock back into his mouth, choosing to focus on that and the way Jackson fucked his finger in and out of him as his other hand worked his cock in a tight, mind-numbingly slow grip.

Minutes passed as Day did his best to give as well as receive, but it was hard when he was fucking down on Jackson's fingers and thrusting up into his tightened fist. It was like he couldn't help himself. He dug his nails into Jackson's ass, relaxing his throat, content to let Jackson fuck his mouth while he took Day apart.

It was all so much. There'd been the odd hookup

here and there, but nothing like this. Nothing like how Jackson was trying to claim Day's body in every conceivable way, penetrating him so thoroughly, Day couldn't think of anything else. It wasn't fair. It felt like Jackson was playing dirty somehow, reading what Day needed and giving it to him without him even asking.

Day could feel his balls drawing up tight to his body, could feel himself losing his ability to control the way he worked his cock up into Jackson's fist. When Jackson pushed a second finger inside him, Day pulled off his cock. "Please. Can I come? It feels so good, Daddy. I need to come," he begged.

"No," Jackson said, tone as casual as if they were discussing the weather. He twisted his fingers inside Day, dragging his knuckles over his prostate until Day moaned like someone out of an adult movie.

"Please, Daddy. You can do whatever you want to me. Fuck my mouth, come down my throat, come on my face. Anything. Please."

Jackson worked him faster, dragging a helpless cry from Day. "I can already do whatever I want to you. I'll tell you when you can come."

Day sobbed, frustration welling up within him. He'd edged himself on camera so many times, but it was nothing like this, nothing like feeling like he was two seconds from exploding into a million little pieces.

"Did I say you could stop sucking my dick?" Jackson asked.

Day tongued over Jackson's balls, sucking gently, before taking Jackson back in his mouth, working his tongue along the thick vein of his shaft, slipping a finger between Jackson's cheeks to tease over his hole.

That earned Day a low growl of warning or maybe of pleasure. Day didn't know but he wanted to find out. He did it again, just ghosting the pad of his finger over the puckered entrance.

Suddenly, Jackson's hand disappeared. "You can come now, you little tease."

Jackson's mouth closed over Day's cock and sucked him down while his fingers twisted inside Day until his knees were shaking and he was sucking Jackson because he didn't know what else he could do. His hands spasmed, fingers gripping the comforter as he fucked into the heat of Jackson's mouth over and over again, each thrust more shallow than the last. He pulled off Jackson to mutter, "I'm coming. I'm coming."

Jackson didn't pull off, just held Day in place as he writhed and cried, spilling over Jackson's tongue, moaning as Jackson tried to suck him dry.

As soon as he pulled off, Jackson said, "Open up."

Day didn't question him, just opened his mouth and

stuck out his tongue, watching as Jackson jerked his swollen cock with long strokes, swiping his thumb over the tip and working his precum and Day's saliva back over his shaft. Day let his fingers find Jackson's balls, massaging them and teasing the spot just behind. Jackson snarled, and then he was painting over Day's lips, his tongue, even his hair and the mattress.

After a minute, Jackson collapsed on the bed, his head still facing Day's feet. Day startled as Jackson laid his head on his belly and pushed his thigh under Day's head. Neither spoke, but it wasn't an uncomfortable silence, which, somehow, made Day feel worse. Uncomfortable was good. Uncomfortable meant it wouldn't happen again. He didn't want to get used to the feel of Jackson's beard on his belly or the way his fingers skimmed along his skin. But even though he didn't want to get used to it, he already knew it was going to happen again and again.

Jackson placed a kiss on Day's belly once more, just over his belly button in that same infuriatingly sweet gesture, and then sat up. "Turn off your cameras and come shower with me."

Day rolled away from Jackson and sat up, facing the wall. "I-I have a lot of editing to do. I'll just take a quick shower in here and then get to it. I don't like to be late putting up my videos."

Jackson was quiet for a minute, then Day felt him stand, and suddenly, he was in Day's space, lifting his chin with a finger. "Okay. Do your edits. Keep that hustle. Whatever you need to do. But, next time, maybe we do this without the cameras. This can be just about sex if that's what you need, but I always get what I want eventually."

Day swallowed the lump in his throat. "And what is it you want?"

Jackson laughed and dropped a kiss on his head. "You, Dayton."

Panic, sharp as a scalpel, sliced through him, causing him to jerk to his feet. "Don't. Don't say things like that. You-You have no-no idea…" Day snapped his mouth shut as he heard himself stuttering over his words. It had taken years to get past that, and now, in less than a day, Jackson was reducing him to an idiot. "Just…just don't. Okay? I don't need that. I'm not that guy."

"Hey, relax. I wasn't trying to freak you out. If you want this to just be about sex, then it's just sex. Good sex. Mind blowing sex."

Day could feel himself breathing hard and tried to pull it together. "Yeah. Sure. The sex was amazing. I'm going to go take that shower now." He left Jackson standing there, staring after him.

With the door closed and locked, he slid down and

sat on the cold tile, bringing his knees to his chest and covering his face with his hands. What was wrong with him? He'd just made himself look so fucking stupid. He'd gone from cool and flirty to a hot fucking mess in less than twenty-four hours. That was a new record for him. He just wasn't fit to be around other people. He was too messed up.

He took deep breaths, trying to quell the tears and anxiety welling up from within. It was just the hookup. That was all. Day had vowed a long time ago that he'd never go down on his knees for anybody ever again. Not after years of dealing with Carl, but he'd done it for Jackson without thought. He'd never even considered saying no. He shoved his thumbs into his eyes, trying to scrub away the memories flooding in on him, but they were relentless. The smell of Old Spice and sweat. The sound of heavy breathing and his weird breathy grunts. The way Carl's gut would press against his forehead as he forced Day down. The feel of his hands in Day's hair. His apartment that always stunk of cigarettes and garbage.

"You're lucky I like you, kid. I'm saving you a lot of money this way. Don't worry, I won't tell your little girlfriend about our arrangement. I don't think she could handle any more bad news. Do you?"

Day jerked forward, just barely making it to the toilet

before his stomach heaved. Thankfully, there was painfully little left in him. He sat there, with his head on the toilet rim, for five minutes until he was sure the nausea had passed then finally turned on the shower. He undressed carefully, making sure not to snag his hose. They were the most expensive part of his outfits. When he was naked, he got under the heavy stream of water, enjoying the pulsing sensation of the shower head as it beat down on his sore muscles. He washed quickly but stayed under the spray until his fingers were pruny and his eyes were heavy.

Once he was safely wrapped in a towel, he stood in front of the mirror, drying his hair and trying to style it with his fingers. His lips and cheeks were red from where Jackson's beard had brushed against him. He trailed his fingertips over the areas, closing his eyes so he could try to relive what it felt like to kiss Jackson.

Day shook his head. He didn't belong there. Jackson was everything Day wanted in a guy, except that he was clearly unhinged. Who looked at somebody like Day and just acted like this could be more than it was? Maybe he was just trying to make Day feel better? Jackson did seem rather old-fashioned. Opening doors and buying Day food. That had to be it.

Hopefully, Jackson had taken the hint and realized that Day wasn't in the market for a hero or a Prince

infuriating

Charming. Just somebody to keep him alive until they caught a murderer. He just needed to find a way to show Jackson that Day wasn't Cinderella, he was the pumpkin.

eight

JACKSON

JACKSON WAS PULLING A WAFFLE FROM THE WAFFLE maker when Day stumbled down the stairs, his platinum hair sticking up in all directions and his glasses perched on his nose. He was wearing a pair of black joggers and a hoodie the same pool blue as his eyes. He seemed out of sorts.

"You hungry?" Jackson asked.

Dayton crawled onto a stool at the other side of the bar, glaring at Jackson's dark wash jeans and fitted t-shirt. He could only smile at the grumpy look on Day's face. He clearly wasn't a morning person, and he seemed irritated that Jackson was already dressed

infuriating

and ready for the day.

Jackson plated the waffle and held it out to him, but Day shook his head, eyes at half-mast. "Coffee?" he croaked, like he had just crawled across the desert.

Jackson leaned onto the counter until he was in Day's space, chucking him under the chin. "You could at least say please."

Day perked up enough to purr, "Please, Daddy?"

Jackson grinned. "That's much better. I should warn you though—"

The door to Jackson's apartment flung open, and three screeching gremlins ran through the door, followed by Jackson's sister, who looked like she was two seconds away from committing murder. Jackson was instantly pinned to the fridge, his two nieces and nephew hanging from his arms as he did curls and roared, garnering squeals of laughter.

The tension in the room shifted when Ruby and Day caught sight of each other. Day looked at Ruby suspiciously, but Ruby looked at Day like he was fresh meat. Her smile looked friendly, but Jackson smelled trouble.

"You didn't tell me you had company. I thought you weren't seeing anybody right now?" she said, her tone letting him know she didn't like being lied to.

Jackson sighed. "Day, meet my younger sister,

Ruby, my nieces, Chloe and Keisha, and my nephew, Isaac. Ruby, meet my newest client, Dayton."

"Day," Day corrected, holding out his hand. "I love your dress. Did you get that at Calico's?"

Ruby's eyes went wide, and she smoothed her hands over her orange sundress before sticking her hands in the oversized pockets and swaying, giving Day a genuine toothy grin. "I did! How did you know that?"

"I know fashion," Day said, his tone a bit smug. "That color is amazing on you. Very few people could pull it off."

Jackson thought his sister looked like she'd just escaped from teaching a kindergarten art class with her bright sundress, oversized cardigan, and her hair in two buns on the top of her head, but the last time he'd commented on Ruby's style, she'd forced him to go shopping with her. So, he said nothing, instead pushing a mug of coffee in front of Day, who took a sip of the black brew and sighed.

Jackson frowned as a thought occurred to him. "I thought you said you were going to call when you were downstairs?"

"Well, there was nobody at the desk, so we just came on up. Besides, if you'd had any warning, you would have just hidden away your new…client, and then I wouldn't have gotten such a nice compliment,"

infuriating

Ruby said, beaming at Day, who smirked at Jackson, his brows somehow looking smug.

"What do you mean there was nobody at the front desk? There's always supposed to be somebody at the front desk. That's why I live here," Jackson said, ignoring the way Ruby and Day appeared ready to tag team him.

"You don't live here. You live in Miami," Chloe reminded him. Jackson snatched the five-year-old up and tickled her until she screeched, "Stop! I'm gonna pee."

That earned a snicker from Day, and it did something funny to Jackson's chest to see him smile at Chloe. Keisha, however, was not one to be outdone by her baby sister. "Uncle Jack, I got a reading award at school."

"You did?" Jackson asked, putting as much pride in his voice as he could muster. "Well, that sounds like you deserve some whipped cream on your waffle."

"Gross. I want peanut butter," Keisha said.

"Now, you're talking," Day said. "Peanut butter on waffles is the bomb."

"Nobody says 'the bomb' anymore," Isaac said, watching Day warily and picking lint off his Spiderman t-shirt.

"Isaac Isiah Harrington. Is that how you speak to

grown ups?" Ruby asked.

"Sorry," he said, not sounding sorry at all. "I'm gonna go play Xbox in your room, Uncle Jack."

Jackson watched as Isaac shot up the stairs and threw open his bedroom door, not waiting for permission.

"Can I take my waffle upstairs and watch Isaac play *Assassin's Creed*?" Keisha asked.

"Yes, you may. Just don't get your sticky fingers all over my bed," Jackson said.

He finished prepping her waffle and handed it to her, watching her walk up the stairs at a much slower pace. Chloe didn't follow. She climbed up onto the stool beside Day and just stared at him while he drank his coffee. When Day noticed her, he frowned at her over his cup before setting it back on the counter. "Hi?" he said.

"Hi," she chirped.

"AJ, can you help me grab something out of my car, please?" Ruby asked.

Jackson knew there was nothing for her to get out of the car. She planned to interrogate him about why there was a client living in his home when there were several safe houses he could have chosen to take Day to. But he honestly had no answers and the last thing he needed was for his sister to see him wavering. She'd have his mother and sisters there before nightfall and

infuriating

Day would run screaming. He was far too fragile to be exposed to the entire Avery clan on the second day of knowing Jackson. Nobody was that strong. He'd seen those women bring Linc to heel with a look. Of course, they loved Wyatt and Day had very Wyatt-like qualities... He was just far more wounded.

"Can it wait a few minutes? I'd like to eat my breakfast," Jackson lied, ignoring the way Day's gaze shot to his, a silent cry not to be left alone with a small child.

"No, actually. It can't. I don't want it to wilt."

Wilt, his ass. Jackson had a black thumb. He couldn't even keep a fake plant alive. There was no way his sister would bring one of her precious babies to Jackson for him to murder. He was lucky she trusted him with her kids. She said it was because the kids were old enough to ask for food and water. He shook his head. She wasn't going to let this go.

Jackson sighed. "I'll be right back. Ten minutes. Don't open the door for anybody."

"Duh," Chloe said, her hand under her chin.

"Yeah, duh," Day said, mimicking her gesture.

Jackson grabbed his keys and followed his sister out the door, locking it behind him. They weren't even to the end of the hallway before she turned on him. "What's going on with you and Wonder Bread in there?"

"Don't call him that," Jackson said, side-eyeing her as they waited for the elevator.

"What? I'm just saying. You never bring clients to the house. Ever. And he's real pretty. Like flawless. I know you're a sucker for those boys with big blue eyes and a sob story. I saw the way you looked at him. You like him. Like, you like him-like him."

Jackson rolled his eyes as they stepped onto the elevator. "What are you, in middle school? You sound like Mom. I met him yesterday morning. He's a client. He's…prickly, and he witnessed something pretty traumatic, so I thought he'd be more comfortable here than in some bare bones safe house."

Ruby narrowed her eyes at him. "So, you're willing to risk the lives of the people in this building for his comfort? Sounds like he's more than a client. Besides, when was the last time you actually took on a client? Ever? You're the boss. You have tons of employees."

Jackson huffed out a sigh through his nose. "Ruby. Stop. He's not a client. Not officially. Jimmy asked me for a favor. As Dad's old partner. What was I going to say? No?"

Ruby shook her head. "You could just tell Mom the truth, you know? It's been a long time. She's ready to hear it."

infuriating

The doors to the elevator opened just in time. Jackson headed towards the front desk where a young desk attendant with brown hair flopping over his right eye was now seated. Jackson stopped at the desk, leaning over it menacingly. "Where were you when my sister got here ten minutes ago?"

"Wh-what?" the boy stammered, looking up at Jackson like he might hurt him.

"I pay an obscene amount of money for a desk that's guarded twenty-four-seven and that's what I expect. This desk is never to be unmanned."

"I just came on shift. J-Just now. I'll tell my supervisor."

"AJ! Stop scaring him. What is wrong with you?" his sister asked, her tone taking on a sharp edge.

Jackson tapped his hand on the desk. "I'm sorry. Please let your supervisor know I want to speak with him. Jackson Avery. Apartment 2501."

The desk clerk nodded, scribbling the details on a message pad. Jackson stomped towards his sister's Mercedes SUV that she'd parked illegally. "What is it you just had to give me?"

"Shit about having a stranger in your apartment. Seriously. Are my children safe here? Is somebody coming after him?"

"You think I'd let anything happen to those kids?

He wasn't the target, just a witness, but it's highly unlikely the killer even knows who Day is or where he lives. Jimmy is just being extra cautious because the victim was a high-level target."

"High-level target? You're not exactly making me feel better here," Ruby said, crossing her arms over her chest and cocking her hip to the side.

"Do you want me to watch your kids or not?" Jackson asked, leveling a stare at his sister. She was the only person who could make him lose his patience. "Just go to your luncheon thing and watch your husband get his award and leave the kids to me."

She snorted. "You can lie to yourself but you can't lie to me. There's something about that boy in there, and you and I both know it."

"Please, get in your car and drive away, woman."

"K, love you, bye," she chirped, using the same voice as his nieces.

Jackson watched her drive off before he started to make his way back up to the apartment, giving another wave of apology to the boy behind the desk as he went. When he reached his apartment, it was weirdly quiet. Jackson went to his office and flipped on the cameras. Keisha and Isaac were lying on Jackson's bed, Keisha munching on her waffle and Isaac's fingers flying on the controller. He flicked to the camera in the hallway just outside Day's open door. Inside, Day sat on the floor with Chloe, who had pulled several items from Day's drawers. She wore huge white sunglasses and a hot pink feather boa over her clothing. He had no idea what Day was saying to her but they were both emphatically gesturing to each other, like two old ladies at a cocktail party.

Jackson couldn't help but laugh. He kept the cameras focused on both rooms as he sat answering emails and checking in with Jimmy on where he was with the case, asking him to send the file so he could look it over himself. He had avenues he could search that the cops couldn't.

By the time Jackson got off his conference call, it was almost lunch time. As he walked up the stairs, he could hear Isaac and Keisha laughing and playing, but Day's room was quiet. When he glanced inside, it looked like the room had exploded. There were feathers and tulle and satin everywhere. It took him a moment to spot Day and Chloe because they sat on the other side of the bed, facing the windows. Day's head and shoulders were visible, his elbows propped on his knees. All he could see of Chloe was her wild curls, bleached a light brown by the sun.

"What's your book about?" Day asked, pointing to what Jackson imagined was the book in question.

Chloe looked down. "It's called *Maddi's Fridge*. Can you read it to me?"

Day was quiet for a long moment. "Uh, I don't have my glasses that help me read. Why don't you read to me?"

It was a lie. Day's glasses were on his face and, unlike Jackson, he was far too young to need reading glasses. Jackson wondered if he should interrupt. Chloe was sensitive about reading.

Chloe's voice dropped, like she was telling Day a big secret. "I don't read so good," she said in a stage whisper.

Jackson's heart ached for Chloe. She was struggling in school. She was only five, but Ruby and Darren had already had to hire tutors to help her. She had some type of processing disorder that required special tutors three times a week. She also read to dogs at a local shelter as part of a program initiative that made it less stressful for kids to read out loud since dogs wouldn't judge them. He hoped Day didn't push her too hard. Chloe was the sensitive one.

Day dropped his head, his whisper conspiratorial. "Can I tell you a secret?"

Chloe nodded solemnly, her big brown eyes wide.

"Promise not to tell anybody? It's a little embarrassing."

Jackson frowned, suddenly feeling like he was intruding but also leery about leaving a stranger to share secrets with his five-year-old niece. Chloe, like most little kids, didn't share Jackson's reservations.

"Pinky promise," she swore.

Day hooked his pinky with hers, leaning in. "I don't read so good, either."

"Really?" she asked, sounding awed.

Day nodded. "Yeah, really. So, why don't you read to me?"

"People make fun of me when I read," Chloe confided.

"I would never make fun of you," Day promised. "When I was your age, I was so bad at reading, I had to have a friend read for me. You can read to me and if you make a mistake, I won't even know, so you won't have to worry."

Jackson had never thought of that approach. Chloe didn't like to read in front of her parents or siblings because she was embarrassed, but now, she saw Day as an equal. She cracked the book open and began to read slowly.

Jackson headed back downstairs to the office and set about figuring out lunch, watching Day and Chloe on the monitor. He'd have to thank Day for that later, maybe with something that involved them both being naked. Day would at least give Jackson that, as long as it didn't seem like anything that resembled a date. Jackson had a feeling he was resigning himself to three months of Netflix and chill, but after seeing what Day had done for Chloe, Jackson was willing to go iceberg slow in the romance department.

Who would have thought Day would be a kid person? Who would have thought Jackson would want a guy who was a kid person?

nine

DAYTON

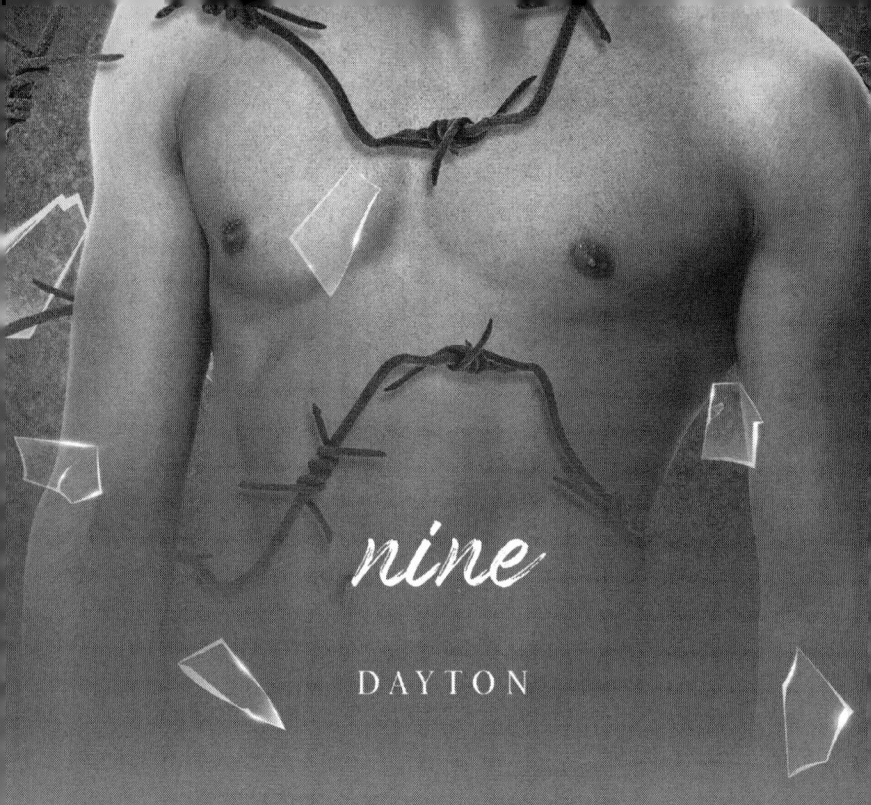

DAY WAITED UNTIL THE KIDS WERE GONE AND JACKSON was busy in the kitchen before he laid down on his bed, pulled out his laptop, and put his ear buds in. He used his voice activated software to log into his accounts. It was probably too soon for Jackson to notice the little things about Day, the things that everybody figured out once they got close. The way he kept his earbuds in all the time. The way he only used voice to text. That he tended to take too long to look over reading material or just signed things without pretending to read them at all.

It was all well and good in the beginning. People

who claimed to be his friends would, at first, think they were just little idiosyncrasies, until they realized Day not only used voice to text but that he also used software created for the blind that would read to him. Then his headphones became an annoyance, and his friends would ask why he didn't just go to one of those literacy schools for adults instead of cheating the system, as if Day had just never bothered to learn to read. He used to try to explain his disorder, that he had a severe form of dyslexia and dyscalculia. That it wasn't just a matter of learning to read but how his brain processed what he did read. That he still had a stutter when he was flustered or embarrassed. The support would eventually turn to annoyance and disbelief. But that usually took months. That's why Day didn't give people months. He didn't give anybody anything. It just wasn't worth the effort.

But Jackson was a different story. For some reason, the thought of somebody like Jackson belittling him or growing frustrated with him hurt far worse than the memory of anybody who'd made it past his walls in the past. Jackson was patient and kind and stable and hot and sexy and made Day's whole body quake with need.

Jackson wasn't like the guys Day had met when he and Sarah had run away all those years ago. Jackson

infuriating

was so far out of Day's league that they weren't even breathing the same air, and watching Jackson come to that realization would be more pain than it was worth. Day shook his head. He'd known Jackson for two days and he was worried about what he'd think of him? He was pathetic. It was just because he was the first guy with his shit together who'd ever shown an interest in Day. That had to be it. It didn't matter anyway. In just a few weeks, this stupid investigation would be over and Day could go back to his lonely little life and Jackson could meet some rich business tycoon and forget Day existed. At least Day had their tape to watch.

Which brought Day back to the task at hand. He hit a button, and the computerized male voice informed him that he had several comments on his latest video and almost two hundred dollars in tips. He smiled. He'd known his audience would love it. It had taken Day twice the usual time to edit and upload last night because he'd stopped to jerk off. Every whine, whimper, and moan Day made while Jackson fingered him on the tape had driven him to distraction until he'd had no choice but to get himself off.

Day closed his eyes and hit the button for the first comment, knowing the software would continue to read the messages one right after the other.

PYT8014: So hot. You two were hot like lava.

Hawt4U: Who's your new man?

Pattycake21: Yum. More please.

DTFU09: Did he win the contest? Is it over? Do we get to watch him fuck you?

Hawt4U: Yes. Please? We want to see you take that huge cock.

Ken4Ken: So pretty.

DannysDaddy666: whore whore whore whore whore whore whore whore whore whore whore whore whore whore wh—

Day pulled his earbuds from his ears and threw them on the side table before slamming his finger down on the spacebar to stop the voice from reading. His heart slammed against his ribs hard enough to make him feel lightheaded, his face burning with humiliation. He pushed his laptop away with shaking hands.

"Day, dinner's ready," Jackson said, leaning into Day's doorway.

"O-Okay," he managed, his tongue tripping over the word.

Jackson frowned. "You're white as a sheet. What's wrong? What happened?"

Day just shook his head. "No-Nothing. I'm f-f-f—" He huffed out a noise of frustration as his brain caught on the 'f,' causing the sound to go on for too long. "Fine," he finally ground out.

Jackson came to sit on the edge of the bed, resting his hand gently on Day's knee. "You're clearly not fine. What's happening? Did somebody upset you?"

Day could barely think past the heat of Jackson's hand on his thigh, as comforting as it was distracting. He didn't want to tell Jackson what it said. It was just a word. It came with the territory. It wasn't the first time somebody had called him a whore, and it wouldn't be the last. He should have just lied, but when he looked at Jackson and his big brown eyes filled with what looked like genuine concern, Day could only pick up his laptop and hand it to him.

"Do you know this guy?" Jackson asked, voice full of gravel, like he was trying to hold back something.

Day gave a helpless shrug. "I don't know any of them, not really. Some of them, like that guy, want to talk with me on Stripversity but he never has a picture. It's just always a dark screen. I talk. I perform. He watches. He never talks. A couple of weeks ago, he sent me a lot of money for no reason. A lot. It freaked me out, so I didn't touch it. I just left it in my cash app."

Jackson pulled his phone from his pocket and punched in a number. "Webster. Jackson. I need you to backtrace an internet user on an app called OnlyFans." Day wished he could quell the shaking of his insides, but it was impossible. It wasn't even the word…it was the rage beneath it. He glanced up at Jackson as he said, "I don't care how hard it is. I need you to track this guy. Now." Jackson's hand squeezed Day's knee again for emphasis, and Day hated that he felt better just from Jackson's touch. "If it's not life or death, drop it and work on this. No, there's no case number. No, I don't have to tell you what it's about. Call me when you have something."

When Jackson ended the call, he looked at Day and gave him a reassuring smile, which he didn't return. "You didn't have to do that. I'm probably just being stupid," Day muttered.

"You're not being stupid. This kind of behavior could be nothing or it could be some kind of escalation. This is what I do for a living, and that kind of response is…abnormal."

"I just mean I get messages like that from time to time," Day said, not bothering to argue Jackson's

infuriating

point about his intelligence, instinctively knowing that Jackson wouldn't allow him to call himself stupid, even if it was true.

"Then why did this one, in particular, upset you?" Jackson asked, his voice that same soothing tone that somehow lowered Day's pulse but doubled his craving to bury himself in his strong arms and just pretend the rest of the world didn't exist.

"I don't know. I guess because I wasn't expecting it on my OnlyFans account. That sort of thing is usually for the guys who show up in my live shows and want something for nothing, never from my supporters."

"Then it doesn't hurt to take a closer look at him," Jackson said. "Can you send me his info on CashApp and his screen name and what sites he follows you on?"

Day's panic swelled within him. "I can't right now," he blurted. "I'll have to look them up. I can get them to you later."

At Day's odd babbling, Jackson once more squeezed his thigh. "Webster's a pro. Your client will never know we were looking at him. I promise."

"Yeah, okay," Day said, letting out a deep breath.

Jackson stood, offering Day his hand. "Come eat dinner with me, and then we can find something to watch on television before you have to start working."

"Does it bother you?" Day said before snapping his

mouth shut. Why would he ask that? They didn't even know each other.

"Does what bother me?" Jackson asked.

Day scrambled to think of another logical question instead of the one he wanted to ask, but he froze, finally just asking what he really wanted to know. "What I do for a living. Does it bother you?"

Jackson's mouth turned down at the corners. "Does it bother you?"

Day scoffed, folding his arms across his chest. "Don't do that. Don't do that thing that shrinks do where they just repeat shit back until they tie you up in knots."

Jackson sat back down on the bed. "No. It doesn't bother me. If this is how you choose to make a living, it's your choice. I do wish you weren't planning on auctioning off your virginity, though."

Day gave him a smirk. "I thought you didn't 'do' virgins."

Jackson gave him an aborted smile. "I don't. But I also think the first person you let enter your body should at least be somebody you can trust to take some care with you."

Day rolled up onto his knees to kneel beside Jackson, cupping his face in his hands and kissing him long and slow. Then he pulled back. "Technically, you're the first person to have 'entered my body,'"

infuriating

Day reminded him, grabbing Jackson's right hand and sucking on the two fingers that he'd fucked into him the night before.

Jackson's response was immediate, his heated gaze melting Day's core and hardening his cock until it tented his joggers.

Jackson pushed his two fingers in and out, watching them disappear into Day's mouth. "Fuck, you are such a little tease," Jackson growled.

Day scrapped his teeth along Jackson's knuckles before pulling free and licking the palm of his hand. "Who's teasing, Daddy?"

"You'll do anything to keep from having to have a real conversation with me," Jackson mused.

Day stopped short, his expression growing stormy. "Is that what you think I'm doing? Using sex so I don't have to try to tax my brain by having an intelligent conversation with an adult?"

"Day—"

"Fuck you, Jackson."

Day rolled off the bed and strode into the bathroom, slamming the door shut like a sullen teenager, locking it behind him as if Jackson might follow. Day looked at himself in the mirror. *Way to fucking overreact, stupid. Now, he's going to think we're insane.*

He was insane. There was literally no reason for

him to have flipped out on Jackson like that. He barely knew the guy and Jackson had been nothing but nice to Day for the whole whopping two days they'd known each other. It was Day who was crazy. Day, who'd decided to invite Jackson into his bed and into his job. Day, who'd just turned a conversation about his safety into one about feelings and his virginity. Christ, he was fucking unstable. This was what came from locking himself away for the last three years, only associating with the outside world via computer.

There was a light knock on the door. "Day, I'm sorry I upset you, but you don't have to hide in the bathroom." Tears sprang to Day's eyes, and he wiped at them, his eyes instantly going bloodshot to match his red face. "I made pasta. If you don't want to eat with me, you can come get it and bring it to your room, or I'll just leave it in the microwave for you for later."

Day didn't answer, just leaned against the wall, shaking his head. He needed to fucking pull it together. It was day two in Jackson's home, and Day was already embarrassing himself by acting like a moody, clingy boyfriend.

Day removed his glasses and splashed some cold water on his face. When he opened the door to apologize, Jackson was gone. He peeked down over the living room to see Jackson on the sofa with his feet propped up on the coffee table, watching something sporty on the television. Day's bowl of pasta sat on the table, a respectable distance from Jackson's bare feet.

Day sighed, padding down the stairs barefoot and plopping down beside Jackson. He didn't acknowledge Day, other than flipping the channel to something that didn't involve watching somebody throwing or catching a ball. Day could have been offended by Jackson's assumption that Day didn't like sports, but he fucking hated sports and didn't want to sit through a game to try to prove that he could like makeup and football when he just didn't.

Jackson clicked onto a movie, and Day waved his hand, trying to swallow his pasta. "Go back. Go back. That's the best movie ever."

Jackson frowned, going back two channels, and laughed. "This movie? You want to watch *Don't Tell Mom the Babysitter's Dead?*"

"You disagree?" Day asked, leveling a stare at Jackson, daring him to disagree.

Jackson's gaze softened, and Day realized that Jackson could see his blotchy face and red eyes. "It was okay, I guess," he teased. "Can we at least start it over from the beginning?"

"Yes, please," Day said, bouncing a bit in his seat as he stuffed another fork full of pasta into his mouth.

When nothing happened, Day turned to find Jackson just looking at him with a strange look on his face. "Whah?" he asked, his mouth still full of bowtie pasta.

Jackson just shook his head with a smile. "Nothing."

A few presses of the remote's buttons and the movie was starting over again. Once they finished eating, Day couldn't help but notice how Jackson moved closer until they were almost touching. Day wanted nothing more than to close the distance between them and just wrap himself around Jackson's arm and rest his head on his shoulder. Somehow, Day knew Jackson would let him, but he just couldn't bring himself to do it. This was all a weird illusion, a false intimacy that came with being forced to play house together. Still, he glanced up at Jackson anyway.

When Jackson's gaze strayed to Day and he saw him staring, he asked, "What? What's wrong?"

"Sorry," Day said, forcing the word past the lump in his throat.

Jackson frowned. "For what?"

"For flipping out on you upstairs. I'm just…I don't know…overwhelmed."

Jackson shrugged. "Don't even worry about it. I have three sisters, an entire team of bodyguards who are bigger divas than the people they're hired to guard, and a slew of friends who make what happened up

infuriating

there seem like a walk in the park."

"I don't know if that makes me feel any better," Day said.

Jackson grinned and slapped a kiss on Day's forehead. "As long as it doesn't make you feel worse."

ten

JACKSON

"I GOT NOTHING."

"Since when is 'I got nothing' an acceptable answer?" Jackson asked, pinching the bridge of his nose as he glanced over to where Day stood on the balcony, phone in the air, making peace signs and smiling into the camera.

"Okay," Webster said. "Will you accept 'I have nothing useful'?"

Jackson sighed. "Then tell me what you found that isn't useful."

Sometimes, it felt as if the people working for him deliberately tried to goad him into losing his shit.

infuriating

That's just not who he was as a person. It never had been. Anger never helped a situation. Ever. It only added fuel to the fire. Years of watching his father and mother argue had taught him that. They had both been stubborn and foul tempered and neither was ever willing to admit fault, at least to each other. Luckily, his parents hadn't taken the same approach with their children.

"I traced the username back to a sockpuppet account and a stolen credit card. They've been using it for months, but the person it belongs to seems to have fallen off the face of the earth, which I'm guessing is a bad sign and also why they haven't reported their card stolen."

Jackson's gaze pulled back to Day, unease tugging at his insides. Would this anonymous stranger be willing to kill to get to Day? Did the district attorney's death even have anything to do with his job, or could this person be trying to take out anybody he perceived as competition? It could explain his fury over Day's video. Or not. It was all just supposition at this point.

"Jack? You still there?" Webster called, his voice taking on a singsong tone.

"Yeah. Listen, I need you to do a deep dive into Day's followers. Cross reference his accounts and make a list of his most active users. Find out which ones live close by. Also, this user sent Day six thousand dollars that's sitting in his CashApp account. See if you can trace it to a bank or credit company and see if it matches our sockpuppet. Also, keep this between us. I don't want Day finding out."

Webster snorted. "Now what will we talk about while we paint each other's nails?" he snarked before adding, "You know I've never even laid eyes on this guy, right? Okay, well, I've definitely laid my eyes on him. All of him." Jackson growled at the thought of Webster laying anything on Day. "Hey, I'm kidding. You and this kid tight or something? I'm just saying, why would I say anything to him?"

"Not him. I'll talk to him. Anybody else. Elite has more leaks than the *Titanic*. You tell Linc and he'll tell Wyatt, and then Wyatt and Charlie will somehow weasel their way into Day's DMs, and my life will become a shit show."

Webster snickered. "I never thought you'd be afraid of the twink and the dink. What do you think they'll do? Trick you into falling in love with your little shutterbug?"

"Shutterbug?" Jackson asked, deliberately ignoring Webster's baiting.

"Yeah. He's having a field day snapping photos of himself on your balcony. Hashtag beautiful day,

infuriating

hashtag smile, hashtag hello sunshine, hashtag hustle," Webster said around a laugh.

Jackson smiled as he looked out on the balcony once more, but his smile died as he noted that Day wasn't smiling at all. He was now lying on one of Jackson's lounge chairs, knees tucked under his chin as he gazed out over the railing, looking like the weight of the world rested on his narrow shoulders. How much of Day's online life was just theatre? Was he ever really happy? Did he love camming as much as he said he did? "Just get it done, and let me know the second you have anything that could help me."

Webster's joking tone disappeared. "You're the boss."

Once Jackson disconnected, he watched Day in profile. He leaned his head back, teeth clamped down on his bottom lip, and gazed out at the clear blue sky. Day had gone upstairs after they'd watched their movie the night before, Jackson following closely behind, reaching the top step only to hear Day's bedroom door lock click into place. Jackson hadn't been surprised, but he had been more than a little disappointed. More than anything, he wanted a chance to catch Day just being himself, not the caricature of himself he played for the audience, even if that Day was surly and argumentative and mercurial. Jackson wanted it. But Day was slippery. Just when Jackson thought Day might be warming up to him, the claws came out.

Jackson wandered to the sliding glass doors and pulled them open. Day looked up, eyes going wide, before he wiggled his fingers at Jackson in a hello. Day wore shorts that barely covered his ass and an old t-shirt with no sleeves that were cut down the sides. He looked sexy as hell, and the coy look and sly smile he gave Jackson told him Day knew it, too.

Jackson took the chair beside him. "Everything go okay online last night?" Did he sound jealous? "No problems with any of your…clients?"

Day's smile disappeared, and he went back to looking out over the city once more. "No. It was slow last night. I only made fifty bucks. None of my regulars were there."

"Maybe you should take some time off?" Jackson regretted the words as soon as they left his mouth. The last thing they needed was Day taking time off, especially if he was the intended target, but Jackson hated the idea of putting a bullseye on his back.

Day scowled. "I can't afford to take time off. Do you have any idea how much my piece of shit apartment costs in rent?"

The offer to pay Day's bills was on the tip of Jackson's tongue, but he knew Day would be furious at such a suggestion. The idea of taking Jackson's money would definitely push him over the edge.

"Do you think your client could have had anything to do with that DA's murder?" Jackson asked, trying to make his tone as casual as possible.

Day's head whipped to Jackson, his pale face turning ghost white. "Is…is that what they think? They think this is my fault?"

Jackson's brows knitted together. "None of this is your fault. This isn't about fault. It's about finding out who's responsible before somebody else gets hurt. Somebody like you."

"Tell me the truth. Do they think this guy killed Jay because of me?" Day asked, breathless.

Jackson shook his head. "No. They still think it has something to do with his caseload. I'm just trying to run down every possible lead, and your client was very unhappy about seeing me in your video."

Once more, Day's face morphed into his sex kitten expression, lids heavy and lips wet, as he uncurled himself from the chair and made himself at home in Jackson's lap, straddling his thighs. His hands came around Day without thought, gripping his ass and dragging him close, flexing his hips upward so Day could feel him harden against him.

Day traced Jackson's lips with his finger. "You're so

fucking hot."

Jackson grinned. "Oh, yeah?"

"Mm," Day murmured, lips finding Jackson's, his tongue briefly slipping inside before darting back out. "Is anybody stopping by today?"

Jackson shook his head.

Day slipped from Jackson's lap onto his knees, pushing a few buttons on his phone before handing it to Jackson. "Start recording," Day said, his hands unbuttoning and unzipping Jackson's jeans. "Up," he demanded.

Jackson chuckled but shifted to let Day drag his underwear and jeans to his ankles. He shifted, slouching in the chair to give Day more access. He hummed his approval, his hand closing around Jackson's shaft, stroking him slowly as he kitten-licked over the head, gathering the fluid there onto his tongue and showing it to the camera.

Jackson groaned as Day played, dragging his lips and tongue up one side of Jackson's cock and down the other, Day's hand massaging his balls. "Fuck. Stop teasing and suck me."

Day dragged his shirt over his head and tossed it aside, looking up at Jackson. "Yes, Daddy."

Day could give a masterclass on blowjobs. The only thing hotter than his cock disappearing down

infuriating

Day's throat was watching it happen through the camera lens. Day was so beautiful on his knees, taking Jackson's dick deeper with each pass until he was buried in Day's mouth, his throat spasming around Jackson in a way that made him crazy. His hand went to the back of Day's head, fingers twisting in his hair as he rocked his cock even deeper. "That's it. Swallow my cock. So fucking good."

Day's fingers flexed, letting Jackson know he needed air. When Day pulled off, his eyes were tearing but he had a smile that showed he was pleased with himself. "Can I touch myself, Daddy?"

"I don't know. You've been kind of a brat. Do you think you deserve to touch yourself?" Day nodded but his expression said something else. "I don't know. Maybe I should just jerk myself off while you suck my balls?"

Day pouted, his tongue circling the crown of Jackson's cock, sucking it until it was slick with his saliva. "Please, Daddy? I'll be good."

"Are you already hard?" Jackson asked, knowing full well he was.

Day nodded. "Yes, Daddy."

"Show me."

Day got up onto his knees and pushed his shorts down, his cock slapping against his belly, flushed pink and already wet at the tip. Day looked up at the camera lens, but he was really looking at Jackson, big blue eyes wide, still wet from tears, as he stroked his flat belly. "See how hard I am for you, Daddy?"

Pleasure spiked through Jackson's blood. Day was an absolute tease, but he was so fucking beautiful. "Lean back so I can see."

Day rested his weight on his left hand so Jackson could see everything. "Mm, you are hard. Show Daddy how you get yourself off at night."

Day licked his palm and then wrapped his hand around his cock. Jackson adjusted his position so the camera caught him stroking his own hard cock as well as Day's body splayed out before him. Day jerked himself slowly, never taking his eyes off Jackson.

Jackson squeezed the base of his cock to keep from coming, already keyed up from Day's hot, wet mouth and now watching him get himself off. "That feel good, baby?"

"Not as good as your hand, Daddy," Day gasped.

"You haven't earned my hand. You were a bad boy last night." Jackson watched Day's nipples harden at the comment, a whimper escaping his lips. "You like being bad, huh? You want Daddy to punish you? Put you over my knee and spank your bare bottom?"

Day whined, his eyes flying open at Jackson's

infuriating

taunt, his hips bouncing as he fucked his fist harder and faster. "Yes, please, Daddy. Oh, fuck. I'm going to come," Day cried, sounding almost surprised, his seed spilling over his fingers as he continued to stroke himself, his bliss evident as his face went slack.

"Come here," Jackson growled.

Day swayed back up onto his knees as Jackson gripped the boy's sticky fist and used it to slick his own dick before gripping Day's hair and tugging him towards his throbbing erection. "Suck me off. Make me come. I want to watch you lick your cum off my cock."

Day made a tiny gasping sound, but then his tongue shot out, licking Jackson from root to tip before taking him back into the warm damp heat of his perfect mouth. Jackson didn't hold back, and neither did Day. He relaxed his throat as Jackson worked himself in and out, unable to tear his gaze away from Day's lips and the soft slide of his tongue. Christ, he was already so close. His hand tightened in Day's hair even as he warned him, "I'm gonna come. You're gonna take it all."

Day whined around Jackson's cock, and that was it—he was shooting down Day's throat even as Day sucked harder, like he didn't want to waste even a single drop.

Day didn't even pull off once he swallowed. He stayed on his knees, his head resting on Jackson's thigh while his dick went soft. Jackson wasn't exactly sure what Day was doing but it felt nice, so he just let Day do as he pleased, stroking his hands through his platinum tresses.

After another ten minutes passed, Day suddenly sat up then stood up, pulling his shorts back into place and walking towards the sliding glass door without another word. "Where are you going?"

"To upload the video to my OnlyFans."

Jackson wasn't one to find himself speechless, but he sat there gaping at Day, his dick still lying soft against his thigh.

"What? You think this guy might be a psycho because he didn't want you touching me. How do you think he'll react when I upload this?"

Jackson gave a startled laugh. "Yeah, you're right. I guess we're going fishing."

Day sashayed into the house as Jackson fixed his clothes and thought about everything that had just happened. Was any of it real? Which Day was the real one? Were any of them real? Jackson walked into the kitchen and poured himself a finger of whiskey, gulping it straight down. Three days in and Day was twisting Jackson into knots. What would a lifetime feel like?

Jackson's stomach burned, but he wasn't sure if it was the alcohol, or the thought of a lifetime with Day.

eleven

DAYTON

DAY MANAGED TO KEEP HIS STEPS SMOOTH AND HIS glide across the living room to the stairs slow and steady. He gripped the banister on either side to keep his hands from shaking. *It was just a scene. It was just a scene.* The camera lens between them was supposed to keep some distance. If the camera was on them, then this was all for show. A way to bring a new audience, to make some money. That's all he needed. Money. Enough money to get out of Los Angeles for good, his promise be damned.

It wasn't like Day hadn't tried. He had. But he wasn't smart or talented like Sarah. When she was on stage, people couldn't take their eyes off of her. Day was pretty enough, and with Sarah around to help him memorize his scripts, he'd even gotten a couple of bit parts and walk-on roles, but it wasn't enough to keep food on their table…or get Sarah the medications she needed.

Day blinked back tears and forced the thought of Sarah from his head. He couldn't let himself think about her. She'd just have to understand that Los Angeles had been her dream, not his. He was her people, she'd been the star. He transferred the video to his laptop. Uploading the video was muscle memory at this point, but he still needed his voice to text options to create a caption that would hopefully get him more tips. He took a deep breath as the video began to upload. Get him more tips and potentially antagonize a stalker, who Jackson thought was willing to kill for him.

Jackson. What was Day supposed to do about him? Jackson was big and strong and just so rock steady. Whenever Day was near him, everything just felt… safe. Day felt safe—safe from the constant turmoil that rocked him almost daily. Did he have food, and if he had food, did he have rent, and if he made rent, could he still pay for the internet and bus fare? Those things still existed. He still needed money to pay his bills,

infuriating

but, somehow, Jackson made all the noise in Day's head go quiet for a little bit, and it was such a good feeling, Day had slipped. He'd stayed on his knees, the concrete balcony floor pushing tiny microscopic grains into his flesh, just to rest his head on Jackson's thigh, just to feel his fingers push through his hair, like somebody gave a fuck about him. Like Jackson gave a fuck about him.

Why couldn't Jackson see that he was tying Day in knots with his strong hands and soft lips and dirty talk that liquified Day's insides? Jackson was perfect. A walking fantasy. Gorgeous, funny, successful. The perfect Daddy. Day's perfect Daddy. Which was why he needed to pull it together. The wall he'd built wasn't nearly high enough for somebody like Jackson. He was too steady, too persistent. He'd patiently erode Day's walls, like water beating against rock, day after day. He could feel that. Jackson looked at Day like he was worthy of somebody like Jackson, but it just wasn't true. Jackson needed somebody who could match his success, who could be his equal. Somebody who could read past a third grade level and not stutter anytime he was overwhelmed.

If Day was braver, he'd just say so. But he wasn't. Instead, he'd hide in his room and work on building better walls. But, in the deepest parts of his core, he knew it didn't matter. If Jackson wanted something from Day, he'd try to give it to him. At least, physically. He'd just come so hard, he was sure his heart was going to explode, but if Jackson walked in there and ordered Day onto his knees again, he wouldn't refuse. If Jackson wanted any part of Day, he'd give it to him. Day could give Jackson his body, even if it broke him in the end. It would be worth it. Something Jackson could tuck away and pull out, like a photograph or souvenir. A tether to something he had almost had.

When the video finally loaded, Day stared at the title line for a while before deciding on *Daytime Fun with Daddy*. If that didn't get his stalker good and pissed then Jackson's theory was wrong and Jay's murder had nothing to do with Day. He really hoped it had nothing to do with him. Day didn't think he could handle being responsible for the deaths of two people. He hadn't loved Jay. Hell, he'd hardly known him, but he'd always been good to Day, sending him money, presents, and checking in on him. Day had never found him particularly attractive, but the attention had felt nice.

He startled when his phone rang. He frowned at an LA number he didn't recognize. "Hello?"

"Day? It's Wyatt. How's prison life at the palace treating you?"

infuriating

Day's shoulders sagged. "I'm so bored. There's only so much television a person can watch, you know?" Day lied.

"Well, you're either driving Jackson up a wall or he's desperate to make you happy because he called to see if Charlie and I wanted to come over and keep you company for a bit."

"He did?"

"Yeah. Who knew we were both still young enough for our Daddies to arrange playdates?"

'W-What?" Day stuttered, his heart rate tripling.

"Sorry, bad joke. Do you want to hang out with us for a while?"

Day forced himself to relax. "How fast can you get here?"

Wyatt gave a laugh that made Day think of floating. "We're already on our way."

"SO, WHAT DO YOU DO HERE ALL DAY . . . DAY?" Charlie asked, her long nails scratching over his scalp, like he was her new favorite pet. Day imagined being Charlie's favorite pet would be a step up from his current life. The gorgeous brunette smelled like suntan lotion and dressed like a pop star, but she had flopped on his bed like they'd been friends forever and then had patted the spot beside her like they'd known each other all their lives. That's how he'd ended up with his head in her lap. Day was a little fuzzy on how Wyatt's head had ended up resting on his thigh, but it felt nice, like having actual friends.

Day's hand played through Wyatt's golden curls, finding the act of touching the other pretty boy as soothing as Charlie's thorough petting. "Nothing much. We watch television. Jackson cooks. Oh, I met his sister and his nieces and nephew yesterday."

Day's sentence was the literal embodiment of a record scratch. All motion ceased. "What? What'd I say?"

"You met Jackson's family? Like, his actual flesh and blood family?" Charlie asked.

Day tipped his head up to look at Charlie. "I mean, I didn't get a DNA test, but that's how he introduced them."

"What's his sister like? Is she tall? Is she hot? Does she look like she could bench press a Buick?" Charlie questioned, her voice both excited and yet somehow conspiratorial, like Day was dishing some juicy gossip.

"She seemed nice. I'm not sure she liked me much. She was really pretty. Kind of tiny. Good fashion sense. She definitely was surprised to see me there, so I'm guessing he didn't tell her about me…I mean, me

infuriating

being a client. She thought I was his boyfriend."

"Oh?" Charlie asked. It was one of those *ohs* that smacked of fake disinterest.

It made Day laugh. "Yeah, oh."

"In her defense, Elite does have a bit of a history of bodyguards marrying their clients."

This time, Day was the one who stopped the petting. "They do?"

"Yeah," Charlie confirmed. "Wyatt down there started the trend by marrying Linc."

"Guilty," Wyatt said, sounding dreamy. "I'm most definitely not sorry."

Charlie laughed. "Then Elijah Dunne married his bodyguard, Shep, and moved out of LA. Though I can't imagine why anybody would want to live anywhere but here to be honest."

"I guess I sort of remember hearing about that. Then his ex-boyfriend ended up in the headlines because he was all heartbroken or something?" Day asked.

"Yeah, until he met Calder, who wanted to do a lot more than guard his body. They now live in the middle of nowhere with a mess of foster kids and rescue animals. Robby became a preacher. Nobody saw that coming. They're happy, though."

"Weird," Day managed, trying not to let jealousy coat his tongue.

Wyatt shifted, shrugging. "Not when you grew up in a cult."

"What?" Day managed.

"Nothing. So, anyway. What do you think of Jackson, really? You said you thought he was hot when we talked the other day. Still think so?"

Day froze. Was this some kind of set-up? "I'm not blind. He's gorgeous. But we're never going to happen." When neither of them responded, he looked up at Charlie then down at Wyatt. "What? I'm serious. There's nothing there."

"Tell him, Wyatt," Charlie ordered softly.

"Okay, like, don't freak out, but when we met the other day, I sort of signed up for your OnlyFans."

Day's pulse pounded in his ears, his mouth a desert. "Yeah?"

"That's totally Jackson in that video. How did you convince him to crawl into bed with you the first night?" Wyatt asked, sounding impressed.

Day had no idea what to say. Should he lie? Tell them it was none of their business? It wasn't but still. "I don't know. We were just super flirty from the jump. I made the offer, he accepted. No big deal."

"Are you kidding? Jackson is the most private person ever. Like, he hardly ever talks about himself. Linc didn't even think he liked guys, which I thought was strange because I was totally convinced they'd hooked up when they were in the military," Wyatt said.

"Maybe you were just hoping they had. I'm sure you wouldn't have had a problem being the meat in that particular sandwich," Charlie snarked.

Wyatt scoffed. "Like you would? You tried to get in Jackson's pants, too."

"You did?" Day asked, hating how indignant he sounded.

Charlie rolled her eyes. "Relax, Daydream. He didn't even accept my friend request on Facebook. He's all yours."

"He's really not," Day swore, the words sounding hollow to his own ears. "I don't do relationships. Neither does Jackson. It's just temporary. Casual. No feelings. Just sex."

"Okay, Day. Okay," Charlie soothed. "Whatever you say."

"Are you going to at least let him punch your v-card?" Wyatt asked, looking at Day expectantly.

Of course, he'd seen that on his OnlyFans. Day sighed internally. He missed this. Friends. He missed Sarah. He missed having somebody to talk to, someone he could tell everything to.

"If he wants to bid on it like everybody else," he lied.

"Damn, you're a savage, Daydream. I like it,"

Charlie said around a laugh.

Day's answering laugh was empty. Jackson could have his virginity with nothing more than a crook of his finger. Day knew it. Jackson knew it. He was pretty sure Wyatt and Charlie knew it, too. But if Day let Jackson in, all the way in, into his body and his soul, it was all over for him. He'd be screwed. Three days. It had only taken Jackson three days to erode his walls enough to make Day care, to make him want things that weren't meant for him. Where would Day be in three months when this was all over and Jackson was gone and Day had to go back to his old life? He didn't want to think about that.

"Don't hate the player, hate the game," Day said.

The three of them burst out laughing all at once, sounding like a bunch of drunken teenagers.

Jackson's voice boomed from downstairs. "What are you guys getting into up there?"

"Oop, Daddy's mad," Charlie said before they all erupted into another fit of laughter.

God, Day *really* missed having friends.

twelve

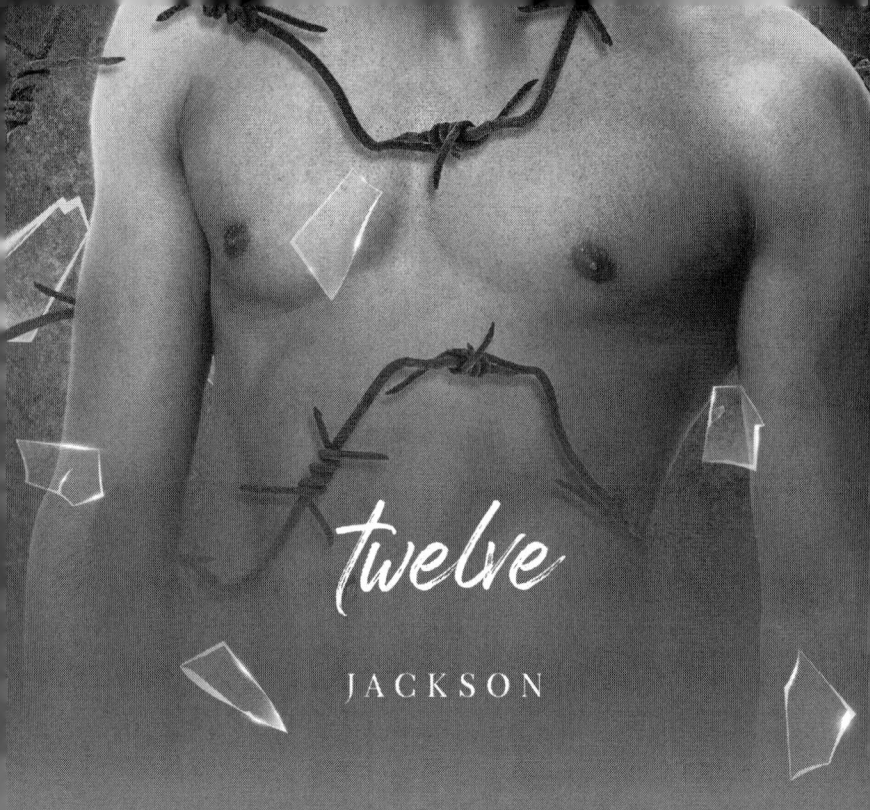

JACKSON

JACKSON COULDN'T BELIEVE HE'D LECTURED WEBSTER about keeping his mouth shut to keep Charlie and Wyatt away only to call them in himself. Setting the two of them loose on Day was a dirty move, but Jackson didn't know what else to do. It was clear to Jackson that Day was conflicted. About everything. He was also lonely. For as much as he had seemed afraid to be alone with the kids yesterday, he'd seemed to enjoy Chloe's company. Jackson only seemed to make Day nervous or upset…or horny.

Jackson didn't mind that last one, except, when it was over, Day immediately ran away. He was hiding something. Or maybe he was afraid. Of what, Jackson wasn't sure. He didn't think it was him. No, Day seemed to thoroughly enjoy teasing Jackson, toying with him, even fighting or verbally sparring with him. But there was something there between them that Jackson just couldn't get past. They'd only known each other for a few days. Jackson needed to be patient. That's all.

Jackson's cell phone vibrated across the kitchen countertop angrily. He sighed, picking it up. "Hello?"

"Hey, boss. It's Hurley."

Hurley was in charge of the Miami branch while Jackson was out of town. "What's up?"

"Angel Fuentes is losing his shit. Says he's pulling his account."

Angel was one of his biggest clients. A small arms dealer who gave Jackson a lot of money to protect his men during transactions. "What? Why? What the fuck happened?"

"Shit went south in Bogotá. Garcia says it was just a misunderstanding, but Fuentes is saying one of his men ended up with a bullet in his knee and is now disabled for life. I tried to appease him, but he only wants to talk to you."

"I'll set up a phone meeting," Jackson said.

"He wants it face to face. He wants you down here

by tomorrow night or he's walking with his whole account."

Fuck.

"Yeah, alright. Call Pam and ask her to book a private charter and a spot on the terrace at La Mar for tomorrow night. I'll start packing my bag."

He hung up as Wyatt and Charlie came bounding down the stairs. "Bye, Jackson," they called out in unison.

"Bye," he echoed, staring up at Day's open doorway.

Jackson walked up the stairs, resigned. He'd see if Linc could come stay with Day for the next few days while he tried to work things out with Fuentes. It was the logical thing to do. If Jackson was going to pull this one out of the fire, he needed to focus.

Day laid on his belly across the bed, those short white shorts he'd worn earlier molded to the generous swell of his ass as he thumbed over whatever he was looking at on his phone. Jackson crossed the room, blanketing Day's body with his own. Day gave a startled breathy laugh before crossing his arms and resting his cheek on them so he could see Jackson over his shoulder. "Back for more already?" Day asked before catching his lower lip between his teeth in a look that let Jackson know Day wouldn't refuse him. The thought had him getting hard once more.

"Don't tempt me any more than you already are in those shorts," Jackson said, his lips brushing across Day's jaw and cheek. Jackson just couldn't stop touching him. It was maddening. He pressed his cock against Day's ass. Day wiggled beneath him invitingly. "Stop distracting me, you little tease."

There was no malice in his words. If anything, the taunt only made Day more flirty, tilting his hips so he was grinding himself against Jackson's throbbing erection.

"If you don't stop that, I'm going to drag those shorts off you and bury myself in that tight little ass of yours, auction be damned," Jackson growled.

Day's answering whimper went straight to his cock. "I love it when you talk dirty to me," he whispered, his voice breathy and strained.

"You'd let me fuck you, wouldn't you?" Jackson asked, his voice like gravel. "You'd let me peel those shorts off you, work you open nice and slow, before sinking my cock into you inch by inch."

"Yes, Daddy."

"Fuck, you're so good for me. Such a good boy for me," Jackson said, his lips finding Day's, his tongue slipping inside, teasing at Day's. The angle was awkward, but Day didn't seem to care. He was gone, melted into the bed, his hips pressing into the mattress before pushing up into Jackson's dick.

Jackson lifted his weight off of Day, and he whined out his disappointment. Jackson reached for the lube that was already on the nightstand, snagging it and tossing it beside Day before dragging his shorts down and out of the way along with his jeans and underwear. Jackson pulled Day back against him so they were both on their sides, Day's ass snug up against Jackson's cock once more. Jackson lubed up his cock, pressing it into the crease of Day's bottom, before his slick hand closed around Day's flushed cock. Day gasped as Jackson began to move, his erection sliding between Day's cheeks, fist jerking Day in time with his thrusts.

It wasn't as good as sinking himself into Day's tight pink hole, but it was close. Day was moaning and whining, rocking back against Jackson even as he thrust forward into his hand. There was nothing coy or teasing about this. This was just about getting off. It was about giving each other some version of what they both needed. "Fuck, you feel so good, Daddy. You feel so good."

Jackson dragged his lips across whatever skin he found—Day's ear, his throat, his shoulder. Day's fingers dug into the arm underneath his head, his nails digging into the skin of Jackson's forearm where it was locked across Day's chest. "You can come whenever you want," Jackson said between gritted teeth, his own orgasm already building in his balls.

"Unf," was Day's only response. He was too far gone, his whole body writhing against Jackson's as he jerked him hard and fast, palm twisting with each upward motion, thumb swiping across the tip to gather the fluid there and work it across his shaft on the way down.

Day clenched each time he tried to thrust into Jackson's palm, cocooning Jackson's cock in a tight slick heat that was just enough to do the trick, just enough to make Jackson crave more.

Suddenly, Day cried out, and Jackson's fist grew wet and sticky with the evidence of Day's pleasure. Jackson pushed Day down onto his stomach so he could straddle his hips and lock his arms around him, burying himself between the slick heat of Day's cheeks, pretending he was thrusting inside as he worked himself against Day, his teeth sinking into Day's shoulder as he felt his release building. He was so close. So fucking close.

"I want you inside me so bad, Daddy," Day panted.

Jackson gripped Day's hair hard as he came, his hips stuttering, his cum pooling in the dip of Day's lower back. Jackson collapsed on top of him, too tired to care about clean-up.

infuriating

"Well, that was unexpected," Day muttered against the comforter. "Should I expect these visits every day?"

"I didn't come up here for this, but then I saw you, and I'd forgotten how hot these shorts look on you, and I just couldn't help myself."

"You're forgiven," Day said, a smile in his voice. "What did you come up here for?"

"I have to go out of town."

Jackson felt Day tense beneath him. "You're leaving me?"

"Come with me."

The words sprung from his mouth before he could even think about it, but he didn't retract his invitation. It might even defuse the situation with Fuentes. Their son was a fairly well known drag queen on the Miami scene. They had no problem with homosexuality. Even if they did, Jackson still would have brought Day. Jackson didn't want to be away from him, not even for three days. He didn't examine the thought too closely.

"You want me to go with you?" Day repeated, almost like he was certain he'd misheard him.

"Yeah. I mean, it's a business trip, so you'll have to sit in my office while I check on the Miami branch and sit through what could be a rather tedious business dinner, but the food is good and the view is amazing."

Day craned his neck around as far as he could manage to look at Jackson. "You really want me to go or are you just afraid to leave me alone here?"

Jackson kissed Day's cheek. "I really want you to go. I have a dozen guys who could babysit you while I'm away if I wanted to leave you here."

"When do we leave?"

Jackson smiled, genuinely happy to have Day along for the trip. "I'm not sure. Pam still has to set up our charter, but I'm sure we can get a jet by tonight."

"A jet? We're taking a jet? Like a private jet?" Day asked.

Jackson frowned. "Yeah, why? Do you have a fear of flying?"

Day shrugged. "I don't know. I've never been on an airplane before."

Jackson rolled off of Day, grimacing at the cum already flaking on his skin, still digesting that piece of news. "Why don't you take a quick shower and then start packing? You don't have to bring much. We'll only be gone a couple of days."

Day rolled over. "I don't have a suitcase."

Jackson rose to his feet, stretching before he straightened his clothing for the second time that day. "I do. Hop in the shower, and I'll leave it on your bed."

Jackson started to walk away when he realized Day

infuriating

wasn't moving. He turned back to find him sitting on the bed, hair adorably rumpled and shorts still caught around his knees. He was so fucking beautiful.

"What's wrong?"

"Maybe I shouldn't go."

Jackson frowned at Day's sudden lack of enthusiasm. "What? Why?"

Day looked away from Jackson. "I don't want to embarrass you."

"Why would you embarrass me?"

"What if your business associate asks who I am to you? What if he asks what I do for a living? What if I wear the wrong thing or say the wrong thing?"

Jackson walked back to Day and pulled him to his feet. "You worry too much," he said, kissing his nose. "The guy we're meeting is a gun runner. He has no business looking down his nose at anybody, least of all you. You tell him whatever you're comfortable telling him. I don't care what he thinks of you. The only opinion I've ever cared about is mine…and my mama's…'cause she scares me."

"Well, hopefully your gun runner friend likes me more than your sister did."

Jackson laughed. "My sister liked you a lot. If she didn't, she would have eviscerated you on sight. She's mean. All the women in my family are."

Day gave a shy smile. "Then how come you're so sweet?"

"Survival. Plus I was the only boy. That helped." Day still looked like he was wavering. "Stop thinking so hard and go shower. Everything is going to be okay. I promise."

Day gave a stilted nod and kicked off his shorts before walking towards his bathroom, naked from the waist down. Jackson averted his eyes, fearing he might change his mind and follow Day right into the shower. There was no way his body would rally again so fast, but he just couldn't seem to keep his hands off Day. Every time he touched him, he just wanted to touch him more. It was both exciting and frustrating.

thirteen

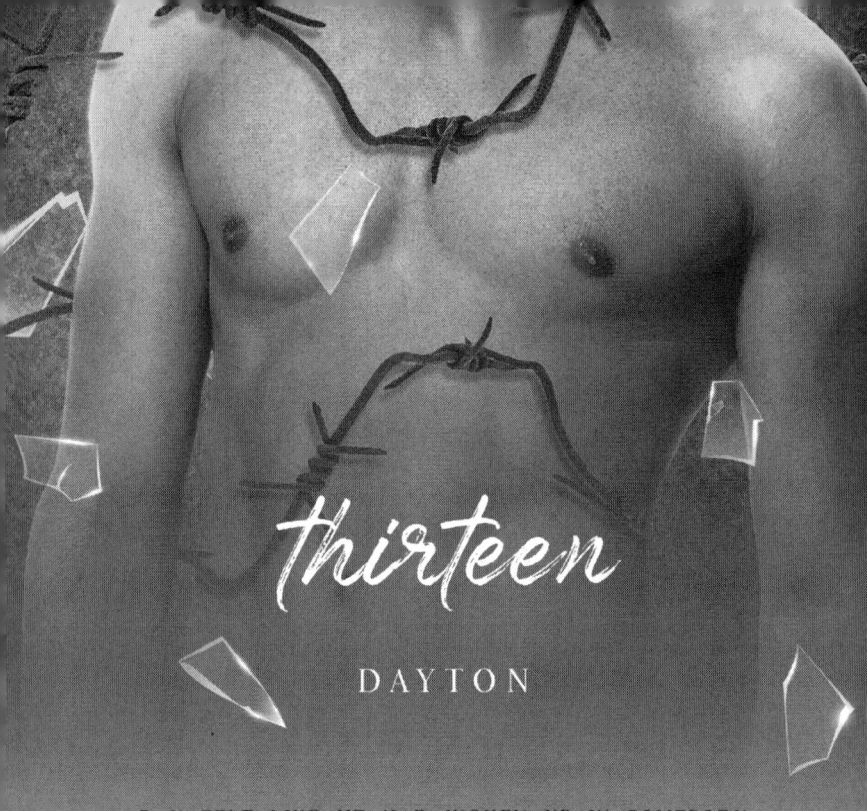

DAYTON

DAY FELT LIKE HE HAD WOKEN UP IN SOMEBODY else's life. Jackson sat beside him in the back of a black Cadillac Escalade while a prim older woman with bright red hair in a navy business suit sat across from him, firing off his itinerary like he was a celebrity. "Before you meet with Fuentes, you need to stop by the office. There's a contract on your desk that Calliope said can't wait for your signature. She was going to overnight it to you, but this will be easier. Also, I thought you'd want to meet up with Hurley to figure out how you plan on disciplining the guys to appease Angel's blood thirst before your seven thirty dinner reservations at La Mar. Ricky picked up your suits from the dry cleaners and left them on your bed for you. Is there anything else you need me to do for you while you're away, sir?" she asked as their car rolled to a stop on the tarmac.

"No, Nancy. I think that's everything. Thanks for taking a ride. I really didn't want to have to do this over the phone."

She gave him a bright smile just as Jackson slid his sunglasses back on. "No problem, Mr. Avery. Anything to get out of the office for an hour or so."

Jackson grinned, and Day swore the older woman swooned like he was Idris Elba. It was that way everywhere they went. Girls and guys couldn't help but smile and bat their lashes at Jackson. Not that Day could blame them. Even now, dressed in what Jackson considered his casual clothes, he carried himself with the confidence of a celebrity. His dark wash jeans molded to his ass and thighs, and his black and gray zip front sweater fit him like a glove. His white sneakers didn't so much as have a speck of dirt on them and had probably cost more than Day's rent. Rent which was due in two days. Day grimaced at the thought. He hated being an adult. He also hated feeling out of his element, and he was way out of his element here.

When Jackson had said dress for comfort, Day had

infuriating

believed him. He'd put on a pair of black joggers, a thin blue cotton Pride hoodie, and a pair of Adidas sandals complete with white socks because his feet got cold. Nancy had looked at him like he was a ridiculous child, but Jackson had simply taken his hand and helped him into the back of the car. He'd also held Day's hand the whole way to the airstrip, right in front of Nancy and her upturned nose. When Day had tried to squirm his hand free, Jackson only clasped it tighter and gave him a look.

Day wasn't sorry to see Nancy leave with the car. Jackson picked up both their bags but was quickly met by a tall, slender uniformed man, with copper skin and perfect snow white teeth, who took them from Jackson. "Let me get those for you, Mr. Avery. I'm Paolo. I'll be one of the attendants on-board with you today. It's just the two of you, so feel free to make yourselves as comfortable as you like," he said, looking back and forth between Day and Jackson until Day became self-conscious and gave Paolo his patented stare down. The attendant gave him a smug smile in return.

Jackson snickered beside him before he put an arm around his shoulders and steered him to the stairs leading up to the door of the plane. "Stop terrorizing the staff. Not everybody has to be your enemy, you know."

"He was looking at me funny," Day grumbled.

"Because you're gorgeous, and he was trying to decide which one of us he wanted to go home with," Jackson said. "After that look, though, I'm pretty sure I just won by default."

"Haha, you're so funny," Day deadpanned, stopping short when they stepped onto the plane and into the cabin. There were eight large leather seats the color of caramel in varying configurations. Jackson led Day to one of the bench seats running the length of the plane before taking a seat beside him.

Paolo boarded the plane, winking at Day on his way to the back of the plane.

"He thinks I'm a pro," Day murmured.

Jackson chuckled once more, wrapping his arms around Day from behind. "He does not. Do I look like the kind of guy who has to pay for sex?"

Day leaned back against Jackson's broad chest begrudgingly, far too comfortable in his arms. "Have to? No. Willing to do it to keep from running into unnecessary complications? Definitely."

"That's what I look like to you? A rich guy who doesn't like complications?" Jackson asked. He didn't sound mad, just disappointed.

"Maybe at first. Now… Now, I don't know what to think," Day admitted.

infuriating

The pilot introduced himself over the speakers and announced takeoff. Jackson and Day put on their seatbelts, but Jackson's arms returned to Day once more. He turned to look out the window as the jet moved faster until the runway was just a black blur, and then they were sailing up into the air. Day's fingers found Jackson's, squeezing hard, as his pulse tripled and his stomach swooped. The ground below became smaller and smaller.

"Are we staying in a hotel?" Day asked when the plane finally leveled out and his heart rate returned to normal.

"No. I figured we'd stay at my place unless you want to stay in a hotel?"

"You have an apartment in Miami, too?" Day asked. Jackson was silent for so long, Day craned his head around to look at him.

Jackson hugged Day close. "Yeah, I live in Miami year round. I keep the apartment in LA because that's where my family still lives, so I do longer stays there when necessary. I have properties all over. Some of them double as safe houses, but Miami is my home."

Day's heart sank. "Oh."

Had Day known that? Had he referenced his life in Miami? Day couldn't remember. He wasn't sure what he thought about that, so he just settled back against Jackson and closed his eyes, ignoring the way Jackson's lips skimmed across his hair.

JACKSON'S MIAMI APARTMENT WAS JUST AS UPSCALE and fancy as his place in LA, but it looked far more lived in. While there was a place for everything, mail was stacked on the counter, there were pictures of his family everywhere, and there were two small dishes on the counter. "You have a cat?"

Jackson shrugged. "Does anybody really *have* a cat? We're more like roommates. I found him outside when he was a kitten. His name is Kevin. He's kind of a dick. I'm almost positive he likes my housekeeper more than he does me."

Day looked around for any sign of Jackson's asshole cat, but it was quiet. "Your cat's name is Kevin? Why?"

Jackson grinned, pulling a bottled water from the fridge, taking a swig and offering it to Day. "You'd have to ask him. We should get ready. I don't want to be late for my tongue-lashing."

"Sounds kinky," Day murmured, setting the bottle aside and wrapping his arms around Jackson's neck, jumping to wrap his legs around Jackson's waist, leaving him no choice but to catch Day or let him slide

infuriating

down his body like a stripper pole. Jackson chose to catch him, capturing Day's lips in a slow, dirty kiss until he was whining.

After a moment, Jackson smacked Day's butt, and he lowered his feet back to the ground. "You go get ready in the other room. You are too tempting."

It was a ridiculous lie, but Day blushed anyway, feeling floaty. Jackson had said there was no dress code for the restaurant, but when Day went to spy on him, he'd swapped out his jeans and sweater for a pair of tight-fitting maroon pants, a thin untucked white button down shirt and another pair of insanely expensive shoes.

Day, on the other hand, had pulled his nicest pair of white jeans from his bag and paired it with a button down Hawaiian shirt covered in cheetah print and flowers before shoving his feet into brown loafers. He'd bought it four years ago for Sarah's luau themed birthday party. It had lived in the back of his closet since. He sprayed his hair back off his face, brushed his teeth, and called himself done. It wasn't like there was anything to shave off his chin.

When Day met Jackson back in the kitchen, a fat ginger cat sat on the counter, Kevin presumably. He eyed Day warily as he ate his food, like Day might steal it. "Your cat is huge."

"Don't fat-shame my roommate. Kevin is his own man. He does as he pleases."

Day rolled his eyes. "Does anybody else know what a dork you are underneath all that swagger?"

Jackson picked Day up and plopped him on the counter, making Day a head taller than Jackson. "Only my family…and you."

Day cupped Jackson's cheeks in his hands, enjoying the feel of his beard on his palms. "Why me? You don't even know me."

"Because I know I'll never get to know you if I don't let you know me. The real me. The dork who likes musicals and names his chunky cat Kevin because that was the name on the delivery bag I found him sleeping in. I also play a mean game of Dungeons and Dragons, and I cheat at Monopoly."

Day's heart squeezed up into his throat, forcing him to swallow hard. "Everybody cheats at Monopoly," was all he could think to say.

"You look really hot tonight," Jackson said, punctuating each word with a lazy kiss. "How about when we get back, you let me peel you out of this outfit."

"We'll see," Day said, leaning down to give Jackson one last kiss before saying, "We're going to be late."

"Nah, the restaurant's only around the corner,"

infuriating

Jackson said, contradicting his own words from earlier.

Day smirked at him, shaking his head. "Come on, Daddy. We can't be late. This guy's already mad at you."

"Come on, you little tease," Jackson growled, spanking Day's ass hard enough to sting, causing him to bite back a moan.

The walk to La Mar was nice. The Florida weather was balmy but not so humid that it made Day sweaty or sticky. They walked hand in hand with nobody so much as batting an eye at them. It was only two blocks, but in that time, the sky shifted from blue to pink and orange fire, and the city lights seemed to spring up around them.

"Have you ever had Peruvian food?" Jackson asked.

"No. I've never been anywhere but LA and Idaho, and I can't afford to get experimental with food choices. If I'm feeling fancy, I eat my ramen noodles out of a bowl instead of the styrofoam cup."

Jackson leaned over and kissed Day's temple. He didn't say anything, but it felt like an apology.

Once they reached the restaurant, Jackson held the door open for Day, and they were met by a bubbly blonde girl. "Welcome to La Mar. Do you have a reservation?"

"Avery, party of four," Jackson said, flashing the

girl a bright smile.

She blushed all the way to the tips of her ears. "Yes, sir. The rest of your party is already here. Follow me."

Day made a googly-eyed face behind the girl's back, mocking her reaction to Jackson. He gave Day a single upturned brow. "Behave yourself."

The soft warning left goosebumps up and down Day's whole body. Before he could respond, they were led to a table looking out over darkening waters where a middle-aged man in a linen shirt and hat smoked a cigar and a woman ten years Day's senior sat wearing a skintight strapless, floral dress with diamond studs in her ears and a diamond ring on her left hand so big it spanned from knuckle to knuckle.

They both stood as Jackson and Day approached. Jackson clasped Angel, slapping his back like they were old friends, before kissing the woman on both cheeks. "Angel, good to see you, my friend. This is Dayton. Dayton, this is Angel and his wife, Sylvia. I hope you don't mind if he joins us tonight?"

"Of course not, *mijo*. He's your *novio, si*?" Sylvia asked.

Day looked to Jackson, eyes wide, but Jackson simply smiled. "*Si.*"

"*¡Es maravilloso!*" Angel said with a laugh.

Was it? Day thought.

infuriating

The server arrived with two more glasses of water. "I'll give you a few minutes to look over the menus. In the meantime, our wine list is right here in the center. Can I get you started with something from the bar?"

Day's heart stopped. The menu. How the fuck was Day going to order off the menu? He could say he'd forgotten his glasses or excuse himself to the restroom and hope Jackson ordered for him. Day swallowed hard. Maybe, by some miracle, there would be some words he recognized simply by sight? He cracked open the menu, biting down on the inside of his cheek until it bled.

"Day?"

Day jerked his head up. "I'm sorry, what?"

"Do you want a drink?"

Day blushed, glancing at the server. "Sorry. Martini, extra dirty, please."

The server smiled, and Day went back to studying the menu until Angel said, "Your man studies the menu like there will be a quiz afterwards."

Jackson glanced over to Day, who slowly closed the menu and set it down. "I've never had Peruvian food before. It all looks so good, I don't know what to order."

Sylvia laughed. "It's all so delicious. You can't make a bad choice."

"Hah, clearly, you don't know me," Day joked,

earning a chuckle from the older couple. "Sometimes, I think I don't make any other kinds of choices."

"I don't know, *miho*. It seems your luck might be changing. Look at this man on your arm," Sylvia said, pointing one perfectly manicured hand at Jackson. "He *es guapo*."

"*Si*," Day said with a sigh.

The server returned with the drinks, and the conversation flowed around Day like a warm breeze. Neither Angel nor Sylvia questioned Day when he said he worked in the entertainment world, and they seemed to have no problem with the way Jackson leaned into him, a protective arm slung over his shoulders.

When the server returned, Day leaned into Jackson, brushing his lips against his ear. "Order for me, I can't decide what I want."

"You sure?" Jackson asked.

Day nodded. Jackson ordered something Day had never heard of, but he didn't care. If it tasted like an old shoe, Day would eat it and smile. He was just relieved he'd found a way around that particular crisis.

When dinner came, the food was amazing, and Jackson beamed as Day excitedly told him how delicious each bite was. But, as soon as the meal ended and the coffee arrived and the bill was paid, the

infuriating

festivities took a decided turn.

Angel cleared his throat as he poured a generous amount of cream into his coffee. "Okay, so let's talk. What are we going to do about what happened in Bogotá? I lost one of my best guys because your guys were sloppy."

Day's temper flared at the accusation. He didn't even know what Angel referred to, but there was no way Jackson hired sloppy guys. That wasn't who Jackson was. As if he could feel Day's fury, Jackson found Day's hand under the table, giving it a squeeze. It felt like a warning.

Jackson leaned back in his seat. "Angel. Be reasonable. Colombia is a dangerous country. We all knew the risks going in. You have my best guys. If they hadn't been there, it could have been a bullet to the head, not the knee. I'm sorry your man was hurt, and I'll, of course, be happy to compensate you for his medical bills, but how long have we been doing business together? Has this ever happened before?"

"It's not unreasonable to expect military trained guards to keep my men alive during these transactions. My men aren't militia. They are businessmen. They wear suits. Perhaps you are spreading yourself too thin, my friend." He looked at Day and smirked. "Perhaps, you're getting a bit…distracted?"

"Does your beautiful wife distract you from your work?" Jackson countered, smiling at Sylvia, who was now playing on her phone, doing her best to be invisible.

Day simply twisted his napkin in his hand until the fabric bit into his skin.

"At my age, I admit, I'm not as distracted as I might have been in my youth. When I was your age," Angel said.

Jackson scoffed. "You're not that much older than me, Angel. Lay it on me. What is it you want here?"

Angel smiled, taking a sip of his coffee. "Reduce my yearly contract by fifteen percent."

Jackson's laugh was loud enough to catch the attention of other tables. "Fifteen percent? For a kneecap? Those are bullet to the head prices, my friend."

Angel shrugged. "He was my best man. He'll be very hard to replace."

Jackson shook his head. "I'm sorry, Angel, but your best man's knee isn't worth 1.5 million dollars a year."

"Is it worth losing a ten million dollar contract?" Angel countered.

Jackson picked up his phone. "Let me crunch some numbers."

Jackson wasn't crunching anything. He opened a gaming app and began to fire projectiles at balloons.

infuriating

Day frowned but didn't ask questions, just sipped his ice water.

Angel grinned, clearly believing he'd won. Day hoped not. Angel and Sylvia seemed nice, but they didn't deserve Jackson's money. Sylvia sighed and told Angel in Spanish that she was bored and to stop playing games because she wanted to go home and watch Jimmy Fallon. Angel responded that he was going to get something for that idiot's kneecap, and if Jackson wasn't smart enough to negotiate, that was his problem.

"You think Jackson's stupid?" Dayton asked in perfect Spanish.

Angel and Sylvia both stopped smiling. Jackson closed out the game on his phone, giving Day his full attention.

"Jackson works really hard and is one of the most honest people I've ever met in my life. He has made an offer in good faith so that he can keep your friendship and your contract, and you think you can just come in here and try to cheat him out of money for a worker you just called an idiot?"

The three of them stared at him in stunned silence before Jackson said, "You speak Spanish?"

"And Italian, Portuguese, French, and a little Creole," Day said, still staring down Angel.

It wasn't a lie. Day couldn't read or write in any language, but he had a knack for mimicry. He picked up other languages easily, something that had always made Sarah jealous.

"Your *novio* is very protective," Sylvia said to Jackson with a smile. "Angel, apologize to your friend, and let's go home."

Angel gave a sigh and an apologetic smile. "I accept your offer to pay for the idiot's medical bills. I'm sorry if I came across as ungrateful. You are a good friend."

"You're a good friend, too. I am sorry for the incident in Bogotá. I'd be happy to compensate his family for a few months' work as well."

"That's more than enough," Sylvia said, already standing and grabbing her clutch. "Say thank you and let's go before you do something else to embarrass me," she said in rapid-fire Spanish. They all stood and shook hands. Sylvia kissed Jackson's cheek and then Day's. She cupped his face. "You're good for him, I think," she told him softly.

They all parted ways at the exit, Jackson and Day walking back to the apartment in silence. Day's mood soured the farther they got from the restaurant. Jackson was clearly pissed that Day had intervened. He hadn't meant to. It just popped out. He wanted to tell him so, but the longer the silence went on, the harder it was for Day to break it.

When they entered the building, the doorman opened the door for them. "Welcome back, Mr. Avery. How's Kevin?"

"Fat and happy," Jackson responded, like it was a longtime joke between the two of them.

Once they stepped onto the empty elevator, Day was fully prepared to plead his case, but when the doors closed, Day found himself shoved up against the glass wall, Jackson kissing him in a way that had every nerve ending lighting up and his cock throbbing against his zipper.

"You're just full of surprises," Jackson murmured, sweeping his thumb along Day's cheek. "You just saved me a lot of money, you know that? I'm starting to think you're my good luck charm."

Day preened, even as some part of him died. He was nobody's anything, but just for tonight, he wanted to pretend he was Jackson's…in every way.

fourteen

JACKSON

JACKSON HAD A HARD TIME KEEPING HIS HANDS to himself on the walk from the elevator to the apartment. Day was brilliant, funny, feisty, gorgeous. He was perfect. Absolutely perfect. Once the door closed, he gently pushed him up against the door, kissing him long and deep, trying to push everything he felt into that kiss. Day's cry of surprise turned into a whimper that went straight to Jackson's dick. He pulled his mouth away so he could place biting kisses along Day's jaw, the shell of his ear, his throat. His fingers were on the third button of Day's shirt when he grabbed Jackson's hands. "Jackson, wait."

infuriating

"What's wrong?"

Day's face flushed pink, and he stared at a spot over Jackson's shoulder, like he just couldn't bring himself to look at him. "I know you don't 'do' virgins…" Jackson watched his Adam's apple bob as he swallowed audibly. "But would you…do me?"

Jesus. Jackson's cock was already leaking at the thought of sliding into Day. But he needed to be sure. "What about your auction?"

"The only person who was even a little close to meeting my asking price might be a murderer. The auction's over. If you don't want to…if it violates some moral code or whatever, I get it—"

"Dayton," Jackson said sharply, cutting Day off mid-sentence.

"Yeah?" he muttered, still refusing to look at Jackson.

"Let's go to bed."

Day's gaze finally slid back to his. "Okay."

This was a different side of Day. Shy. Nervous. Timid. But equally compelling. Jackson kissed him gently, picking him up to carry him. Once more, Day's legs came around him, clinging to him, his mouth exploring Jackson's throat before resting his head on his shoulder.

"You should just carry me everywhere."

"Oh, yeah? That's how it is, huh?" Jackson asked, kicking the door closed behind them so Kevin didn't disturb them.

"Mm," was Day's only reply.

"From bossy bottom to pillow princess in three days. That has to be some kind of new record," Jackson said, setting Day on his feet, his fingers reaching for the buttons on Day's shirt.

Day's brows went up, and he pushed Jackson's hands away. "Oh, you want me to be more take-charge, Daddy?" Day asked, leaning in to run his tongue along the hollow of Jackson's throat. "I can do that."

Day's nimble fingers worked the buttons on Jackson's shirt open, lips dragging across his skin as it was revealed. Jackson reached for Day, but he batted his hands away before letting them trace over the muscles of Jackson's abdomen. Day's tongue flicked out, teasing at Jackson's flat nipple, before scraping his teeth over it until Jackson hissed in a pleasure/pain response that had his cock straining against his zipper.

"Day." He said it like a warning, hoping to convey that he wasn't sure he could take much more of Day's teasing.

Day pushed his shirt off his shoulders, letting it fall to the ground, before dropping to his knees in front of him. "Can I, Daddy?" he asked, rubbing his cheek

infuriating

against Jackson's obvious erection.

"You better," Jackson murmured, watching Day's pupils blow wide at his words.

Day opened Jackson's pants, pushing them down to his thighs so he could mouth over Jackson's cock through his boxer briefs. "I love your dick, Daddy. It's so big."

"Yeah?"

"Fuck, yeah."

"Show me how much you love it," Jackson crooned, petting his hands through Day's hair.

Day peeled Jackson's underwear down, running his lips up and down the length before sucking the crown into his mouth. Jackson's eyes rolled back at the perfect heat and suction, but then it disappeared. He looked down to find Day sitting back on his heels, gazing up at Jackson obediently.

He smiled. So, Day wanted to play. Jackson could do that. "Open up, baby. Stick out that pretty tongue for Daddy."

Jackson watched goosebumps erupt along Day's skin at the command. He did as Jackson asked, pink tongue just waiting for him. Jackson gripped his cock, slapping it against Day's tongue, holding his head in place as he worked it in and out of Day's mouth.

"You look so pretty sucking my cock. You know that?"

Day whimpered, the sound going straight to Jackson's balls. "You like the way I taste?" Day hummed, closing his lips over Jackson and taking him to the root, sucking deep on his way back up. "Good boy."

Jackson stepped out of his pants and underwear and walked to the bed, sitting in the center against his padded headboard, leaving Day on his knees.

"Undress for me…slowly."

Day rose in that way of his, where he sort of just unfolded in one easy move. He turned around and began to unbutton his shirt, his gaze locked on Jackson, who stroked his cock as he watched Day strip.

"You're so pretty," Jackson said again.

He meant it. Day was gorgeous, could easily have graced the cover of any magazine, but Day flushed to the tips of his ears, even as his nipples hardened to tight peaks. Jackson had wanted to play with Day, but the longer it took him to undress, the more Jackson wanted to just throw him onto the bed and work him open with his tongue, his fingers, his cock. He just needed to be inside Day's tight little body.

Once Day was naked, Jackson crooked a finger at him. Day crawled up the bed and right into Jackson's lap, melting into him. Jackson kissed him slow, his tongue dipping between Day's lips. He still tasted of coffee. Jackson gripped Day's ass, spreading him open, letting his cock slide against his hole, but making no effort to enter him. He wasn't ready. But Jackson wasn't ready to stop kissing him, either. He slicked his fingers with the lube on the bedside table without even breaking their kiss.

"Lift up a little for me, baby," Jackson said against Day's lips.

Day did as Jackson asked, stuttering out a sigh. He rubbed his fingers against Day's entrance. He buried his face against Jackson's throat and sank down on his two fingers, moaning as he went. Jackson had thought he'd play with him a bit first, but Day was clearly as impatient as Jackson.

"Oh, fuck," Day whispered against Jackson's throat as he crooked his fingers inside him, grazing the bundle of nerves. "Oh, fuck, Daddy. Oh, God. That feels so good."

Jackson let Day ride his fingers, his boy's cock already leaking as he put Jackson's fingers just where he wanted them, chasing his pleasure without apology. Jackson used his other hand to play with Day's nipples, and give the occasional stroke to his cock, gathering the precum and feeding it to Day on his thumb. His dick throbbed as Day sucked Jackson's thumb clean.

Day was so tight, but when Jackson went to add

another finger, Day shook his head. "No. Just you. I'm ready."

"Are you sure?" Jackson asked.

Day gave him one of those looks, the one that said he didn't want to be argued with. "I know my body. I've used toys before. I'll be fine."

Jackson was reaching for the lube when he stopped short. "Condom?"

"We're both negative," Day said, then bit his lip.

"They say it's easier with a condom your first time," Jackson said.

Day cupped his face. "I don't want it to be easy. I just want you. I want to feel you come inside me. Please?"

Jackson nodded, his chest tight. Had they really only known each other four days? If so, why did this feel like so much more? Why did this one thing hold so much weight? Day was the one who reached for the lube, his hand slicking up Jackson's cock and placing it against his entrance, looking him in the eye as he sank down, sucking in a pained breath as the head of his erection slipped inside.

Jackson's hands found Day's hips, squeezing tight.

Day shook his head. "I'm okay. You're just…bigger than I expected. You feel so much bigger."

"We don't have to do this," Jackson said, hating the tight pinched look on Day's face and the way he'd

infuriating

squeezed his eyes shut.

"Just kiss me," Day said. "I'll be fine if you just kiss me."

Jackson slanted his lips over Day's, and his hand wrapped around Day's softening cock, stroking it as he explored Day's mouth, hoping to distract him from the pain. It must have worked because Day rocked himself in tiny aborted movements, taking Jackson farther inside an inch at a time until he was panting and making soft little cries against Jackson's lips.

"Fuck, I feel so full," Day said, sounding almost awed by it. "You're definitely better than any silicone toy."

Jackson chuckled as he flexed his hips, slipping even deeper into the tight heat of Day's body. "Christ, you're so tight."

Day came up onto his knees before sinking all the way back down. "Does that feel good, Daddy?"

"So good. Do it again, baby," Jackson murmured.

Day did as he was told—once and then again—until he found a rhythm. "Oh, fuck. God, why does that feel so good? You feel so good inside me." Jackson wrapped his arms around Day, holding him still so he could fuck up into him. "Oh, my God," Day moaned. "I want more, Daddy."

Jesus. Day might literally be the end of Jackson. He

didn't think he'd refuse him anything. If he said he wanted a wedding ring, Jackson probably would have dropped to one knee, he was so gone on Day. Jackson stayed inside Day as he made his way to the side of the bed, holding him close. "You want more?" Jackson asked, biting Day's bottom lip.

"I want all of it," Day begged. "Fuck me, Daddy."

"Put your arms around my neck."

Day's eyes went wide, and for just a moment, he looked a bit apprehensive, but he wrapped his arms around Jackson anyway, locking his hands behind his neck. Jackson slipped his arms under Day's knees and stood. Day moaned, gripping Jackson tighter as his cock slipped all the way inside. "Oh, my God," Day moaned.

Jackson lifted Day, pulling almost all the way free before dropping him down again. Day gasped, "More."

Jackson gave Day what he asked for, grateful for Day's slight frame as he lifted him up and slammed him back down until Day's head was thrown back and he was all but wailing at Jackson.

"Harder," he begged. "Please."

Jackson walked forward until Day's back rested against the wall and he had the leverage he needed to drive up into him, hard and deep, burying himself to the hilt, driving Day's breath from his lungs with every thrust. Day was hard again, his cock leaking between them as Jackson fucked into him again and again until his thighs burned and they were both slick with sweat.

Day's eyes were closed, his head back, words spilling from his swollen red lips. "I need to come, Daddy. I need it. Please. Please."

Jackson could listen to Day begging forever, especially if it meant being buried in the tight warmth of his hole.

He walked back to the bed and dropped Day on the mattress, pushing his legs up into his chest before sliding back into him. "Touch yourself. I want to feel you come on my cock."

Day's gaze was glazed, and he bit down on his lip in a moan as his hand closed around his cock, and he began to stroke himself hard and fast, only worried about his desperate need to get off. Watching Day touch himself only drove Jackson closer to his own release. When Jackson shifted, Day gave a cry of surprise that turned into a long, low moan. "Oh, God. Right there. Right there. Oh, my God. Please don't stop. I'm so close. I'm so close. Oh, fuck. I'm gonna come, Jackson. I'm gonna come."

Day painted his stomach and chest with his release,

his hole spasming around Jackson's cock in a way that shot heat into his belly, that spread to his limbs, his balls tightening until his hips stuttered off rhythm and he was grinding into Day's ass, cock throbbing as he came deep inside him.

Jackson stayed where he was until his brain came back online. When he went to withdraw from Day, he wrapped his legs around Jackson's waist and whined. "No, not yet."

Jackson chuckled, leaning down to kiss Day's forehead, his nose, and finally his lips, his softening cock slipping free. Day groaned. Jackson padded naked into the bathroom, relieving himself and then wetting a washcloth, wiping himself down and then taking it to Day who was now on his belly, eyelids at half-mast as he watched Jackson come towards him.

Jackson cleaned him gently, checking to make sure he hadn't hurt Day. He could see his cum leaking from Day's hole. If Jackson could have gotten hard again, he would have. He gently slipped a finger back inside Day, who gasped at the unexpected intrusion. "You liked coming inside me," Day said, voice muffled. "Do you have a breeding kink, you big perv?"

Did he? Jackson had never thought so before, but he couldn't help the feeling building in him as he fingered Day's loosened hole, feeling the wetness inside him. He pulled free, wiping his fingers off before gently cleaning Day once more and gathering him into his arms.

Day wiggled like a child trying to escape a parent's embrace. "Is this cuddling?" he said grumpily. "I hate it."

"You do not," Jackson said. "Besides, I demand post-coital cuddles. Fight me."

Day didn't fight. If anything, he wiggled closer, molding himself against Jackson's side and resting his head over his heart. "Fine. I guess this isn't so bad."

Jackson shook his head, smiling. "You don't always have to be so prickly, you know."

"My spirit animal is a porcupine," Day muttered, sounding sleepy. "Was it okay?"

Jackson looked down at the top of Day's head. "Was what okay? The sex?"

Day craned his head up. "No, my interpretive dance. Yes, the sex. Was it okay?"

So prickly. Jackson smiled. "It was perfect. You were perfect."

Day rubbed his face against Jackson's chest. "I thought I did pretty good, but it's nice to hear. Everybody likes compliments."

Jackson laughed. "You are one of a kind, Dayton. I'll give you that."

"I'll take it," Dayton murmured sleepily.

"Go to sleep, Day. We have to be up early."

Day didn't respond. A moment later, the sound of soft snoring reached Jackson through his haze of sleep. He wrapped his arm around Day tighter, knowing that sleepy, cuddly Day wasn't who Jackson would wake up with. Day might have decided that Jackson was worthy of his virginity, but he still wasn't ready to trust Jackson with his heart. But Jackson was patient. He'd wait him out.

Day couldn't stall forever. Could he?

fifteen

DAYTON

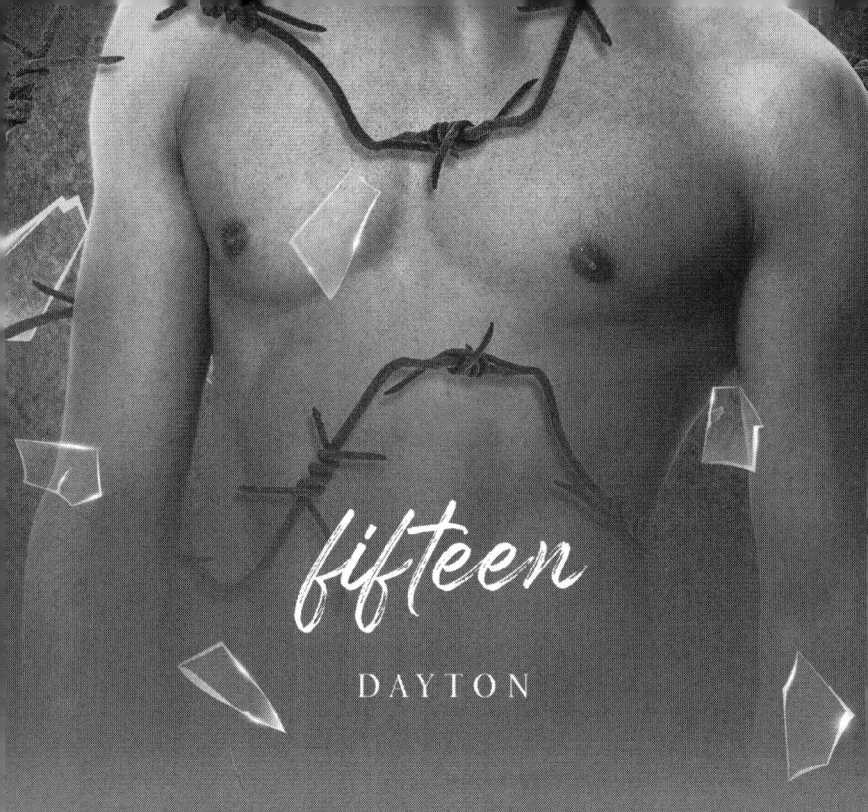

DAY SAT IN HIS OWN SEAT ON THE PLANE HOME, HIS socked feet tucked beneath him, clutching his venti quad shot mocha latte in his hands as he gazed out the window at the world below. Jackson sat across from him, his laptop open, typing furiously with just two fingers. Day took a sip of his coffee to hide his smile. He might not know how to type, but he knew it required more than just hunting and pecking with your pointer fingers, but Jackson seemed to have adapted just fine.

Jackson had woken him that morning with a gentle kiss on the cheek. Kevin had woken him up by plopping his fat furry ass on his chest and swishing his tail across his face. The ginger terror was now purring in his carrier on the seat beside Jackson, giving Day a supercilious look. Kevin was a smug cat. Day decided he didn't like smug felines. He shifted to reach for his earbuds and winced as he put his full weight on his ass. No matter how good Jackson's cock had felt last night, Day was paying for it this morning.

"Are you alright?" Jackson asked, brows knitted together in concern.

Day gave him a half smile. "I'm fine. Nothing a bit of time won't fix."

Jackson pushed a button on the chair. "I'm going to be taking a conference call for the next hour. Please don't disturb us."

"Yes, sir," Paolo said, his tone making it clear that he didn't think there was a conference call.

The look on Jackson's face made Day think there was no conference call, either. What was Jackson up to? He stood, pulling Day up with him and leading him over to the bench seat. "Kneel."

"W-What?" Day said, flushing at the way he stuttered.

"Kneel on the seat. Now."

Day shivered at Jackson's authoritarian tone, but he did what he asked, feeling ridiculous. "What are you—"

infuriating

Day gasped as Jackson dragged Day's joggers and underwear down to his knees, his traitorous cock semi-hard just from Jackson's barking tone. Jackson spread Day's cheeks apart. Day dropped his head to his forearm, equal parts humiliated and turned on. Jackson's finger probed Day's entrance, but there was nothing sexy about it. He was almost clinical in his inspection.

"I'm just a little sore. You want to kiss it and make it better?"

Jackson's finger disappeared, and there was some movement behind him. Day was about to shift to look over his shoulder when he felt Jackson's beard scrape against one side of his ass, then the other. Before he could fully understand Jackson's intent, the broad sweep of his tongue licked across Day's entrance.

"Jesus, Jackson."

Jackson's palm cracked against Day's bare ass, ripping a gasp from his lungs. "Is that how you address me?"

Day moaned, spreading his legs without thought, his cock hanging heavy between his legs. "No, Daddy." Jackson bit Day's bottom on both cheeks, hard enough to leave impressions, and Day pushed back, wanting more. "Spank me again, Daddy," he begged, voice breathy.

Jackson's palm came down hard on Day's other cheek, and then Jackson was burying his face between his cheeks, his tongue laving over his entrance until Day's nails were digging into the leather seat before him, moaning like he was performing in one of his shows. But this wasn't an act. Jackson was dragging the sounds from Day with every touch until he heard himself mewling. Maybe they'd blame Kevin for the sounds Day was making?

Was this seriously happening? Was Jackson eating him out on a private jet with six other people on the opposite side of what had to be a not very sturdy divider? Jackson gripped his ass, pulling him apart so he could tease the tip of his tongue against Day's abused hole. The ache combined with Jackson's soft tongue had Day pushing himself back against Jackson, desperate for more.

Jackson pulled back, but before Day could protest, Jackson was pulling Day's cock back between his legs, licking him from his tip all the way back to his hole. Day moaned as Jackson teased and played with him. It was so dirty, but so hot. When Jackson spit in his hand and wrapped it around Day's cock, he was already so close to coming. Jackson's tongue returned to his hole, fucking his tongue into him, as he jerked him in long, slow pulls that made Day's eyes roll back

infuriating

from pleasure.

"Daddy..." Day managed before dropping his head to his forearm and burying his teeth in the flesh there. He couldn't talk. His whole body was hot and flushed, his legs shaking, and he whimpered out pathetic sounds as he tried to force himself not to come.

Jackson pulled back. "That feel good, baby?"

"Nff," was all Day could manage, all brain function ceasing until only pleasure remained.

"You can come whenever you want. You've been so good for me these last two days. My perfect boy."

Jackson jerked Day faster, his mouth still teasing his entrance, sucking and nibbling at the tender skin until Day's balls were tight against his body, his orgasm building like a spring winding tighter and tighter. He gave a hoarse cry, his cum spilling onto the leather bench seat below. Day stared at the evidence of his release, idly wondering if cum stained leather as he dragged air into his lungs.

Jackson pulled Day's clothing back into place and gave him a chaste kiss on the back of the neck, leaving Day on his knees and returning to his abandoned laptop. He walked to the back of the plane where the restroom was, locking the door and closing the toilet seat, sitting heavy on the lid.

Day had no idea what he was doing...what they

were doing. Some part of him felt guilty. Jackson was fun and sexy and he thought Day was great, no matter how surly and prickly he tried to be. But Jackson didn't know everything. He hardly knew anything. There was a difference between being a grumpy person and a bad person. Day was just a bad person.

An image of Sarah swam into his mind, her skin sallow, a tube between her lips. Los Angeles had been her dream. She was the one who was supposed to wind up jet setting around the world in private jets. Day was always going to be her people. The one who just did things to make her life easier, whatever that entailed. It wasn't fair that he was there, riding in a private jet, having mind-blowing sex with a gorgeous rich man. He didn't deserve any of it.

Day tried to tell himself that he and Jackson weren't a forever thing, no matter how good he was at making Day feel that way. This wasn't a whirlwind romance. It was a fling. He just needed his heart to get on board with that. Maybe he deserved to have his heart broken. Maybe that would somehow level the score between him and Sarah. Was a broken heart the equivalent of murder? Probably not. Day splashed water onto his face and flushed the toilet, even though he hadn't done anything.

Once back in his chair, he popped in his earbuds and

connected to the plane's wi-fi. Jackson's gaze flicked to him as if to make sure Day wasn't about to open the plane's door and dive out, but then he went back to his typing, clearly satisfied with whatever expression he saw on Day's face.

Day clicked the button that autosaved his email login information and clicked on the first of several emails, closing his eyes as he listened to notifications for everything from fifteen percent off botox to a reminder that he needed to pay his internet bill.

Day was half dozing when the voice began to read a text that stood out from the rest.

You fucking whore. Day gasped, his hands fumbling with the phone, dropping it to the floor and somehow turning off his earbuds. The computerized male voice filled the room, sounding shrill and hysterical to Day's ears in what was once the silent vacuum of the cabin.

How dare you let him touch you like that? How dare you kneel before him like he's good enough for you? Have you let him inside you yet? Have you? Has he tainted you with his filthy hands and cock? You best pray the answer is no. I'll slit his fucking throat just like I did that pig district attorney. How fucking dare you? Do you know the lengths I've gone to in order to be the first to make love to you? Do you? You best hope you're still clean and that he hasn't defiled you with his seed, you dirty slut. You disgusting whore. Whore. Whore. Whore.

Day was shaking by the time Jackson put his laptop aside and reached for the phone, silencing the speaker. "Another message? Is that a message from the site?"

Day shook his head, tears pricking the back of his eyes. "That was my puh-personal email," Day said, hating that his brain hung on the p for too long, hoping somehow Jackson didn't hear it. "He knows my real name, Jackson. He knows who I am."

"Come here."

Day shook his head, clenching his hands into fists to try to quell the shaking, but he couldn't stop the feeling like his organs were quivering with fear.

"Dayton, come here."

Day stood, walking the two short steps to Jackson. He pulled Day into his lap, cradling him. He hated himself for dropping his head on Jackson's shoulder and letting himself be held. "He said he killed Juh-Jay. He killed Jay because of me. This is all my fault."

Jackson kissed Day's forehead. "Stop that. It is not your fault that some lunatic imagined some connection with you. He's clearly unstable. Maybe now that he's used your personal email, we'll be able to see where he's sending them from." Jackson flipped through Day's other emails while he held his breath. "As soon as we touch down, I'll get my guys working

infuriating

on this. He's clearly devolving. He's bound to make a mistake."

Day shook his head. "What if he hurts somebody else to try to get to me?"

"Then it still won't be your fault, but I'm going to do everything I can to make sure that doesn't happen. I won't let anything happen to you, Day. I promise."

"Don't make promises you can't keep."

sixteen

JACKSON

"NO. NO FUCKING WAY," DAY SAID, STOMPING HIS FOOT like a toddler.

"Day, be reasonable."

"It's reasonable to expect a certain level of privacy, Jackson," Day countered, his head wobbling back and forth, hands on his hips, like he was ready to fight until his last breath.

Webster sat with his ass half on the arm of the sofa, arms crossed over his chest, his blond hair flopping into his eyes, his glasses perched on his nose, watching Jackson and Day's exchange with some amusement. It was the first time Jackson had contemplated punching the tech wizard.

"Not when somebody wants to murder you!" Jackson growled through gritted teeth.

Day pushed his way into Jackson's personal space, standing on tiptoe until they were almost nose to nose. Jackson could literally feel his breath puffing against his lips. Day smelled like toothpaste. "Don't think you can just go all 'grr' on me and I'm going to wilt like some fucking flower, Jackson Avery. I'm not afraid of you."

Jackson threw up his hands. "I don't want you to be afraid of me. I want you to be reasonable, which it seems is something you're completely incapable of doing, even when somebody might be trying to murder you."

"I'm sorry that I won't just hand over my laptop to a total stranger, but I need it to work. You know what work is, right? I don't have houses around the world and employees who jump when I snap my fingers. I have to pay my rent. I have to keep my lights on. Just because I'm living here doesn't mean my other life ceases to exist. I can't work without my laptop."

"I'll pay your bills!" Jackson shouted, his tone somewhere between exasperated and infuriated.

He never got mad. Ever. It wasn't something he considered worthy of his time or energy. There was nothing that couldn't be fixed if you just came at the problem logically and with an open mind. At least, that's what he'd thought before Day had steadfastly refused to hand over his laptop so that Webster could check it to see if it was being monitored remotely somehow. That was an hour ago.

"If I might interject," Webster finally said, holding up a hand. "I don't actually need the laptop to come with me. I can just mirror the hard drive and check it that way. Even though it would probably be better if you weren't using it until we know for sure whether it's got a virus or spyware on it. We don't want him tracking you."

Day blew air out of his nose, his face sullen. "Why didn't you just say that then?"

"Who could get a word in edgewise?" Webster asked.

Day's expression was mutinous as he handed over his prized laptop and pointed at Webster. "You. I don't like you." He turned on his heel before stopping to glare at Jackson. "You, either."

Jackson tried to bite back a smile as Day walked up the stairs, regal as a Queen, Kevin hot on his heels. Jackson's roommate had clearly chosen a side, and it was not Jackson's.

"So, that's your type?" Webster asked when they

were alone. "That twinky ball of rage?"

Jackson gave him a look. "I'm still your boss."

"Then fire me, but you know you'll never find anybody else willing to do the sketchy shit I do for you and your crew of misfits," Webster said.

"And you'll never find another boss willing to fund your little passion projects, so we're even."

Webster opened Day's laptop and connected it to the small piece of hardware he'd pulled from his bag. His hands flew over the keyboard at warp speed, far faster than Jackson's own hunt and peck typing.

"Seriously, are you violating your own rules? Weren't you the one who said no more canoodling with the clients or we're fired?" Webster asked, his eyes never leaving the screen.

"I'm the boss and he's not paying," Jackson said, already irritated with the direction of the conversation.

"So, the loophole is, you're doing him *pro bono*?" Webster said, emphasizing the last word by wiggling his brows.

It was on the tip of Jackson's tongue to say he wasn't 'doing' him, but that would be a lie. Day had been done quite thoroughly by Jackson. At the hotel, on the flight home. Twice in the shower. Once on the back porch. Then, in the shower again. Day had even blown Jackson in the kitchen fifteen minutes before Webster had shown up. They hadn't really been able to keep their hands to themselves for the last two days. So, he said nothing, instead choosing to glower at Webster. After all, it was his fault Day was mad.

Webster mirroring Day's hard drive came after two days of frustrating dead ends where Day's stalker was concerned. Whoever he was, he was either incredibly smart or terribly lucky. Either way, if Jackson found him, he was going to tear his arms off and beat him to death with them. He was caught up in a rather vivid fantasy when Webster cleared his throat.

"Uh, Jack."

"What? Did you find something?"

"Uh, I'm not sure. Does Day have vision problems?"

Jackson frowned. "He wears glasses, but he doesn't fall down the stairs without them. Why?"

"His computer is wired for software that's most often used by people who are blind or, at least, legally blind. Voice to text software. Software that close-captions webpages."

"I—" Jackson cut himself off, running through a series of memories rapid-fire. Day staring at the Elite contract for ten minutes. Day telling Chloe he didn't read so well. Day asking Jackson to order for him at the restaurant. Day's phone reading his emails to him out loud. Jesus. Was that what Day was trying to hide

infuriating

from him? Was Day losing his vision? He didn't think that was it.

"Is it pertinent to the case?" Jackson snapped.

Webster's gaze went wide. "I don't know. Probably not."

"Then mind your own business."

Webster gave him a mock salute and went back to clacking away on his keyboard. Jackson looked up at Day's closed door before heading up the stairs and knocking gently on it.

"Go away," Day shouted from the other side.

Jackson pushed the door open to find Day lying across his bed staring up at the ceiling. He kicked the door closed behind him and sat at the head of the bed.

"Guess I should have known better than to expect any privacy. If I can't have it on my laptop, why would I have it in my room?"

"Dayton," Jackson said softly.

Dayton's gaze darted to him, and he rolled up onto his forearm, frowning. "What? Did Webster find something on my computer? Is that person spying on me or something?"

"No, it's not that. I need to ask you something."

Day shook his head, hand flailing. "What? Why are you looking at me like you're about to ask me for one of my kidneys? You're freaking me out."

"Webster asked if there was a reason that you have software on your computer that helps the blind better use their computers… Is there?" Jackson asked.

Dayton's mouth formed a perfect O, and then he flushed from his throat to his hairline, the tips of his ears turning bright pink. He snapped his mouth shut and looked away, rolling off the other side of the bed to pace. "So, what? I'm just lazy. I like to have stuff read to me. It's not a big deal."

"Day…"

Day stopped dead in his tracks, his arms crossing protectively in front of his chest as he sneered at Jackson. "What? Stop looking at me like that."

Jackson frowned. "Like what?"

"Like you feel sorry for me. Like I'm some one-eyed homeless cat Sarah McLachlan wants you to fucking adopt. I'm fine. There's nothing wrong with me. I pay my bills. I buy my own groceries. I've been making my own way in life since I could tie my own shoes. Stop looking at me like I'm defective."

Tears streaked down Day's cheeks, but Jackson wasn't sure Day even noticed. He was too mad. Too humiliated. Jackson had done that. Jackson had made him feel stupid and small and helpless. "I don't think you're defective."

"Oh, well, that's a relief," Day choked out around

infuriating

a sob.

"Day, stop. Please," Jackson tried. "Just tell me what the problem is, and we can try to fix it."

"I don't need to be fixed, Jackson!" Day shouted, turning on his heel and going into the bathroom. Jackson heard the lock click, his heart breaking as he heard Day dissolve into tears on the other side of the door.

"I got what I need," Webster called from downstairs. "I'll show myself out."

Jackson didn't even bother to answer. When he heard the door click behind Webster, he went to the bathroom door and knocked. "Day, please… I didn't mean you needed to be fixed. You're perfect. That's not what I meant at all."

"Go away," Day said, voice thick with tears.

Jackson sighed. "I can't do that. Not until we talk this out."

Day sniffled. "There's nothing to talk about. I'm fine."

"You're obviously not fine. I didn't mean to upset you or make you cry. Can I please come in?" Jackson asked. There was no answer. "Day?"

Jackson listened intently at the door, but all sounds had ceased from the other side. Suddenly, Jackson thought of Wyatt lying in the hospital bed, white as a sheet, after he'd almost bled out from when he was a cutter. What if Day was hurting himself?

"Day?"

Jackson took a step back and kicked the bathroom door with enough force to drive the hollow door off its hinges. Day sat in the empty bathtub, now staring at the remnants of the bathroom door and Jackson in shock.

"What in the actual fuck?" Day asked, dabbing at his eyes with a washcloth. "Did you hit your head or something? Can't a guy get five seconds of privacy to have a meltdown in peace?"

Jackson felt his face grow hot. "I just thought… Never mind."

Day sniffled once more, his eyes red-ringed and bloodshot, his nose running. "You just thought… what? I was drowning?"

"Nothing. It was stupid."

"So, I have to bare my soul to you, but you can't even tell me why you just pulled a shock and awe on my bathroom door?" Day said before blowing his nose loudly with the roll of toilet paper he'd taken into the bathtub with him.

"It was stupid. I thought… I thought maybe you were upset enough to hurt yourself."

Day's mouth fell open, but then he scoffed. "You

thought I'd slit my wrists in the bathtub because you figured out I'm fucking stupid and can't read? Please, if people thinking I'm stupid was all it took to make me off myself, I'd have never made it past the third grade. My grandmother called me stupid so much, I was convinced it was my given name."

Jackson stepped over the shattered remnants of the door and stepped into the bathtub, grateful it was a soaking tub and not the standard one in his Miami apartment. He picked Day's legs up so he could sit, then refused to let them go, half thinking Day might run again. "I don't think you're fucking stupid. Don't say that. You're one of the smartest people I've ever met."

Day snorted. "Look, I know we're sleeping together, but you don't have to give me empty compliments."

Jackson's nostrils flared, and he ground his teeth until the muscle in his jaw popped. "Just stop, okay? Stop acting like I'm the kind of person who would give you fake compliments because I want to keep sleeping with you. That's not who I am. It's like you just said. You pay your own bills. You've found a way to get around not being able to read. Jesus, Day. You speak four fucking languages…"

"Five," Day said, wiping his nose with his forearm. "Six if you count American sign language."

"You're not stupid. You're…" Jackson floundered for the word. "You're incredible."

Day looked like he was trying to hold back a laugh, but it suddenly broke through, a high-pitched almost hysterical giggle. "Incredible? Wow. You really do love this ass, huh?" Day said.

"You're such a brat," Jackson snarled, but there wasn't any heat behind it because Day pitched himself headfirst into Jackson's arms, hugging his neck and kissing his mouth.

Jackson gathered him in his arms until they were both sat fully clothed, Day between Jackson's thighs, his arms around him. Day tipped his head as Jackson kissed his way down Day's throat, giving him more access. "I'm really not worth all this effort, Jackson. I don't say this because I feel sorry for myself, I say it because it's true. There are too many things about me you don't know. I know you think my illiteracy is something that can be fixed, but it can't. I'm not just dyslexic. I have a sensory processing disorder that just doesn't allow the pieces to line up for me. I had a speech impediment and a stutter, too, but those are things I outgrew. My dyslexia, combined with whatever other problems I have…up here…" He tapped his temple. "That's never going to go away. I'm never going to be able to sit down and read a book or write anything that doesn't look like a preschooler wrote it. That's just how it is."

Jackson didn't necessarily believe that was true, but Day clearly did, and, for right now, Jackson had to accept that. "I don't care if you can't read. I don't care if you ever learn to read. You've clearly figured out a system that works for you. I just want you to let me in."

Day rested his head against Jackson's shoulder. "The optimist in you is going to leave us both broken if you don't learn to listen to me. Run now, Jackson, before it's too late."

"I'm not going anywhere." Jackson looked at his watch. "Actually, that's not true. It's Sunday. So we're both expected at my mother's house…for dinner. In two hours."

seventeen

DAYTON

"I CAN'T BELIEVE YOU JUST DECIDED TO SPRING THIS whole dinner with your family thing on me at the last minute."

"I wasn't trying to spring it on you last minute. If I'm in town, I do Sunday dinners with my family. I can't leave you alone with some crazy stalker looking for you here in LA. Also, I'd rather keep you close after what happened between us earlier."

Day shook his head. "No. I'm not going. I'm not meeting your family. This is too much. It was bad enough meeting your sister—who hated me, by the way. Now, you want to parade me around to your

infuriating

whole family? Why? I keep telling you this thing between us is temporary, and you just keep acting like we've been dating for a year instead of fucking each other for a week."

Jackson looked at Day like he was crazy. He *was* crazy. He was acting crazy, but he couldn't stop himself. Ever since Jackson figured out his secret, he'd felt like he was trapped outside with a tornado bearing down on him. Having to sit with Jackson's family while Jackson's mother asked him a million questions and his sisters watched made Day sick to his stomach.

Day had just wanted the fantasy for a few more days. Was that too much to ask? A few days to pretend he was a normal guy without a warehouse full of baggage. A few days to pretend there was a world where he and Jackson fit together, but it just wasn't true. But then Jackson had gone and ruined everything because he just didn't see Day for what he really was: a lost fucking cause. Why couldn't Jackson see that? Day needed to make him see that.

"Day…"

"No. It's fine. We'll go. As long as you know this is going to be a disaster, right?"

Day turned on his heel and marched up the stairs. As soon as he closed the door, he leaned against it and took a few deep breaths, grimacing as he noticed the remains of his bathroom door. Jackson had literally kicked down a door because he'd thought Day might be hurt. Who did that? Jackson. Only Jackson. He was a goddamned superhero. Too bad Day wasn't leading lady material.

It was time Jackson saw who Day really was. He found his tightest pair of jeans, donned his bubblegum pink crop top and a full face of makeup, leaving his hair wild and just a little unkempt, like he'd spent a day at the beach…or rolling around in bed with Jackson.

Jackson met him downstairs, looking Day up and down. "You look beautiful, but you didn't have to get dressed up for my family."

Day looked at Jackson's two hundred dollar jeans and his D&G white t-shirt and arched a brow. "You look pretty fancy to me."

Jackson shook his head. "I'm not the one wearing enough holographic highlighter to be seen from space," Jackson said with a chuckle. "But I see your point."

The drive to Jackson's mother's house passed in silence, Jackson playing the audiobook they'd started the day he'd brought Day home. His mother didn't live far, just outside the city in a quiet subdivision, but everything in LA took at least an hour to get to.

Jackson pulled up to a modest craftsman style home

infuriating

with a trellis over the walkway. The exterior was painted a buttery yellow with a pale blue door and white trim. Flowers bloomed all around the steps and the railing of the porch. Jackson's mother clearly loved her home.

The overwhelming scent of night blooming jasmine hit Day like a fist, his stomach swooping like he was on a roller coaster and plunging to the bottom. He wasn't sure he could go through with his plan. As much as he hated to admit it, he desperately wanted to be somebody Jackson's mother would approve of, to be somebody who could be part of a real family. But that wasn't ever going to happen. It was better Jackson saw that now. There was no world where Day would ever fit into his life or his family.

Jackson walked around and opened Day's door. He couldn't help but notice the two late model luxury SUVs and a four-door Mercedes crossover. Were all the Avery children successful, or was Jackson just generous with his money? Day suspected it was probably both.

Jackson didn't knock, just opened the door and called out, "Hello."

A series of high-pitched screams erupted in response to Jackson's greeting, and then six children came running from the back room, surrounding Jackson and Day, all of them talking over themselves to get Jackson's attention. All but Chloe. Chloe approached Day with her finger in her mouth. She beckoned him with a wave of her little arm, her big brown eyes wide, like she thought he might refuse. When Day leaned down, she whispered, "Do you like my dress?" She twirled, her fluffy skirt flying up around her.

"It's beautiful. You look just like a princess."

"Where's my boy?" a voice boomed over the noise of the children. A heavyset woman with warm chestnut skin and long wavy black hair approached wearing a pair of perfectly tailored slacks and a butternut yellow sweater set. She used a cane when she walked, but she moved at a pretty good clip, cutting through the children like a knife through warm butter.

"Hey, Mama," Jackson called, meeting her halfway to lean down and kiss her cheek. "You haven't been standing up while you were cooking, have you? Dr. Schneider said you need to be careful until your surgery."

She scoffed, waving a hand at him. "What am I supposed to do, wait for one of the girls to cook a meal? Those girls are smart but not one of them can so much as boil water." She turned and narrowed her eyes at Day. The children abandoned Jackson, running back to the back room now that all the excitement was over. All except Chloe, who grabbed Day's hand with her own, the fingers from her other hand still stuffed in her mouth. Jackson's mother stepped closer. "You must be Day. My granddaughter had a lot to say about you. My daughter, Ruby, too. I tend to trust Chloe over Ruby, though. She gives people too much credit."

Day had no idea what to say to that, but luckily—or not—two more people emerged from what appeared to be the kitchen. Ruby and another woman Day had never seen. She was clearly one of Jackson's sisters. She looked almost identical to Ruby, though she had a more curvaceous figure and her mother's shrewd look in her eye.

"Mama, leave that boy alone. Can't you see he's scared?" the woman said, holding out her hand to Day. "I'm Della. I'm the nice one."

The other three adults scoffed at her statement, but then Jackson's mother was waving them into the dining room. "Come in, come in. I'm Beverly, but everybody calls me Bev or Mama. I answer to both. Dinner's ready. We just been waiting on you."

Chloe let go of Day's hand and ran off to join the other children. Day had to fight the urge to run after her. He didn't want to be left alone with the grown ups. Apparently, the kids were eating chicken nuggets and mac and cheese in the back room by the television.

That sounded alright to Day.

Day had hoped to shock Jackson's family with his clothing or makeup, but he was disappointed to see none of them so much as gave it a second glance. Was everybody in Jackson's family just that liberal? It seemed hard to believe, but then Day had spent his early childhood in Idaho. Maybe people who were born and raised in LA were used to people dressing more…flamboyantly.

"So, where are you from, Dayton?" Bev asked, placing her napkin in her lap.

"I was born in a small town in Idaho, but I moved to LA when I was fourteen."

Everybody helped themselves to barbecued chicken, cornbread, and macaroni and cheese, but Day put just a little of each on his plate, far too nervous to eat. Bev smiled warmly at him. "That must have been a bit of a culture shock. Are your parents still here in the city?"

Day shook his head. "I moved here with a friend. I never knew my dad, and my mom took off when I was three or four. I can't remember now. My grandmother raised me until she OD'd behind the tire shop. Then I came here."

Day had imagined that his answer would infuriate Jackson, but he was looking at Day like he had earlier when he'd figured out that Day couldn't read. It

infuriating

was a look Day couldn't quite place. Pity? Sorrow? Confusion? Maybe he thought Day was making the whole thing up.

"How did you take care of yourself at fourteen? I'm thirty-six and my husband and I can barely afford to feed all my damn kids," Della said.

"Della!" Jackson said, voice low.

Day shrugged, ignoring Jackson. "Let's just say I found a landlord who was willing to let me work off the rent in trade." He made the crude hand signal for a blowjob. Ruby gasped, Della stared, and Jackson looked like he was going to be sick. Bev, however, didn't bat an eyelash.

Bev gave a tight smile. "So, Day. Ruby tells me you're one of Jackson's clients?"

"Yes."

When he didn't offer any more information, Bev prompted. "Are you an actor or a musician? One of those dot com billionaires Jackson babysits all the time."

"Nope, I'm just a camboy," Day said before stuffing a bite of macaroni into his mouth and chewing it while he watched his answer hit his targets.

Della and Ruby gaped at him, but Bev just took a sip of her white wine. "That's one of those boys who gets naked over the computer, right?"

"Mama," Della said before giving a shocked laugh.

"What? I think it's clever. Back in my day, if we were gonna try to bring in some extra cash with our bodies, we had the street corner or the pole. Day's way seems much safer."

Day scoffed. "Tell that to the guy who got his throat slit in front of me."

"No way," Della gasped. "You saw it happen? Like, were you there?"

"Day," Jackson said quietly, his warning clear.

Day ignored him again, leaning in, like he was dishing the hottest of fresh gossip to his new friends. "I saw it happen on camera. I didn't know he was some fancy assistant district attorney until I called the cops."

"No shit?" Ruby said. "You were cyber-banging that ADA who got taken out? They said it was, like, gang related or something. His wife is in my yoga class. No wonder she always looks so miserable. Probably wasn't getting any from her hubby if he was getting it with you."

"Ruby Jean," Bev snapped, exasperated. "Watch your mouth."

"Sorry, Mama," she said, not sounding sorry at all.

When Day looked her way, she winked at him, and he dropped his gaze to his plate. What the fuck did it take to freak these people out? An idea came to him

infuriating

in that moment, and Day opened his mouth before he chickened out and changed his mind. They couldn't ignore this.

"They thought it had something to do with one of his cases, but after I put up a video of me and Jackson, one of my regulars went completely nuclear and took credit for the murder. That's why Jackson's stuck with me. Detective Jimmy thinks this guy is going to try to kill me or kidnap me."

They all gaped at him.

"Jackson made a sex tape?" Ruby said at the same time Della said, "Dad's Detective Jimmy?"

Jackson was glaring daggers at Day now, but he continued to eat his dinner like he'd done nothing wrong, even though embarrassment was eating a hole in his belly. Jackson hadn't deserved this. Nobody's family should know about their sex life. Hopefully, Jackson understood now. Day wasn't good enough for him.

"No, I didn't make a sex tape. It was just a decoy to make Day's potential stalker make a mistake," Jackson said.

Bev looked relieved, but Della narrowed her gaze in confusion. "How did you even know Day had a potential stalker if he didn't flip out until *after* you loaded the sex tape?"

"Drop it, Della. I'm serious," Jackson said.

"Fine. You're the one who said to make Day feel welcome," she muttered, taking a bite of her cornbread and chewing angrily.

"Excuse me. I'm not feeling very well," Day said, bolting from his chair back into the living room. He didn't know where to go, so he just headed out the front door. He stopped short on the welcome mat, realizing he had no idea where he was and that his phone was locked in Jackson's car. He couldn't even call an Uber. Without any other options, he took a seat on the front porch swing and buried his face in his hands, praying he didn't do something even more embarrassing like start crying again.

When the front door opened, Day didn't look up. "Look, Jackson. I'm sorry—"

"It's me you should be apologizing to, young man."

Day's head snapped up at the sound of Bev's voice. She walked towards him, her cane clicking on the wooden planks below as she moved. She took a seat beside him on the swing, using her good leg to set it swaying gently.

"I'm sorry," Day muttered. "That in there…that wasn't about you. Any of you. I was just… I was just trying to prove a point to Jackson."

Bev made a noncommittal sound. "I believe you. To

tell you the truth, I'm surprised you managed to get the words out at all. The whole time you were talking, you looked like you were gonna be sick all over my great grandmother's lace tablecloth."

"That's why I came out here. Thought it might be better to throw up on your azaleas instead," Day said, face hot with embarrassment.

Day jumped as Bev's hand came to rest on his back. "No need for that, but if you do throw up, do it on the gardenia bushes. They like acidic soil." Day couldn't help but laugh. "You got my boy fit to be tied in there, you know."

Day stared at his hands. "I know."

"He texted me earlier that you were probably going to come here and act as outrageous as you could. Said you were just scared and I should ignore it."

Day's gaze shot to hers. "He did?"

"Yep. He didn't want us thinking you were always this…outspoken."

Day shook his head, frustration leaching into his voice. "I am, though. Maybe not as bad as I was in there, but I pop off on people all the time, and everything I said in there was true. My mom was a stripper who left me when I was four. My grandmother was a raging addict who hated me. I don't tell that to everybody but it doesn't make it any less real."

Bev rubbed soothing circles on his back. "I know. Nobody can make up that kind of story off the cuff and sound believable."

"I keep telling Jackson I'm not worth all this effort. We don't even know each other. I don't understand why he can't see that."

Bev smiled. "My boy is a romantic, just like me. I knew I was gonna marry his daddy the moment I laid eyes on him. I just…had a feeling. His daddy always said the same about me. He just knew. My Jackson's been waiting almost thirty-eight years to feel that feeling, and he clearly felt it with you. He's never brought anybody home to meet us before. Ever. You might not think you're worth all this effort, but my boy does, and he's rarely wrong. Don't let fear cheat you out of something amazing."

"Why are you being so nice to me?" Day asked, bewildered.

"Because we are all more than our past mistakes, and if my boy wants you, there's clearly a reason why."

Day dropped his head in his hands once more. "I can't believe I mimed a blowjob in front of you."

She laughed, pulling Day close in a side hug. She smelled like roses. She smelled like a mom. "Let me tell you a story. When I was young like you, I met Jackson's daddy. I was a hot little number back then

infuriating

with my fancy beehive hair and my perfect figure and this down to there and up to here gorgeous green dress that would have made Jennifer Lopez blush. Jackson's daddy was up for a promotion, so we're having dinner with his lieutenant and his wife at this fancy supper club that has entertainment. Right up front by the stage. Now, I've had more than a few drinks because this is an important dinner and I'm nervous about us being the only brown people in the room. Then here comes this belly dancer out on the stage, and well, she's just not very good. She's sweaty and heavy footed and stinks of cheap vodka...so I tell her so. Loudly. In front of everybody. She tells me if I think I can do better, I should show her. Day, honey, I did. I crawled up onto that stage in my gorgeous green gown and I proceeded to belly dance in front of my husband's boss. Not well. The next morning, I was mortified. But my husband got the promotion."

Day stared at her, wide-eyed. "Really?"

She laughed, delighted. "Yes, sir. If you help me do the dishes, I'll tell you about the time I accidentally ended up in the men's room by mistake and how Jackson's daddy thought I'd ditched him."

Day nodded. "Yeah, okay."

JACKSON DIDN'T SPEAK THE WHOLE WAY HOME, AND the more the silence grew, the more nervous Day became. Part of him hoped it would be like their dinner the other night when Jackson kissed him silly in the elevator, but after Day's performance, that was hard to imagine.

On the elevator, Jackson stood beside Day, hands in his pockets, staring straight ahead as Day tried to make himself as small as possible. While his sabotage had seemed like a good idea hours ago, having to face the real possibility that Jackson was done with him, that he'd kick Day out and leave him alone to not only face a potential murderer but also a broken heart, caused a panic Day hadn't felt in a long time.

All he could do was try to triage the situation, stop the bleeding and hope Jackson would give him another chance to at least say he was sorry. As soon as the door to the apartment closed, Day turned on him. "Jackson, I know you're mad—"

"Day," Jackson said, cutting him off, voice a barely-there rumble. "Go upstairs to my bedroom, take off your clothes, and wait for me."

Day's stomach did that swooping thing once more, but, this time, for an entirely different reason. "What?"

"You heard me."

Day licked his lips, swallowing hard. "Jackson—"

infuriating

"Go. Now."

Day shivered at the lack of emotion in Jackson's voice, but he was already half-hard before he made it to the staircase. The trek to Jackson's room seemed to take forever, like he was trudging through quicksand. What was Jackson going to do to him?

Day undressed, but then he wasn't sure what to do. Did Jackson want him on the bed? On his knees? Both? Neither? He paced the room, wondering if he should fold the clothes he'd left on the floor or just leave them. The not knowing was causing a giant knot behind his diaphragm, which Day suspected was part of Jackson's plan.

Day was facing the bed when he heard the door push open. He turned to look at Jackson, who gave Day a long thorough once over as he undid his belt and tossed it on the bed, sitting on the mattress beside the leather strap.

"Jackson, I know you're mad..." Day tried once more.

"I'm not mad," Jackson said, tugging Day closer. "But you've been begging for this punishment for a very long time."

Jackson pulled Day over his knees, and the reality of Day's situation hit home. "You can't be serious," Day said, his words passing his lips in a breathless rush. Jackson didn't answer, but his hand cracked over

Day's ass cheek hard enough to drive the air from his lungs. "Jackson, I'm sorry."

"I know," Jackson said, voice resigned. "I know you're sorry, but the only way you're getting out of this is if you use your safeword."

Day didn't want to use his safe word. The truth was, he was rock hard just from Jackson's first blow, and there was no way Jackson didn't feel Day's erection pressing against his thigh, even through his jeans.

"I'm sorry, Daddy," Day murmured, forcing himself to relax.

The next blow landed on Day's thighs, pulling a pained hiss from him. Jackson didn't react. He didn't speak. He brought his hand down three times in rapid succession, leaving a trail of fire in his wake. Day bit down on his bottom lip to try to keep from crying out, but it was almost impossible. Jackson was brutal and thorough, spanking Day until there was no part of his thighs and ass that weren't burning. Day squirmed, tears filling his eyes and dripping to the floor, but Jackson didn't stop. Day was so hard, his cock throbbed, leaking precum through Jackson's jeans, but Day didn't care. He was too far gone to care.

After two more hard slaps, Jackson's big hand rubbed over Day's bruised flesh, teasing his legs apart to skim his fingers across Day's balls and the cleft

infuriating

of his ass. His shoulders sagged in relief, certain the punishment was over. When Jackson's hand came down once more, Day's whole body bowed upward, his hands flying behind him to cover his abused backside. "Please, Daddy. I'm sorry. I'm so sorry. No more. I promise, I'll be good. I'll do anything. It hurts."

Jackson tipped Day upright and he slid to his knees, too weak to hold himself up at the moment. Jackson's thumb rubbed across Day's bottom lip, dark brown eyes almost black in the dim bedroom lighting. Day sucked his thumb into his mouth.

"Anything?" Jackson asked, rubbing his spit slick finger over Day's tongue before removing it.

"Yes, anything. Anything, I swear."

"Stand up."

Day righted himself, his legs wobbling like he was a baby deer. Jackson went to the nightstand and tossed Day the lube.

"I want you to get yourself ready for me," he told Day before going to sit in the chair in the corner.

Day flushed. It wasn't like Jackson was asking for anything new. Day had been fingering himself in front of a camera for almost three years, but he'd never done it with somebody in the room.

Jackson opened his pants and pushed his jeans and underwear out of the way, stroking his cock. "Don't make me wait. You're already in enough trouble."

Day crawled onto the bed, putting his ass in the air, his chest on the bed. He lubed his fingers and slid them between his legs, turning his head so he could see Jackson's reaction as he slipped one lubed finger inside. Day moaned. The feeling of being penetrated combining with the way his bottom throbbed and the knowledge that Jackson was watching him had Day's thoughts feeling pleasantly fuzzy, the outside world fading away as he fucked his finger as deep as he could in his current position.

"Another," Jackson said.

Jackson was already hard, his thick cock jutting up from a nest of curls. Day sank another finger inside himself, rocking back into them. "Oh, fuck, Daddy. Like this? Is this good?"

"I think you need one more. I want my cock to slide right into that tight little hole."

Day's cock leaked as he pushed a third finger inside himself, hissing at the burn as his body attempted to take another finger.

"Are you nice and wet for me? I want your hole good and sloppy."

Day whined at Jackson's words. "Oh, fuck. Yes, Daddy."

"Then come over here and show me." Day pulled

infuriating

his fingers free, wiping them on the comforter, before crossing to Jackson, who looked at Day in a way that made his core melt. "Spread yourself open. Show me how ready you are for me."

Day blushed to the roots of his hair and he was sure his heart stopped, but he did as Jackson asked, feeling both dirty and more turned on than he'd ever been before. Jackson pulled Day back until he was straddling Jackson's thighs, still facing away from him. Day wasn't sure how he felt about doing it this way. Without seeing Jackson's face, it left Day feeling untethered. But this wasn't about Day, it was about Jackson. Day lowered himself slowly until he felt Jackson's cock snug against his entrance.

Day cried out as Jackson's cock impaled him in one hard thrust, his hand coming up around Day's throat, not cutting off his air but clamping down on the side of his neck until that woozy feeling intensified and Day felt like he was floating away. "You like that, baby? You like Daddy's big cock stretching your hole?"

"Oh, God. Yes, Daddy," Day said around a sob. "Please."

Jackson snarled, biting at Day's shoulder. "Then put your feet up on the chair and show me. Make me come. Show Daddy how much you love this cock."

Day gripped the top of the chair, maneuvering his

feet on either side of Jackson's thighs using the back of the chair as leverage so he could work himself up and down on Jackson's cock. The sounds he was making would be humiliating if Day had even one fuck left to give, but he didn't because Jackson was filling him up and holding him tight, and Day felt like he was penetrating every cell in his body, fucking into the very core of him.

"Fuck, yeah. That's it. You're so fucking tight," Jackson said against Day's ear, his voice like gravel.

Day sobbed. Jackson's fingers were playing with Day's nipples, and his thighs were burning from the effort of working himself on Jackson's dick. He was also so hard he might be able to come just from this, and he might have even said so out loud.

Day suddenly found himself upended. Jackson turned them both. "Knees on the chair, brat."

Day did as Jackson commanded, his fingers trying to find purchase on the back of the chair as Jackson gripped Day's hips and slammed back into him, ripping a cry of surprise from him. Jackson gripped Day's hair in his hand, craning his head back for a sloppy kiss that had him fucking his tongue into Day's mouth in time with his cock thrusting into Day's slick hole. There was nothing soft about this. Jackson wasn't worried about protecting Day, and he loved it. This

infuriating

was feral, animalistic, damn near a fucking felony, and Day never wanted Jackson to stop. He wanted to wake up with bruises on his hips and Jackson's handprints on his ass and an ache inside that let him know Jackson had bred him hard and deep.

Jackson gave a hoarse shout, biting down on Day's shoulder hard enough to pull a cry from his lips as Jackson spilled his release inside him. Jackson draped himself over Day, both of them fighting to suck air back into their lungs. Just when Day was sure Jackson was about to tell him this was a goodbye fuck, Jackson kissed the nape of his neck, his shoulders, his spine.

"You know you had that coming, right?" he asked, his voice no longer devoid of emotion.

Day hated the feeling of relief, the way his insides untwisted knowing Jackson wasn't ready to throw him away yet. "Yes, Daddy."

Jackson placed another gentle kiss on Day's shoulder, right where he had bit him. "Good. Let's go take a shower. If you're a good boy, maybe I'll let you come tomorrow."

Day looked down at his painfully swollen erection. "Tomorrow?" he pouted.

Jackson side-eyed him. "You're lucky I didn't say next week. Is that what you want?"

Day's heart felt like it was floating, orgasm or no.

"No, Daddy."

Jackson slung a heavy arm over Day's shoulders. "Good. Now, let's go take a shower."

eighteen

JACKSON

DAY HAD BEEN QUIET SINCE HIS PUNISHMENT. QUIET, but not upset. He seemed dazed or maybe just contemplative. He'd let Jackson wash him in the shower and he'd eaten the food Jackson brought to the bedroom without a word. When they laid down in bed and Jackson had rolled onto his side to wrap his arms around Day, he didn't put up a fight. If anything, he snuggled deeper, resting his head on Jackson's bicep, interlocking their fingers in a death grip.

Jackson didn't know what was happening in Day's head, but whatever it was seemed to be eating at him in a way he wasn't ready to share with Jackson yet. Maybe he regretted what happened at Jackson's mother's house. Part of that was on Jackson. He should have known better than to spring his whole family on Day like that. He clearly had no experience with that level of socialization. Jackson wasn't even entirely sure why he'd done it other than maybe to see if his mom saw in Day what he did.

"What's it going to take?" Day asked, his voice a step above a whisper.

Jackson frowned. "For what?"

"For you to see I'm not worth all this effort you're making?" There was a thickness to Day's words that nearly broke Jackson.

"Is that what you've been thinking about for the last two hours? What you can do to get me to run?" Jackson asked, holding Day tighter.

"You have to see by now that I'm not worth all this. My brain is broken. My heart is broken. That's never going to change," he said.

"I don't care," Jackson said, pressing his lips to Day's hair. "I don't care if you never learn to read. I don't care that you make your living in sex work. I don't care that you yell at old ladies in grocery stores or you try to come out swinging even when nobody's looking to fight you. I don't care."

"Why?"

infuriating

"Because my instincts tell me you're the one for me."

Day wiggled until Jackson loosened his grip enough to turn in his arms and look at him. Jackson used his thumbs to wipe Day's tears even as he said, "You're crazy. We've only known each other a week. I could be a serial killer. I could be somebody who knocks ice cream out of a toddler's hand." Jackson smiled at that, earning a frown from Day. "I could be a horrible, selfish person who only cares about myself."

"But you're not," Jackson murmured.

"You don't know that," Day said, his voice persistent, his tears still breaking free to slide down his nose and onto the pillow.

"I've trusted my gut for thirty-eight years, and it's never once been wrong. I'm not wrong about you."

Day's distress was tearing at Jackson's heart. "I have a gut, too."

"And what's it saying?"

Day shook his head. "It's telling me to run!"

Jackson tilted his head. "Is that your gut talking or your fear?"

"You think I'm afraid of you?" Day asked.

"I think you're afraid to think I could be right and we could be meant for each other."

Day scoffed, sniffling. "Why would that scare me?"

"I'm not a psychic or a therapist." Jackson ran his

thumb along Day's lip. "But, if I had to take a guess, I'd say it's because you're afraid of letting yourself feel something for me and then it being taken away from you. Which is a valid fear, but not worth never trying."

Day just shook his head, bewildered. "I'm not a good person, Jackson."

"You'll never convince me of that, Dayton."

Day took a deep breath and looked Jackson in the eye. "I killed my best friend."

Jackson blinked at Day, processing his words. It was on the tip of his tongue to tell Day that even murder wasn't enough to keep Jackson away from him. His hands weren't exactly clean, either. He'd made his fair share of kills both on and off the battlefield. "Explain."

"It's a long story, but she's dead and it's my fault. Just trust me."

"You have to trust me first. I've got nothing but time as far as you're concerned. Tell me what happened."

Day rolled back over, facing away from Jackson, and, for a minute, he thought maybe Day was done with the conversation. But then he said, "Her name was Sarah. We grew up together. Her family owned this restaurant, and Sarah would always sneak me food."

Jackson's stomach churned at Day's simple statement. Sneak him food? "Was your grandmother strict about your diet?"

infuriating

"My grandma hated me. To be fair, she hated my mother, and I was just an extension of her, and she never let me forget it. My mom was a stripper, and my grandma used to say, 'At least your mother could shake her ass to make a living. What are you gonna do, Dayton?' Guess I showed her," he said, giving a hollow laugh.

Jackson pressed his hand over Day's heart, but he didn't interrupt, no matter how badly he wanted to tell Day that his grandmother was clearly a damaged person, who took out her own insecurities on him. But maybe she was right about Day's mother. Who runs and leaves their child behind with a woman like that?

"Grandma liked to go next door and get drunk and high with the guy in the next trailer over. Nothing heavy at first. Just weed, sometimes pills. I never liked him. I hated the way he looked at me. He was always touching me, pinching me, looking at me in ways that made my stomach sick. She thought it was funny. So, any chance I got, I would go stay with Sarah in her tree house. When we were older, she would do my homework for me, so I didn't get any notes sent home. Those always set my grandma off, and believe me, nobody wanted my grandma pissed off."

Day shuddered, like he was right back there in his past. Jackson wanted more than anything to make it better somehow, but he knew Day had to get this off his chest. Whatever this was that was eating a hole through him.

"Sarah had a disease. Cystic fibrosis. She needed new lungs. She was on oxygen almost for as long as I could remember us being kids, but she never let it stop her from doing anything. She was always the first to audition for plays, even musicals. They never gave her singing parts, but they always gave her a role. She said it was because they felt sorry for her, but I think they just saw what I saw. She was this…I don't know… radiant light. She was just always happy and positive, and she would tell me that, as soon as she got her new lungs, we were going to move to LA and she would be a star and I would be her agent."

Jackson could feel Day's dread. He spoke each word like it was being pulled from him, like a splinter buried deep. Nothing could convince Jackson that Day had killed this girl, a girl he described as radiant, but he'd let Day pull the splinters out. It was the only way for him to heal.

"My grandma started doing heavy drugs when I turned thirteen. That's when things got real bad. She didn't care about whether I ate or whether we had power or water. She only cared about heroin and then the meth. When she started hinting about selling me

infuriating

to get her drugs, when she started making jokes about how I might be more useful than she first thought, Sarah threatened to tell her parents."

Good. Somebody should've told an actual adult, somebody who could've saved Day from that woman. But obviously nobody had or Day wouldn't be lying in Jackson's arms bearing his soul to him.

"But before Sarah could tell, she became really sick to the point where she couldn't leave the hospital anymore. That became our new playground. There were toys and video games there. Puzzles, coloring books, even a dog that would come once a week. The hospital became my escape. I stayed there for hours every single day. I think the staff felt sorry for me. They would bring me meal trays when they brought hers. They would bring us cookies and ginger ale. When I showered in her room, they pretended not to notice. It felt like a vacation to me, even with my best friend hooked up to so many machines. There were always cupcakes and even superheroes showing up to entertain. And then one day, she got the call. She was getting her transplant.

"She thought that would make her free, but getting the transplant meant she had to take a ton of drugs to keep her body from rejecting her new lungs, and they made her feel really sick, so she wouldn't eat and when she did eat, she'd vomit for hours. She was wasting away, and we all thought she'd die before she ever got to enjoy her new lungs.

"But then she got better. By the time we were fourteen, it was almost like she was a different person. By then, I was sleeping in the treehouse in her backyard to avoid my grandma's house. I didn't want to turn tricks so she could pay for her meth. And then she died. Just like that. They found her behind the tire store… OD'd." Day said it with no feeling. No joy or sorrow, no anything. Just the facts.

"Jesus," Jackson whispered. Day's grandmother had overdosed behind a tire store and that's not even the part that had broken him.

"I told Sarah I was leaving. I wouldn't let them put me in foster care. Everybody knew what went down in those places. I told her I was running away to LA, and that she could meet me there when she graduated. I imagined by then, I would have a place to live and a real job. I was so fucking stupid," he said, so disgusted with himself. "I packed my bag and the food Sarah stole for me, and I hopped on a bus and took it all the way to LA. That's where Carl found me. At the bus station. That's where they all go to hunt for their fresh meat. Stupid kids like me who don't know any better.

"He said I was pretty. Prettier than any girl he'd

ever met. He said I was so pretty that I was sure to be somebody's new meal within a week, but he could help. Carl owned this disgusting pay by the hour motel, riddled with every infestation imaginable. It was all junkies and pimps and girls and boys working to feed their drug habits. There was one room Carl kept for himself. He didn't live there or anything, he just said he couldn't rent it out. I never thought to ask why. So, he let me stay there. All I had to do was blow him whenever he wanted."

Rage poured over Jackson like warm water, his nostrils flaring. What kind of piece of shit scumbag forced a fourteen-year-old to trade oral sex for a roof over his head?

"Ow," Day muttered.

Jackson realized he was gripping Day tighter, fingers digging into Day's hip. "Sorry."

"It wasn't so bad. It was better than getting fucked. Most of my money would have gone to whatever pimp decided I was his to turn out and they would have gotten me hooked on drugs, just like my grandma. Carl was the lesser of two evils. Instead of doing drugs, I ran them. It wasn't exactly a financial windfall, but it was enough where I could get food and necessities from the bodega. I was too young for a real job, and I didn't have a birth certificate or a social security number anyway. I would write letters to Sarah and tell her how great I was doing, but I think she knew it wasn't true."

Jackson had imagined Day's childhood had sucked. Nobody as prickly as Day had come from a happy place. That level of self-protection usually came from years of emotionally insulating yourself from the next disappointment or heart break. But Jackson still hurt for Day. Life had been kicking him in the face pretty much since birth and Day still hadn't gotten to the part where he'd supposedly killed his best friend. Jackson wasn't even sure if Day knew he was just vomiting up his entire past to him. Maybe he thought Jackson would see his ugly past as a reflection of himself. He was wrong.

"She showed up on my doorstep one day. She had her bags with her. By then, I'd been there for almost two years, just treading water. I could tell she was shocked at how bad I looked, but she just smiled and dropped her bags and acted like we were staying at the Ritz and not in some disgusting motel with mold on the ceiling and stains on the mattress. I tried to convince her to leave, to go home. But she said there was nothing left for her in Idaho, and she couldn't handle her parents and their constant babying of her. She said she had enough meds to last her six months,

infuriating

and if she hadn't made it by then, she'd go home. I should have tried harder to make her go back, but I was just so fucking lonely, and it felt so good to have her there with me, to have somebody sleeping next to me every night. She made everything better."

Jackson wished there was something he could do or say to lessen the anguish in Day's words. The guilt was clearly weighing on him in ways Jackson would never understand. He had his own burdens to bear, his own wounds that hadn't healed, just closed. Whatever Day was about to confess, it couldn't be worse than the things Jackson had been forced to do in the name of fighting a war he hadn't even believed in. But none of that mattered. Day was all Jackson cared about. He just needed Day to be okay.

"For a while, we were fine. Sarah even managed to get work as an extra from time to time. Then she started getting plays in small theatre productions. Nothing that paid, but good experience. We would eat pizza and go bowling with her theatre friends. That's when I learned about camming. I was too young, but nobody knew that. Her friend, Lola, told me all about the money she made and how even guys, especially gay guys, could make good money, too. Sarah said it was illegal. That we could get in trouble for child porn, so I just let it go. But then Sarah got sick. Really sick. It happened so fast. We thought it was just the flu. Maybe bronchitis. But we didn't have insurance. Sarah was a runaway and I was underage. She was afraid if she went to the hospital, she'd get sent home and I'd go into foster care. She was always looking out for me.

"One day, after a visit with Carl, I came back to the apartment to find Sarah struggling to breathe. She was so pale and her lips were blue and she wasn't responding to me. I was so scared I called 911. But there was nothing they could do for her. She had a horrible infection throughout her whole body. A fungus had destroyed her new lungs because her anti-rejection meds had left her too immuno-compromised to fight it. She was only in LA for five months and she'd managed to live more than I had in the two years I'd been there…and it killed her. I killed her. She'd come out there to be with me because she knew I was miserable and lonely. That's what her mother told me at her funeral. Right before she told me she was sorry I'd ever met Sarah and that she regretted ever letting me into their home and that I was no better than my good for nothing trailer trash family. And she was right."

Jackson shifted until Day was on his back. "She was not. She was angry and hurting because she lost her child, but she wasn't right. No matter the reason your friend came to LA, she chose to stay. Even if it was a bad decision, she chose it. Not you. You were doing everything you could to survive while adults were taking advantage of you at every turn. Sarah wasn't your fault. Carl wasn't your fault. The fact that you managed to find a way to crawl out of that life is amazing, no matter how you had to do it. Do you know how many people never manage to do what you did?"

"It was the room," Day said, his cheeks flushed, his eyes dull and bloodshot. "The room was full of mold called aspergillus. It was growing on our carpet. It's why the room was empty. Carl wasn't allowed to rent it out because it could potentially cause people to get sick. It's why he let me stay there. There wasn't any payment exchanging hands, so he figured he wasn't doing anything wrong."

"It's a miracle you didn't get sick."

"I wish I had. By the time the health inspector made it out to figure out how a sixteen-year-old girl had gotten so sick, I'd managed to buy a fake ID. I went to Sarah's theatre friend and asked her to help me get set up. It took a long time to figure out what worked, but it kept food on the table and a roof over my head. Carl moved me to a room, once I could afford to pay, but he still expected to be serviced whenever he asked. Luckily, once I could get online and Carl helped me find a way around not being able to read, I realized that I could order my birth certificate online. When I turned eighteen and was legal, I found better sites and other ways to hustle guys out of their money. I've been doing it ever since. And that's it. That's my whole life story."

Day was staring at Jackson's chest, so he just kissed his temple. "It didn't work."

Day flicked his gaze to Jackson's, his confusion obvious. "What?"

"You didn't chase me off. I'm still here. If anything, I am honestly just upset that not a single person tried to help you without wanting something to gain for themselves. And that Carl guy is a pedophile and ought to be put in jail for his crimes."

Day shrugged. "Without him, I'd have been doing things a lot worse than blow jobs."

Jackson shook his head. "That doesn't make him a hero, Day. He took advantage of you. He hurt you. He put you in a dangerous situation, and it cost your friend her life. It could have cost you yours."

Day looked up at him. "You really don't care, do you?"

This time, it was Jackson who was confused. "What?"

"You really don't care about my past."

"We all have a past. You're not the only person with

infuriating

regrets and things they feel the need to atone for," Jackson said with a sigh before he reached up and switched off the lamp.

Once they were blanketed by the darkness, Day pressed kisses into Jackson's chest, his throat, and finally, his lips. It wasn't a kiss that was meant to go anywhere.

"Jackson?" Day whispered in the darkness.

"Yeah, baby?"

"If you break my heart, I don't think I'll survive it."

Jackson's chest tightened at the raw desperation in Day's words. "Your heart is safe with me, Day. I promise."

nineteen

DAYTON

"SO, WYATT OVERHEARD JACKSON TELLING LINC THAT you have some creepy stalker who is, like, killing people to prove he loves you. Is that true?"

Day looked up at Charlie from his spot in her lap. "You just totally say whatever pops into your head, huh?"

"So do you. Jackson told Linc that, too," Wyatt said. "He said you'd fight the wind if it whistled by you the wrong way."

Day couldn't even argue the point. Jackson wasn't wrong. It was just easier to swing first and ask questions later, even if his jabs were of the verbal kind.

infuriating

"I guess so. Yeah."

Wyatt sat on the floor, painting Day's toenails a coral color. He hadn't asked him to. They had just shown up out of the blue with face masks and nail polish and told him they were there for a self-care night. Day suspected Jackson had called them, but Day couldn't even be mad about it. Even though a few days had passed since he'd opened up to Jackson, the truth was, he felt like somebody had skinned him alive, like he was one big open wound.

"So, do you? Have a stalker, I mean?" Charlie asked just before she plucked another hair from between Day's brows.

"Ouch. Yes. I mean, I think so anyway."

"That's so cool," Charlie said before attacking his brows with far more force than Day deemed necessary.

"Charlie," Wyatt admonished.

"What? You know what I mean. I'm not saying I'd want somebody dead, but having a stalker is, like, A-list celebrity type status. I want to get to a level of fame where some crazy loser, who sits in his mother's basement, jerks off to my movies and imagines us in a fictitious relationship until it drives him mad. But, you know, without being murdered and becoming another Hollywood cautionary tale."

Day's eyes went wide, but Wyatt just shook his

head. "Ignore her. She was dropped on her head as a baby. She was super excited to find out our friend Robby grew up in a creepy cult, and she almost wet her pants when we learned our friend Elijah's husband is a card carrying sociopath, who we're almost positive has literally killed somebody. Maybe more than one somebody."

"Who are you people?" Day managed. "Ouch! I think my brows are plucked enough. I'm going to look like Joan Crawford in *Whatever Happened to Baby Jane*."

"That might be the gayest thing I've ever heard somebody say and I'm surrounded by them every day," Charlie said, delighted.

"Do you know how offensive that is?" Wyatt asked, shaking his head.

Charlie snorted. "I'm a card carrying family member, boo. I put the B in LGBT, baby."

"You do know the B doesn't stand for bitch, right?" Day asked.

Charlie gaped at him, and Wyatt howled with laughter. She held Day down and tweezed another hair, so he reached up and pinched her. She slapped him on the forehead, and then they all dissolved into fits of laughter.

When they finally settled, Wyatt asked, "What are you going to do? Just live with Jackson forever?"

infuriating

"Not like he'd mind. You've got him wrapped around your little…finger," Charlie added with a smirk. "You must have a magical ass. Jackson hasn't so much as dated since we've known him and you've got him two seconds away from proposing in a little over a week."

"Shut up," Day said, even though his heart was doing cartwheels behind his ribcage.

Wyatt threw a pack of cotton balls at Charlie before directing his questions at Day. "Do you think this guy will come after you? Do they have any leads about who he is?"

"No. Whoever it is seems to know enough about computers to hide their tracks, or maybe they're just lucky. I honestly just can't imagine anybody giving that much of a shit about me. It doesn't make sense. Like, it's all just fantasy, and he never even talked to me. He would just keep the screen black, which was hella creepy and made it really awkward for performances."

"Maybe he was afraid you'd recognize his voice?" Wyatt said, shaking the clear nail polish in his hand.

Day froze. Could that be it? "Maybe… Do you think? But I don't really know anybody. You're the closest thing I've had to friends in four years."

"It doesn't have to be a friend," Charlie said. "It

could be anybody who sees you on the regular. If binge-watching *Discovery Investigates* has taught me nothing else, it's that danger lurks around every corner and being married is a hazard to a woman's health." Wyatt scoffed, but Charlie didn't back down. "What? It's true. Marriage makes men stabby. The husband always did it."

"So, you think my stalker could be anybody I've ever met?" Day said, disappointment seeping into his voice.

"I mean, yeah, kind of. At least, every man you've ever met. A bank teller? Your yoga teacher? The guy who sells you your weed?" Charlie said.

"Who exactly do you think I am in this scenario? I can't afford a yoga teacher or weed, and my bank is PayPal and CashApp," Day said, shaking his head.

"I'm just saying, everybody is a suspect until proven otherwise. But, if I were you, I'd make a list of legit everybody I know and make Jackson run them down one by one. Besides, you just said you don't know that many people, so how hard could it be?"

Day didn't know how hard it could be. Could it be somebody from his gym? The laundry mat? The Chinese takeaway place? It made Day's blood run cold to think he could be having casual conversations with somebody whose obsession with him ran deep enough to kill.

infuriating

"Yeah. You're right. How hard could it be?" he said, voice dull.

BY THE TIME CHARLIE AND WYATT LEFT, JACKSON WAS in bed, but the door was open and the lights were on, and he could hear Jackson pecking away on his laptop. Day stripped off his clothes, fully prepared to join Jackson in his bed when a much better idea occurred to him.

He went to his drawer and pulled out a pair of pale blue thigh-high stockings, a brocade corset of the same color and a pair of lace shorts that hugged his ass. He laid on the bed and grabbed his phone, opening his FaceTime app and dialing Jackson's number.

It barely rang before Jackson's face appeared on the screen. Day's cock hardened the moment he saw Jackson's gorgeous face and noted he was shirtless. "Day?"

Day bit down on his lower lip, letting his teeth slide over it before he purred, "Hi, Daddy."

Jackson's brown eyes widened, one brow hiking up. "Hi, baby. What are you doing?"

"Thinking about you," he said, turning the screen so Jackson could see Day rubbing his semi-hard cock through his lace panties. "See?"

Jackson's response was a low rumble. "I do see. What is it you're thinking about me doing to you?"

Day sank into the pillows, pulling the phone back enough for Jackson to see the corset that stopped just below his chest, before pinching one of his nipples and moaning. "Touching me here…and here," he said, giving his other nipple the same treatment.

"Lick your fingers and do it again," Jackson ordered, his voice sliding over Day like silk. God, what Jackson did to him…it shouldn't be legal.

Day did as Jackson asked, sucking in a breath as his nipples tightened into stiff peaks. "That feels so good, Daddy."

"I bet you'd feel better if you slid those panties down just enough for you to show Daddy how hard you are for him."

Day wiggled the lace panties down and his cock sprang free, already rock hard and throbbing just from Jackson's few commands. "Now what, Daddy?" Day asked, holding his phone near his thigh so Jackson could see his erection and his face.

"I want you to jerk yourself off. Nice and slow. You're not allowed to come. This is all for me."

Day whined, his hips arching before his hand even closed around his cock. He bet Jackson could make him come untouched with only his words. Day fucked up into his fist, playing his thumb over his slit and rubbing it over the head of his cock, teasing the notch just underneath before coming back down. He could hear Jackson's breaths and knew instinctively Jackson's thick cock was already hard just from watching Day play with himself.

"That's good, baby. So good. I want you to go get a toy from your toy box and get it all nice and wet. Then I want you to get on all fours and set your phone on the bed between your legs so I can watch you open yourself up for me. Can you do that, baby?"

Day bit back a moan. He'd started a game that Jackson was fully prepared to finish. "Yes, Daddy."

Day found his favorite toy, a bright pink plug with a pink jewel on the base. He slicked it up with lube before sticking his ass in the air, his head on his pillow and his phone between his knees.

When Day pressed the tip against his hole, Jackson made a noise that went straight to Day's balls, a low hum of appreciation. "That's it, baby. Put it in nice and slow."

Day pressed the toy in until it was about a quarter of the way inside before his body protested, and he slipped it back out before trying again.

"That's it. You can take a little more for Daddy, can't

you?" Jackson asked.

Day moaned, pushing the toy a little deeper. "Yes, Daddy."

"That's my good boy."

Day's eyes rolled in pleasure, the combination of Jackson's voice and the toy pressing against his prostate almost too much to take. "It's so big, Daddy," Day whimpered.

"Bigger than Daddy?"

"No, Daddy."

"Then relax and show Daddy how you play with your toy. Once it's nice and deep, I have something for you."

How long had Day longed for somebody who wanted to play with him like this? Jackson was perfect. Too perfect. But Day didn't want to think about that. He didn't want to think about anything other than what was happening between them at that moment. "Yes, Daddy."

Day forced himself to relax, and stretched himself with the toy, pushing it deeper with each pass as Jackson uttered filthy words of encouragement until Day was leaking onto the bed and the plug was fully seated inside him.

"Now what, Daddy?"

"Now, you hang up and come show Daddy what

infuriating

you've done."

The phone disconnected, and Day stood, groaning as the plug shifted. He slid the lace panties back into place and walked the fifty steps to Jackson's room. Jackson was sitting up in bed, his cock tenting the covers over his lap.

"Hi, Daddy," Day murmured again, biting his lip and doing his best to look innocent.

"Come here," Jackson growled, crooking his finger.

Day took his time, his hips swaying as he made his way to stand beside the bed, just out of Jackson's reach.

"Show Daddy what you did," Jackson commanded, looking at Day with a heat in his gaze that made Day shiver. He turned, catching the top of his panties with his thumbs and sliding them down and off before spreading himself to show Jackson the plug. "Good boy."

Jackson peeled back the covers and once more beckoned Day. He licked his lips as he saw Jackson's perfect cock, so flushed with blood it was almost purple. Day climbed onto the bed, throwing a leg over Jackson's thighs but staying up on his knees. Jackson pressed on the base of the plug, forcing it against Day's prostate until his cock leaked. "Mm, Daddy…" Day whined.

"What baby? What do you want?" Jackson teased,

tugging on the plug just enough to put pressure on the muscles holding it in place.

"You Daddy. I want your big cock inside me. Fuck me."

"Say please," Jackson said, leaning forward to capture one of Day's nipples, licking and sucking it until Day was trembling.

"Please, Daddy."

Jackson gave Day's other nipple the same treatment, once again teasing the plug in and then out. "Say it like you mean it," Jackson told him, lips dragging along Day's throat to his ear, his voice raspy as he said, "Beg me."

Day didn't even hesitate. He looked deep into Jackson's eyes. "Please, Daddy. Please. I've been such a good boy. I want your cock so bad. I want it deep inside me. Fuck me, Daddy. Please," he pleaded before his lips found Jackson's, his tongue pressing between his lips, tasting toothpaste and mouthwash.

Jackson kissed Day back, one arm coming around his waist and the other jerking the plug free, ripping a gasp from Day's lungs that ended in a long low moan as Jackson thrust into him even as he dragged Day down.

"Is that what you wanted, baby?"

Day gripped Jackson's face on either side. "More," he begged. "Fuck me until I can't think of anything

infuriating

but you inside me. Fuck me so hard I still feel you there tomorrow. Please, Jackson."

"Fuck," Jackson growled, and then Day was on his back, his knees over Jackson's shoulders, practically folded in half, as Jackson did just as Day asked, wrapping his arms around his shoulders so he could hold Day in place as he drove into him again and again, every thrust driving the air from Day's lungs until he was light-headed and his body ached.

"Oh, fuck. Can I touch myself, Daddy. Please? I need to come."

"No," Jackson snarled against Day's ear. "You want to come, you can do it untouched."

Day whined, but the truth was, he wasn't exactly untouched. His cock was trapped between their sweat slicked bodies and, with just the slightest bit of adjustment, Day had the friction he needed each time Jackson thrust into Day. "Oh, fuck. You feel so good, Daddy. So good."

Jackson shifted, tilting Day's hips higher, and, suddenly, each roll of Jackson's hips sent a glancing blow across Day's prostate, driving whimpers and half-bitten moans until his orgasm barreled into him and his cock was shooting his release between them.

Jackson sat back on his heels, dragging Day's hips into his lap to drive into him, gripping his thighs tight and holding them open so he could watch himself disappear inside Day's body. If Day hadn't already come, that might have pushed him over the edge. Jackson's thrusts fell off kilter, and his body shuddered before he gave one last deep thrust inside Day, grinding his hips in aborted little thrusts as he emptied himself. He then collapsed on top of him, breathing heavy against his ear.

Day laughed, pushing at Jackson's shoulder. "You weigh a ton. You're crushing me."

"Deal with it," Jackson said, burying his face against Day's neck and holding him tight.

Day ran a hand over Jackson's bald head and down his back, not willing to fight Jackson when the truth was, he was more than comfortable beneath the heavy weight of his frame, even if the man was a furnace. The truth of the matter was that Day would happily spend the rest of his nights like this, and that scared the shit out of him.

"Jackson—"

Whatever Day was going to say was interrupted by the shrill scream of the alarm system going off, sending his heartbeat into the stratosphere.

twenty

JACKSON

JACKSON SLIPPED FREE OF DAY'S BODY AND ROLLED into a sitting position in one smooth move. "Get in the bathroom and lock the door," he said.

Day sat up. "Jackson, wait."

"Now, Dayton."

Jackson grabbed the gun from his drawer and thumbed off the safety, chambering a round, as he made his way out through the bedroom door, scanning the floor below for any sign of the invader. He could see the front door sat askew but there was no movement below. He crept down the stairs, his gaze sweeping the open space as he went. It was part of the reason he'd picked this apartment, aside from the twenty-four hour security downstairs and the alarm systems in each room. It was an open concept, giving Jackson a view of the whole apartment with nowhere for any assailant to hide.

Once Jackson realized there was nobody inside, he walked to the front door, keying in the code to turn off the screeching of the alarm just as his landline rang. He opened the door and stuck his head out, cognizant of the fact that he was still naked. His neighbors were in the hallway in various states of undress, glaring at him as if he had attempted to break into his own apartment. "Sorry, folks."

Jackson closed the door but stopped short, realizing there was an envelope on the ground. Jackson picked it up, locking the door before answering the phone.

"Hey, boss, it's Webster. The security company called. The alarm was triggered. You good?"

"Yeah, but somebody managed to break in. Call downstairs and have them get you the security footage. If they give you a hard time, you know what to do."

"I'm on it."

Jackson frowned as he opened the envelope and something fell out. He felt it bounce off his foot with a slight metallic clink, but he ignored it, focusing on the neatly folded piece of paper still inside. He flipped on the kitchen light and snagged the thin disposable gloves the housekeeper kept under the sink before pulling it free and opening it up.

I FOUND YOU.

DID YOU THINK YOU COULD JUST TAKE HIM FROM ME WITHOUT A FIGHT? YOU TOOK SOMETHING I LOVE, AND YOU BETTER GIVE HIM BACK BEFORE I RETURN FOR SOMETHING YOU LOVE.

HERE KITTY, KITTY.

Jackson's heart hammered against his ribcage as he leaned down to pick up the object that had fallen out of the envelope. It was a cat collar. Kevin's cat collar. It was bloody.

"Kevin?" Jackson called, his voice taking on a slight panicked sound. "Here, boy."

"Jackson?" Day called, standing at the top of the stairs in a t-shirt and a pair of threadbare shorts. "What's wrong?"

Jackson wanted to yell at Day for not listening to him but he had bigger things to worry about. Besides, the immediate danger to Day had passed. "We need to find Kevin."

"Why? Do you think he got out?" Day asked, closing

the distance between them. "Did you hurt yourself? Why are you wearing bloody gloves? Did he hurt Kevin?" With each question, Day's voice became more frantic.

"I don't know," Jackson barked. At Day's shocked look, Jackson softened his voice. "I don't know. Let's just search the house. Can you just look and see if he's hiding under one of the beds upstairs? And maybe throw me down my gym shorts?"

Day nodded, turning to do what Jackson asked, even though it was clear he didn't understand what was happening. Jackson stripped off the gloves and slid them inside the envelope. Could this fucking prick have gotten to Kevin? Did he have enough time after triggering the alarm? Had he somehow managed to trigger the alarm after he'd entered? If so, how long had he been in the fucking apartment? Christ. Jackson had been so distracted, he'd let this fucking psycho get close enough to hurt them. Dammit.

"Jackson!" Day shouted from upstairs.

Jackson glanced up to see Day holding Kevin in an awkward grip, the fat cat spilling over Day's arms. Jackson sighed with relief, meeting Day at the top of the stairs. He took the gym shorts Day held, slipping them on before taking Kevin from Day to look him over. He was unharmed. Not only was he unharmed, but his collar was still in place. Jackson glanced down to the collar on the counter. It was the same color, the same name tag. Everything identical. He placed Kevin on the floor, heading to his room. He snatched his phone and dialed Linc.

"Hey, brother. What's up?" Linc said, voice gruff from sleep.

Jackson dropped onto the edge of the bed, digging the heel of his hand into his eye. "I think this fucker may have finally made a mistake. I think he can see us."

At Day's sudden intake of breath, Jackson pulled him close. Day dropped onto Jackson's knee, and he wrapped an arm around him, grateful to have him close.

There was the rustling of covers and Wyatt's sleepy voice asking, "What now?"

"Go back to sleep," Linc muttered before a door closed. "You think he's got eyes on you in your own apartment?" Linc asked, fully alert. "How?"

"I don't know, but I want a team in here ASAP to sweep for cameras or any kind of remote access devices. I have Webster pulling footage from the security feed, but this fucker probably wouldn't be stupid enough to show his face. Maybe, if we can figure out how he's watching us, we can trace it back somehow? I also want to know where this guy showed up the first time. What site? Once we've got a company name, I want a meeting with their IT people, like yesterday."

"Yeah, I'm on it."

Jackson disconnected without saying goodbye. He tossed the phone on the bed and wrapped both arms around Day who said, "Do you really think he's finally made a mistake?"

Jackson kissed Day's shoulder. "I don't know for sure, but I hope so."

"Do you really think he's watching us? Even now?" Day asked, looking around with a shudder.

"Either that or he's found a way to Houdini himself in and out of my apartment. I'm not sure which idea I like less."

"Me either," Day mumbled. "I'm really sorry about all this."

Jackson gripped Day's chin gently, forcing his head upwards. "Hey, none of this is your fault. Keeping you safe is my job."

"I'm not even paying you," Day reminded him.

Jackson caught Day's lips in a fierce kiss. "It's not my job because you're paying me. It's my job because you're mine, and I protect what's mine."

Day dropped his head to Jackson's shoulder. "Did you think he hurt Kevin?"

infuriating

Jackson smiled, not because of Kevin, but because, for the first time, Day hadn't argued that he and Jackson were a thing. "Yeah, I thought it was possible. But he's fine. You're both fine, and you'll both stay that way."

"Charlie and Wyatt think I know him," Day said after a few minutes.

"Why do they think that?"

Day looked at Jackson, his pool blue eyes wary, like he was almost too exhausted to be afraid. "Because he never speaks or shows his face. Do you think it's true? That it's somebody I've met? Charlie said it could be anybody I've ever talked to, even in casual conversation."

"Is there anybody you talk to on a regular basis who knows about you camming?" Jackson asked.

Day shook his head. "No. It's not something I talk about to people. Not that I even talk to people. I don't have friends. I don't even have casual acquaintances anymore. Not since Sarah died. Like, the only people I ever talk to are bill collectors, my cable provider, my new gross landlord, and the guy who works in the payroll department for my camming site," Day said, sounding annoyed. "They screw up my pay constantly. He says there's some kind of glitch with my account. Every time we think it's fixed, it happens all over again."

Jackson looked at Day, frowning. "It's always the same guy you talk to?"

"Yeah, his name is Oscar. He's always making really bad jokes."

Jackson reached for his phone. "Do you know Oscar's last name?"

"No, we're not exactly BFFs or anything."

Jackson called Webster and relayed this new information before hanging up. "It can't hurt to at least run a background check on the guy."

Day went quiet, his top teeth digging into his bottom lip until Jackson tugged it free, rubbing his thumb across it.

"I don't want to spend my whole life looking over my shoulder, Jackson," Day said, his voice one step above a whisper.

Jackson could see the toll this was all taking on him. Day was good at hiding, good at making a joke out of things that he couldn't fix. Good at using sex as a shield to protect himself from everything he'd been through in his life. But this was all wearing on him. He had slight bluish purple shadows under his eyes, and he looked pale under the dim bedroom lights. Jackson wondered if Day was eating enough. He certainly wasn't getting much sleep. That was Jackson's fault.

infuriating

"You won't. We'll figure this out. He's going to make a mistake eventually. He might have already. Okay?"

Day nodded. "Yeah, okay."

Jackson stood, bringing Day with him. "No use going to sleep. Let's take a shower before the guys get here to sweep the place. Then I'll make you breakfast. You need to eat something." Jackson sighed. "Besides, I gotta call Jimmy and let him know what's been going on. I haven't spoken to him since you got the email."

Day grimaced at Jimmy's name. Jackson didn't blame him. He had no idea how his father had been friends with Jimmy, much less partners. He always struck Jackson as being greasy. There was just always something off about the guy.

"Can we have sex in the shower?" Day asked, jumping into Jackson's arms, fully confident Jackson would catch him.

Jackson rolled his eyes as his hands found Day's ass and squeezed. "You are insatiable. We don't have a lot of time."

He wrapped his legs around Jackson's torso, grinding his semi-hard cock against Jackson's. "I don't need a lot of time, Daddy. Promise."

"You're such a little monster," Jackson murmured, catching Day's lips in a dirty kiss.

"I just have a weird fear response… It makes me

horny," Day said between kisses before leaning back and giving him an exaggerated pout. "It's not my fault. I had a bad childhood."

Jackson chuckled. "I'm sure that's what it is. Your bad childhood. Not that you're just a giant ball of hormones."

"I could make a really corny joke here about making this whore moan but it's beneath me," Day said, still actively rubbing his cock against Jackson's now equally hard erection through the thin material of their shorts. "This is good, too, you know? You could just put me up against the wall and we could rub off on each other."

Jackson placed biting kisses over Day's mouth before teasing his tongue between Day's lips. "What am I going to do with you?"

"I have an alphabetized list," Day assured him. "We're at F for frotting."

Jackson gave Day what he was begging for, quick and dirty, setting him down on the bathroom counter and pushing their shorts out of the way so their cocks could slot together. It felt amazing, but Jackson was enthralled with Day and the blissful look on his face while he worked himself against Jackson, head thrown back, lips parted, breathing heavy. He was just too fucking beautiful. When Day came, Jackson used his

infuriating

release to jerk himself off hard and fast, kissing Day deep before spilling between them.

Day fell back on his hands, grinning at Jackson, and his heart did this funny skipped beat thing. Yeah, Day was definitely it for Jackson. He couldn't imagine not having him in his life. Now, he just had to convince Day of that.

twenty-one

DAYTON

GROUPS OF PEOPLE MOVED IN AND OUT OF JACKSON'S apartment all day, checking every nook and cranny for the cameras he was certain were there. In the end, he was right. Somebody had managed to slip into his home without detection, replacing the smoke detectors downstairs with ones containing a tiny camera as well as one in the upstairs hallway. Luckily, there were none in the bedrooms.

Day had sat on the sofa, legs pulled beneath him, chewing on his thumbnail as strangers pretended not to look at him as they moved around their boss's home. He did his best to stay quiet and out of the way,

infuriating

but when three strangers entered his room, he jumped up, suddenly realizing they intended to go through all of his things. His personal private things. Day already felt like his life wasn't his own. He had already bared his soul to Jackson.

Before Day could even get the words out to protest, Jackson was pulling them out of Day's room, taking the equipment from them and re-entering the room on his own, bringing only Linc with him. Somehow, that was better. Linc was Jackson's best friend. Wyatt and Linc had lots of kinky sex. There was nothing in there that would shock Linc or cause him to look at Jackson differently. Day never wanted to be an embarrassment to Jackson.

By the time the team was gone, Day's nerves were frayed. Jackson made them a quick dinner and put on a movie, but the moment Jackson set his plate down, Day was on him, stripping him bare and riding him right there on the sofa, channeling all his nervous energy into the one thing he could control, the one thing that made him feel good. Jackson let him control the speed, the intensity, jerking Day in time with his thrusts, until they got off and Day's head was quiet for just a little while.

"Why didn't he put cameras in the bedrooms? Do you think he was interrupted?" Day asked Jackson when they were lying naked and sated on the couch. The only light in the room was a random scenic picture on the television screen saver.

Jackson gazed down at Day where he was lying between Jackson's splayed legs, head on his thigh, Jackson's soft cock close enough to feel Day's breath each time he spoke.

"Maybe. He clearly knows we're in a physical relationship. Maybe he didn't think it was necessary since we've been uploading to your website. Maybe he didn't want to interrupt his fantasies about being your first."

Day shivered at the idea. How could somebody he barely knew become so fixated on him? "Do you think this is my fault? Do you think I brought this on myself?" he asked, finally voicing the thought that had been circulating in his head since Wyatt and Charlie had implied he might know his stalker.

Jackson ran his fingers through Day's hair. "No. Of course not. You didn't do anything wrong. Just because some psycho has an imaginary relationship with you, it doesn't mean you did anything to provoke it. It's no different than a stalker imagining a relationship with a celebrity." Day pushed his head up into Jackson's caress, not satisfied with his answer. "Celebrities don't tweet about needing somebody to use their hole. They don't call their clients Daddy. I put myself out there. I let them think they stood a chance."

Jackson shook his head. "You're offering clients a fantasy, an escape. No sane person out there thinks that the person on these chat services is actually offering up their bodies. Not unless explicitly stated."

Day's stomach twisted. "Except, I did explicitly state it. I offered up my virginity to the highest bidder, knowing full well nobody would ever really be able to meet my price. I knew there was nobody on that site I would be willing to have sex with, on or off camera. I just wanted to make enough money to get out of LA. I hate it here."

"You do?" Jackson asked. "You never told me you wanted to leave LA."

Day shrugged. "Why would I? I never expected us to be…whatever this is. I never expected to meet somebody who gave a shit where I lived or what I did for a living. I know what I am to people. A body to use. A hole to fill. They don't care about my day or if I eat. They don't care if I can't pay my rent or if I need to go to the doctor. And that was fine. It *is* fine. It was just an exchange. They gave me money, and I gave them my time. I gave them the fantasy. It was a way to keep a roof over my head or food in my stomach without having to trick on the street. I never anticipated you."

Jackson dragged his blunt nails across Day's scalp. "If it makes you feel better, I never anticipated you, either. And you are so much more than just a hole to fill or a body to use. I wish you could see you the way I do."

Tears pricked behind Day's eyes at Jackson's words, but he didn't press. He wasn't sure if it made him feel better or worse that Jackson saw him as something more. His words kicked up a tornado in his head, a whirlwind of emotions making him feel like he might just fly apart into a million pieces.

He scooted closer, taking Jackson's soft cock into his mouth, not actively trying to get him hard again but just needing to be closer, needing Jackson inside him somehow. Day had done this to Jackson once before, after he'd given him a blowjob on the balcony. Just like then, Jackson didn't protest, just kept petting his hands through Day's hair.

Day wanted nothing more than to believe in Jackson's notion that there was a happily ever after for them, but Day had twenty-two years of anecdotal evidence that said otherwise. Day didn't think people like him got to live out their happily ever afters. Maybe he was working off bad karma. Maybe he'd just lost some universal lottery system before he was born. Either way, he didn't know how to wrap his head around what a life with Jackson would even look like. If Day wasn't camming, what would he do? Flip burgers? He couldn't even fill out the application without help.

Jackson was worth millions, but Day didn't want to live off of him. He didn't want to feel like he was just some trophy husband. *Husband.* The thought made Day's stomach slosh. Is that what Jackson saw for them? A house with a white picket fence and a mess of kids, like his sisters? Would Day be expected to stay at home with their kids? They'd have to hire tutors. Day couldn't even help them with the most basic of homework assignments.

Their kids… Jesus. Day was so far down the rabbit hole, he could no longer see daylight.

Jackson shifted his hips slightly. He was hard again just from being in Day's mouth. He never second guessed this. They were so good at this. Sex came as easily as breathing; their bodies fit together like puzzle pieces. Jackson was the most perfect Daddy, and there wasn't anything Day wouldn't do to be his good boy. He teased his tongue around the head of Jackson's thick cock, sucking him leisurely as his hand massaged his balls.

Fingers threaded through Day's hair, and then Jackson was dragging him upwards, shifting on the sofa so that he spooned Day. His head rested on

Jackson's bicep, Jackson's arms locked around Day's body, like he was afraid Day might run. When Jackson pushed his knee between Day's thighs, he sighed, moaning when Jackson's hard cock slipped between Day's cheeks, catching on his slick and leaking hole. Jackson slid inside Day in one smooth contraction of his hips, forcing a whimper from Day.

"You okay, baby?" Jackson asked, the concern in his voice tearing Day up inside.

"Yeah, Daddy," Day managed, voice thick.

Day wasn't okay. He was overwhelmed. Jackson was wrapped around him, buried within him, lips dragging open mouth kisses along his shoulder, his throat, running his tongue along the shell of his ear. It was almost lazy in comparison to their earlier session where Day rode Jackson hard and fast, begging him to breed his hole, to choke him.

This time, Jackson held Day's arms hostage against his body as he just rolled his hips, working himself into Day, slow and deep. "Do you have any idea how fucking beautiful you are? How happy I am that you were just dropped into my life?"

Day couldn't speak past the sudden lump in his throat. He hadn't signed on for this. He didn't know what to say, so he just tilted his head back and captured Jackson's lips in a kiss that he hoped

infuriating

somehow conveyed to Jackson that he heard him, even if he couldn't bring himself to speak.

The kiss didn't stop Jackson, though. He kept murmuring words of praise against his ear as he used Day's body, jerking him in time with every movement. "You're so sweet, so open. I love waking up next to you every day. I love your big heart and the way you tell off mean old ladies in grocery stores and even the way you yell at my clients to protect me. You're so sexy and so confident in your sexuality. It's so hot. I love that you wear makeup and soft lacy things, and I love when you wear your glasses and your holey sweatpants, too."

"Jackson," Day managed, tears streaming down his face. If Jackson saw it in the dim light of the living room, he was kind enough not to say anything.

"It's true. I'm never going to stop telling you the truth. You might not see it, but I do. You're smart and funny and fierce, and I need you in my life, Day, just as you are. I'll do whatever is necessary to protect you and keep you forever. I mean it." Jackson suddenly pulled free of Day's body. "Roll over. I want to look at you."

Day hesitated, wiping at his cheeks before doing as Jackson asked. He caught Day's leg with his arm before slipping back inside. Jackson's tempo quickened, and the slow rolls of his hips became hard thrusts as he captured Day's mouth, his tongue moving in time with his cock.

When the kiss ended, Day stayed as he was, their lips almost touching, both of them panting hard, Day thrusting down each time Jackson drove upwards until each motion caused Day to moan Jackson's name, begging him for more, even though there was really nothing more he needed from him. It was all just too much. He'd never imagined this level of intimacy with another human being. He'd never thought there'd ever be a single soul who looked at him and saw anything worth looking at.

Day held Jackson's face in his hands, their foreheads pressed together, lips pressed together, his cock trapped between their bodies, rubbing against their sweat-slicked bellies, as warmth began to pool low in his belly. "I'm close, Jackson."

Jackson growled at the sound of his name on Day's lips. "You can come, baby. I wanna feel it. Come for me."

Day moaned low and long as his second orgasm hit him, his whole body shivering as he came between them. Day dropped his head to rest on Jackson's arm, too blissed out to help Jackson find his pleasure. But Jackson didn't need help. He gripped Day's hips, driving his cock deep three more times, before he was shouting, his hips grinding against Day, emptying himself inside for the second time in as many hours in a way that made him feel claimed...even loved.

Neither of them made any attempt to move; Jackson stayed buried in Day, even soft. Day pressed kisses into Jackson's chest, his eyes drifting shut as sleep began to overtake him. Jackson cuddled Day close, and even though they were sweaty and sticky and covered with drying cum, Day wanted to stay just as he was, safe in Jackson's arms.

"I know you don't believe me, Day, but I love you just as you are."

Jackson's words were so quiet, Day almost thought he imagined them. He burrowed closer. "I don't know how to trust that, not after two weeks. Maybe not even after two years. You just have to give me time, Jackson. If you love me like you say you do, you'll give me time to see that you can love me no matter how bad I get."

"I'm a patient man, Day. I'll wait forever, as long as you're here with me."

"Your mom was right. You really are a romantic."

Jackson kissed Day's forehead as he drifted off to sleep.

twenty-two

JACKSON

"I GOT SOME INFO ON YOUR GUY," WEBSTER SAID BY way of greeting.

Jackson dug his palm into his eye, grunting in response, his phone tucked between his face and his shoulder. Day was sound asleep on top of Jackson's chest, head tucked right up under his chin and hands tucked under Jackson's back. They'd stayed up late and then fallen asleep on the couch and Jackson was feeling it.

"You know it's, like, eleven in the morning…right, boss?" Webster asked, tone chipper.

"You know I can fire you and hire five guys just like

infuriating

you for the cost of your salary…right, employee?" Jackson grumbled.

Webster snickered. "But would they be as pretty as me? I think not."

Jackson wasn't in the mood to play games. "Just tell me what you got before I do fire you, pretty boy."

Day stirred at Jackson's slightly elevated voice, wiggling his naked little body against Jackson in a way that he definitely wasn't mad about. "Who are you calling pretty boy when I'm right here naked, hard, and horny?" Day pouted, voice sleep soaked.

"Hush," Jackson said before adding, "You know I think you're the prettiest boy."

"Uh, should I call you back, boss? Sounds like your pro-bono client has some additional duties for you to attend to."

"Webster…" Jackson said, his voice a warning.

"You tell him, Daddy," Day grumbled, stretching his limbs with an audible groan before snuggling deeper into Jackson with a sigh that puffed into his face, his morning breath making Jackson grimace, then smile. Day didn't seem in any hurry to wake up, and if Webster didn't have anything concrete, Jackson had no interest in leaving this spot until he was good and ready. He'd be more than happy to spend every day waking up with his arms full of sleepy, snuggly

Day, bad breath and all.

"Dad—" Webster started, the question in his voice evident.

Jackson cut him off. "If you finish that word, I will not only fire you, I'll blacklist you to every security firm in the entire world," he warned.

There was another snicker from Webster before he said, "Yeah, yeah, yeah. Fine. So, the guy you're looking for, Oscar Delgado, is in charge of the payroll for Day's main camming account, which is interesting because while Oscar Delgado doesn't have a record, Oscar Salazar does."

"Who the fuck is Oscar Salazar?" And why should Jackson give a shit?

"A two-time felon who's done two short stints in prison. One for attempted rape and another for second degree murder, which got bumped down to manslaughter. He got eight years but only served four before he was paroled for good behavior."

"Are you trying to tell me that Oscar Delgado and Oscar Salazar are the same person? Because if they're not, I might still consider firing you," Jackson murmured, wishing this conversation had happened after coffee.

"I'm telling you that Oscar Salazar has reinvented himself as Oscar Delgado, and Oscar Salazar no longer exists. It takes skill to disappear and reappear as a completely separate person. Like, it takes technical skills or Fed friends. I suppose he could have turned state's evidence on somebody but I sincerely doubt it. It would take me a lot longer than two days to dig up information if the Marshalls had shoved him in witness protection. This was thorough but by no means Fed thorough."

"So, you think this Salazar guy could be Day's stalker?"

There was a creaking on the other side of the line as Webster moved in his ancient office chair. Jackson hated it, but Webster was weirdly superstitious about the chair. "I'm just saying if he managed to disappear himself and reappear a year later with a new life, he definitely has the skills to hide his location. Also, he seems to have frequent phone meetings with Day, which your boy said seemed contrived. He's local. His home address is less than five miles from Day's apartment, and the cam headquarters is right here in LA. Maybe he wasn't trying to hide his face but his voice?"

"I can't do much with maybe," Jackson rasped.

Webster sighed. "You could hand it over to the cops, let them interrogate him. It just seems like one too many coincidences."

"I'm going to go down there and question him

myself," Jackson said. "I'll take Day. If we surprise him, we might be able to get his knee-jerk reaction to seeing Day there in the flesh."

"That's a bad idea, boss. What if he flips and pulls a weapon?"

"I'm not leaving Day alone and I'm not leaving this up to Jimmy. We have the element of surprise on our side and the fact that he's at his place of employment where nobody knows him as anything but an upstanding citizen. If anything, he'll try to play dumb and act innocent. If he's lying, I'll be able to tell."

"You're the boss, boss, but if you end up on the six o'clock news, don't say I didn't warn you."

Jackson shook his head. These idiots had no respect. "Shoot me everything you have including his home and business addresses and his previous record."

"Yeah, on it. But how are you going to get to him if he's working? Are you just gonna waltz in there with your little Kewpie doll cupcake on your arm and demand to see the payroll guy so you can interrogate him?"

"I have one nerve left, Webster. And you're getting on it."

The truth was, Jackson had zero idea how he was going to convince the cam service to let him talk to Oscar, the head of payroll, but that wasn't going to

infuriating

stop him. He'd think of something on the way. All he really wanted was to see the man's reaction to being confronted with Day there in person. If he was as obsessed with Day as his stalker was, Jackson would see it on his face no matter how hard he tried to hide it. He'd conducted countless interrogations in the military. He was great at reading people.

"The details are in your inbox. Watch your six, boss."

Jackson didn't say goodbye, just disconnected, setting his phone back on the table and wrapping his arms around Day. "Time to wake up, sleepyhead."

"Just five more minutes, Daddy," Day groaned.

"We got a lead on who might be after you. Don't you want this to be over?" Jackson asked, sliding his hands up and down Day's spine.

"And then what happens?" Day asked, voice quiet.

Jackson frowned, staring down at the top of Day's head. "What do you mean?"

"I mean, do I just go back to my apartment? Back to camming? Are we dating? You said you think I'm the one for you and that you'll wait until I'm ready, but do you really want to be this forty-year-old captain of industry type with your sex worker boytoy at work functions? Wouldn't that be embarrassing for you?"

Jackson caught Day under the chin. "If you want to keep camming, I'm fine with it. I don't want to control your life. But if you don't, we'll find you something else. Something different, something that meets your skillset."

"Like what? I can't fill out applications. I can't read or write. Hell, I can't even sign my name. There's nothing else out there for me, Jackson. I don't want to cam, but I don't want to sit at home while you pay my bills, either."

Jackson kissed Day's lips. "As much as the idea of you being here and naked every night when I get home sounds appealing, you are so much more than just a body. You're incredibly smart. I can count on one hand the number of people I know who can speak more than two languages, much less five. You have a gift. You also have a disability that probably hasn't been re-examined since you were a child. You have more options than you think, Day, I promise, but I didn't get where I am in life by worrying about what other people think. My inner circle knows me and my values, my family knows me and my values. It's their opinion that matters, and they see in you the same things I do. Stop acting as if loving you is some kind of act of charity. I promise you, between the two of us, you're the catch."

That brought Day up onto his forearms, his elbows digging into Jackson's ribs hard enough to make him grunt. "How do you figure that?"

"I'm really boring, Day. I go to work. I go to the gym. I come home, take a shower, eat my dinner on the couch while watching football or whatever else happens to be on. I like to walk along the water. I like to eat Cuban food in hole in the wall places. I hate clubs. I hate fancy parties. I hate concerts and fireworks because the noise and the lights trigger flashbacks to a time I've worked hard to put behind me. My idea of a big night out is maybe going to a restaurant that won't make me wear a jacket, but nobody cooks better than my mom, so honestly, I would rather just eat at her house."

"To me, that all sounds like a vacation. I'll take boring any day. I don't think there's ever been a time in my whole life when I wasn't afraid. Ever. There was always some kind of impending doom hanging over me. Every decision was mine to make and every failure mine to claim. Except here. I like that you just make dinner without making me pick what to eat. I like that you just tell me what to do and I do it. Sometimes, at my old place, I wouldn't eat all day because the simple act of deciding whether to eat a Pop-Tart or ramen seemed like too big a decision. It's sad that there's somebody who wants me dead and this is still the most relaxed I've ever been."

Jackson frowned. Did he make the decisions? He

supposed he did. It wasn't intentional. He was just used to being in charge. Getting shit done. Day had never voiced a complaint, so Jackson assumed he didn't mind. It had never occurred to him that it was something Day wanted or even needed for his own peace of mind. "I like taking care of you. I like that you let me take care of you."

Day's smile grew flirty. "You can take care of me now."

Jackson knew Day was deflecting with sex. When things got too intense, the conversations too heavy, Day always went back to being the sex kitten. Jackson cupped Day's face, tugging him close until their lips met, then pulled back before Day could deepen the kiss. Day whined, but Jackson shook his head. "No. Uh-uh. We need to track down this guy once and for all and get this figured out so we can figure *us* out without the fear of somebody trying to hurt you looming over us. Okay?"

Day folded his hands on Jackson's chest, dropping his chin on top to give Jackson a sullen look. "Fine, but Webster's right. If we end up on the six o'clock news, I'm going to be real mad."

"Oh, please. You'd love it if you ended up on the six o'clock news. Hell, you dress like you anticipate being followed by paparazzi."

"It's not my fault I have an eye for fashion and a need to be visually interesting. We can't all live our lives in mostly monochromatic color pallets," Day countered.

Jackson rolled his eyes. "Well, when this is all over, you can pick me out an entirely new wardrobe if you like. My sisters would love it."

"I'm going to hold you to that," Day said before sliding off of Jackson, making sure to pause to rub against Jackson's morning erection on his way by.

"You're such a tease."

Day shrugged one shoulder. "You're the tease. I offered, you refused. That's on you."

Jackson lurched from the couch, crouching low and snagging him behind the knees and upending him over his shoulder, smacking his ass as Day yelped indignantly.

"What are you doing? Put me down."

"You wanted me to take care of you, right?" Jackson asked as he marched up the stairs. "We're going to take a shower and you're going to take care of me first, and if you stop squirming, I'll make sure I take good care of you, too."

Day sagged against Jackson, all the fight leaving his body as he played Jackson's butt cheeks like bongos. "Yes, Daddy."

twenty-three

DAYTON

THE HEADQUARTERS OF WPI SAT IN THE HEART OF LA in a glossy, mirrored building that stood head and shoulders above the surrounding buildings. The interior of the lobby smelled like canned air and lemon scented cleanser. A waterfall took up the entire east wall and provided a white noise to mask the calls the three receptionists fielded behind the shiny pale wood lacquered counter.

"They own this entire building?" Day asked Jackson. "Like, all this is for Camscape?"

"No. WPI is a holding company. They own several cam companies, a few of the larger adult film companies, some adult toy sites, and other various entertainment companies of the less adult varieties."

Jackson had called Detective Jimmy to ask him to arrange a meeting with WPI's head of security but told him not to tell them what it was about. Jackson's plan had seemed crazy at first, but even if Oscar was a crazed stalker and a murderer, Day found it hard to believe he would whip out a gun and start firing in the midst of all these people in their fancy business clothes, surrounded by ten foot palms and greenery that made Day feel like he was in some sort of arboretum.

Day wiped his sweaty palms on the knees of his black jeans and once more shifted in his seat. He felt underdressed beside Jackson, who looked like he belonged in a place like this with his perfectly tailored gray slacks, black cashmere sweater that clung to his muscles, and sleek black loafers. He looked more than like he belonged. He looked hot. The moment they'd entered, the women behind the front desk had exchanged knowing glances and sly smiles. Jackson really was everybody's type.

Jackson leaned in, his lips moving against Day's ear. "Relax, baby. You know I won't let anybody hurt you, right?"

Day gave a hesitant nod but that wasn't really his concern. Here, in this huge business lobby, somehow, the idea of Oscar being his stalker seemed almost too absurd to consider. He knew it was a bizarre thought to have. It wasn't as if all stalkers lived in darkened basements, moving through sewers or darkened city streets like cartoonish super-villains, but he couldn't shake the feeling that this was all wrong. "Something's off about this."

Jackson frowned as he looked at Day. "About what?"

Day twitched, his hand spasming in a sort of aborted gesture. "This. All of this. I just don't think he's our guy," he finished with a whisper.

"Well, if he's not, we'll keep looking. This is the first solid suspect we've found, so we've got to let it play out and see how things go."

"Yeah, I guess. I'm just so ready for all of this to be over. It's like being followed by a ghost. I can feel him around me all the time, but he hasn't made a direct threat against me, so it feels surreal, impossible even that somebody would think I was worth killing for. I know that sounds crazy, but my brain can't make the leap from a guy I've talked to once a month on the phone being somebody so obsessed with me he's willing to kill."

"People who are this level of psychotic have no problem achieving the level of mental gymnastics that allows them to imagine a relationship with a total stranger. There have been several cases of stalkers killing over people they've never even met face to face. That is what makes them so hard to catch. It's why often nobody even knows the obsession was there at all until it's too late to save the victim."

Day shivered at that but shook his head. "But does this Oscar guy have a history of stalking or some kind of history that makes him a more likely candidate than any random guy off the street or even in this building?"

"He's got enough of a history to make me think he's capable of this, yes." Day gave Jackson a flat stare at his lack of an answer. He sighed. "He has a history of rape and manslaughter."

Day swallowed audibly. "Jesus."

"That's not going to happen to you. Nothing will happen to you. I promise."

Day didn't have a chance to answer. A man in gray slacks and a pale pink button down shirt walked towards them with purpose. He was fit, mid-fifties with snowy white teeth and a widow's peak. He wore black framed glasses. He looked like everybody and nobody, but when he extended his hand, first to Jackson and then to Day, he gripped both their hands with a friendly confidence that made Day feel even more certain they were on the wrong track.

"Mr. Avery. Marcus Lane, head of security. I spoke with your detective friend, but I'm afraid he gave very little information on the phone. How can I help you?" The man spoke to Jackson, but his eyes kept moving back to Day, his gaze questioning.

"My client, Mr. Daniels, has been working with one of your employees in payroll regarding a recurring error on his payments, and I was hoping we might be able to speak to him."

Lane's eyes widened then narrowed. He was clearly not expecting this to be a money issue. "Are you inferring that this employee has in some way committed a crime in regards to your client's pay?"

"No, not at all. We're investigating another matter entirely, and we have reason to believe that your employee might be able to offer some insight into this separate matter. I assure you that this has nothing to do with anything that might be a liability on the part of the company. I just thought it was better to reach out to you before I asked to speak with an employee on company time so as not to upset anybody."

Day did his best not to gape at Jackson as he smoothly navigated around any potential verbal icebergs, speaking without really giving any information away.

"Employee name?" Lane asked.

infuriating

"Oscar Delgado."

The man reached behind him, and for a split second, Day had visions of the man pulling out a weapon. Instead, he pulled a phone from his back pocket and pressed some buttons. "Hey, Ben. Marcus. Is it possible for me to steal Oscar for about thirty minutes?" There was a brief pause as Day assumed Ben was answering. "No. Nothing to worry about. Just some routine security stuff. Yeah, that should be fine. Thanks, man."

Lane disconnected and smiled. "Oscar is at lunch for another ten minutes. The department heads usually go to lunch later so that the support staff can take their lunches on time. Ben said he'd put a note on his desk to head down as soon as he's back. I'll have Debbie open the first floor conference room for you and show you in as soon as he arrives."

"Thank you, Mr. Lane," Jackson said, giving him his best smile.

"Not a problem at all. If you need anything further, just let Debbie know and she'll get a hold of me."

With one last long look at Day, the older man disappeared back into the bank of elevators on the right, leaving Jackson and Day alone in the cavernous lobby once more. Day tried not to fidget but as ten minutes turned into fifteen then twenty, Day's stomach began to churn. The idea of meeting Oscar face to face suddenly seemed less like a notion and more like a reality, and he wasn't sure he could stand there and look at a man who may have slit Jay's throat right in front of him. "Maybe this was a bad idea," Day muttered.

"What's wrong?" Jackson asked.

"Uh, I am two minutes away from standing in front of a guy who might have murdered another guy for me. I don't know if I can do this."

Jackson gave him a reassuring look. "You are one of the fiercest, scariest people I know. You're always ready to fight, even when nobody's challenging you. You're tougher than you know."

"This isn't exactly the same as me telling some crotchety old lady at the grocery store to get fucked. This is somebody who might potentially want to kill you and/or me."

This time, it was Jackson who was left without a chance to respond as a man in his thirties made his way from the elevators towards them. He was dressed in khakis and a black polo shirt with a WPI logo. He did not have the same confident air as Marcus Lane. If anything, he seemed to walk with his head down, eyes on his shoes. This was Day's supposed stalker.

"Mr. Delgado?" Jackson queried when the man was

infuriating

in earshot.

"No, sir. I'm Ben. Mr. Delgado is my manager. I'm not sure what you needed to see him for, but when he got back from lunch and saw the note on his desk, he grabbed his stuff and bolted. He didn't even take his laptop," the man said, seeming confused and apologetic.

"Can you tell me what the message said?" Jackson asked.

"Only that he needed to go speak to Mr. Lane in security, sir."

Both Jackson and Day exchanged looks, but then Jackson nodded. "Tell Mr. Lane that we thank you for his help and that we'll attempt to reach out at another time."

With that, Jackson was wrapping his arm around Day's waist and guiding him towards the glass doors.

Once they were back in the car, Jackson hit the bluetooth directing the system to call Linc, who answered on the first ring. "Hello?"

"Hey, Delgado's in the wind. A message from security spooked him. Since it didn't mention Day or me directly, maybe he thought the company was onto his identity swap. I'm going to head directly to his last known address. Can you swing by and pick up Day?"

"What? No! I'm coming with you," Day snapped.

"What about the plan to see how he reacts to me?"

"That was when we were in a busy well-lit building with lots of witnesses and it was highly unlikely he was armed," Jackson said, his voice infuriatingly calm.

"Well, I'm not letting you go in alone," Day fumed, crossing his arms over his chest.

Linc chuckled. "I'll meet you there, regardless," he said before disconnecting.

"Fifteen minutes ago, I was the fiercest person you knew. Now, I'm some fragile, delicate fucking flower who needs a babysitter?" Day said, glaring at Jackson.

"Fifteen minutes ago, you were terrified of meeting this same guy in an office building full of people. Now, you want to go storming into his house where he may have a whole stockpile of weapons?" Jackson countered, tone just a little too fucking smug for Day's liking.

"Sometimes, you can be a real asshole," Day muttered, setting his jaw and turning to look out the window, giving Jackson the silent treatment the rest of the way to their destination. He seemed perfectly fine with that arrangement, which only irritated Day further.

When they pulled into a nondescript apartment complex that looked like beige blocks of concrete with Spanish tile and brown shutters, Jackson called Linc once again and confirmed he was ten minutes out.

infuriating

They parked in front of what Day could only assume was Delgado's apartment building.

"Hey," Jackson said softly. Day craned his head farther away from Jackson, feeling both childish and justified. "Oh, so that's how it is, huh? You don't get your way and you're just gonna pout about it? I'm trying to protect you. That *is* my job, remember?"

"It *was* your job. Now, you're my boyfriend, not my bodyguard, and I don't need you to protect me."

"That's not what you said this morning. You said you like that I take care of you. You said you like not having to make decisions for yourself. You're giving me whiplash here, baby. I'm never going to put your life at risk, Day. No matter how much you pout or stomp your foot or cry about it. If you don't like that, then I don't know what to tell you. This is who I am."

Day's face turned bright red, humiliation flooding through him. He had said that. After telling Jackson just last night that he needed time to trust him, not twelve hours later, he'd vomited all his deep, dark longings and how much he needed Jackson to take care of him. No wonder Jackson had whiplash. Still, Day didn't want to give an inch. Maybe he was trying to sabotage himself, or maybe he just wanted to get his way, but he couldn't stop himself from saying, "I finally trust you enough to tell you my feelings and you're going to use that against me to get your way? Wow. That's really shitty, Jackson."

"You know what?" Jackson said, sounding angry for the first time since they'd met. Angry with Day. Day's chest burned. "I'm sorry if you're mad, but I'm never going to let you risk your life. Never. You can get over it or not, but you're mine and I protect what's mine. And I'm sorry if you don't like that either, but it doesn't change the facts, so if you want to sit here and be a brat and give me the silent treatment, go ahead. It won't change my mind because I'm a grown-ass man who isn't easily manipulated. But, if you want to play this game, I'll be happy to show you what happens to brats as soon as we get home."

Day's head whipped around to look at Jackson whose stubborn expression and flared nostrils made his heart skip a beat. He didn't know why Jackson's words put a lump in his throat but they did. Still, he didn't say anything.

Jackson's gaze strayed away from Day to look out the windshield toward where a man was dumping a duffle bag and a garbage bag into the trunk of an older Dodge. "That's him."

Day squinted. The man wore a ratty blue t-shirt, well-worn jeans, and converse. He didn't look like a stalker…but he also didn't look like a rapist and a murderer, so Day supposed looks could be deceiving. Jackson reached across Day and opened the glove box, removing a gun and tucking it into the waistband of his pants before smoothing his black sweater over it.

The man left his trunk open but jogged across the parking lot and back up the stairs that led to the next floor. "Linc should be here in a minute. Do not get out of the car. I'll see you back at the house."

Jackson didn't give Day a chance to respond, just leaned over to pop a kiss on his slightly open mouth, and then he was gone, bounding up the stairs after a potential murderer, leaving Day behind to try to wrap his head around what had just happened. Had he really made Jackson mad right before he ran off to confront a killer? What the fuck was wrong with him?

A car pulled up beside theirs, and Day's heart sank. Linc was there to whisk him away. Day unlocked the car door and stood, turning to greet Linc. But it wasn't Linc. He had just enough time to process that information before lightning rocketed through him, paralyzing his muscles. He felt himself falling, but he never hit the ground. Instead, he was being dragged, his shoes bouncing along the pavement before he was forced into a trunk, leaving him semi-conscious in motor oil and gasoline soaked darkness.

Day tried to keep his eyes open, but even though his

assailant no longer pressed the taser against his skin, his muscles still twitched and his brain still felt like scrambled eggs. "Jackson," he whispered before he lost consciousness.

twenty-four

JACKSON

"SALAZAR," JACKSON CALLED, USING THE MAN'S ALIAS so as not to alarm him.

The man stood in the doorway of his apartment, a trash bag in each hand, gaze darting back and forth, like a squirrel deciding if he should run home or continue on his current mission.

Jackson held up both hands. "Listen, man. I just need to ask you a couple of questions about Dayton Daniels."

The dark-haired man frowned. "Who?"

"Dayton Daniels. He goes by Danny on the cam sites." Before he even finished the sentence, he knew Salazar wasn't his guy. The man clearly didn't recognize Day by name.

Delgado slowly lowered the trash bags, his gaze shifting to the right as he appeared to rack his brain. Jackson saw the moment the man recognized Day for who he was. "The kid whose paycheck is always getting screwed up in our system? What about him?"

Jackson shook his head. "Never mind."

"Wait," Delgado cried. "Did you tell security about this at my job? Is that why they wanted to see me?"

Jackson didn't bother to answer the man. Let him sweat it out. He was halfway down the front steps of the building when he saw Linc's SUV parked in the middle of the lot. Linc crouched beside Jackson's open passenger door. His fingers swiping across something and rubbing it between his fingers before he wiped it on his jeans. Jackson's gaze shot to Linc's passenger seat, his heart skyrocketing when he saw it was empty. He started to run.

"Where is he?" Jackson shouted.

Linc stood. "I just got here," Linc said. "He's gone."

Jackson shoved Linc hard, slamming him back against the car. "What the fuck do you mean he's gone? He can't be gone. I've been gone less than five fucking minutes. He's got to be around here somewhere. Did you check to see if he tried to follow me? Maybe he's walking around the complex. Or lost."

It sounded ridiculous to Jackson's own ears. Linc let Jackson grip his shirt and shake him like a rag doll before settling his hands on his shoulders. "Stop. I think somebody took him. Stop reacting and listen."

Jackson slumped, trying to force his brain to stop with the endless loop of horrible outcomes hammering holes into his rapidly beating heart. Day was gone. Jackson had turned his back for five minutes and somebody had snatched Day right out from under his nose. No, not under his nose. If he'd just brought Day with him upstairs, or at least waited for Linc to get there, this wouldn't have happened. Jackson gave a hoarse shout and slammed his fist through his back passenger window, pain knifing through his hand and forearm.

Linc gave him a hard stare. "You feel better now? You good? I need you to fucking focus."

Jackson's hand was throbbing, but he nodded. "What did you find?"

"Blood, but not enough to think he's mortally wounded."

Linc presented his hand to Jackson so he could see the slight remnants of Day's blood on his fingers. Maybe it was Day's blood. Maybe it was the stalker's blood. Too bad that would be zero fucking help figuring out who had him. "His phone," Jackson barked. "Is his phone in the car?"

Jackson didn't wait for an answer, diving into the car and searching the passenger seat and underneath it before snatching his own phone and pulling up the app he'd installed on Day's phone. His heart sank with relief when he saw the blinking green circle with Day's smiling face inside.

"I've got him."

"Where?"

"Skid row."

Linc frowned. "What? Did he kidnap Day and take him back to his tent on the row? That doesn't sound right. Wait, isn't that old hotel there? The one The Night Stalker stayed at while he was killing people?" Jackson gave him a startled look. "Sorry. You know what I mean. It used to be fancy, but now, it's like a rent by the hour or night kind of place."

"The Cecil Hotel. It's called something else now."

"Yeah, that's the one."

Jackson checked the map, zeroing in until he had an address. "Yeah, that's where he is."

"Why would he take Day there? How would he get him past the front desk? Even if he does, I don't know how we're going to find him. There's got to be six hundred rooms in that hotel."

infuriating

"We'll find him on the security footage. If that's where he's taken him, he can't be that far ahead of us. Let's go."

Jackson started for the SUV, only to realize Linc wasn't following. He closed the passenger door with his jacket over his hand. "There's evidence here. Get your detective friend to send a forensic tech out here to collect it. We'll need it if there's a trial."

"If that fucking scumbag has so much as smeared Day's lipstick, he won't live long enough to see the inside of a courthouse," Jackson vowed.

"Noted. But, until then, call him."

Jackson climbed into the passenger seat of Linc's car, making his calls as Linc drove. The old hotel was only three blocks away, and Day's face still blinked on top of it, which made Jackson's stomach ache. Why would this psycho take Day to a hotel? To kill him? It wouldn't be the first murder that hotel had ever seen. Hell, it wouldn't even be the first that year.

When Jackson shoved open the doors to the lobby, they rocketed back on their hinges hard enough for them to protest, causing a racket that caused most everybody to stop and stare for a brief moment before going back to what they were doing. Linc was right behind him, but Jackson went straight to the front desk where a uniformed man with graying hair and out of control bushy black brows glared across the lobby at a group of rowdy twenty-somethings all huddled together.

When Jackson approached, the man pulled his gaze away, taking in Jackson's elegant clothing with confusion. "May I help you, sir?" the man asked, though his tone implied something along the lines of 'are you lost?'

"My name is Jackson Avery. I own Elite Protection Services. One of my clients' cellphones pinged here. Have you seen him?" Jackson showed a pic he'd taken the day he'd met Day.

The man frowned as he gazed at the picture then shook his head. "I've never seen him before, but another man came in here about fifteen minutes ago and handed that group of idiots a phone and walked off. I suspect it might be the phone you're looking for, but the guy was definitely not your guy."

Jackson took off towards the group of kids. "Hey, let me see that phone."

One look at the glassy-eyed group told Jackson they were all high on something. As twitchy as they were, it was likely meth. Jackson recognized Day's Care Bear case immediately. "It's ours. Get out of here. Find your own, creep."

Jackson didn't have time for this. He reached into his

wallet and pulled out a hundred dollar bill. "Phone. Now."

The ginger-haired girl who clutched the phone squealed in delight, trading the phone for the money without so much as another look. Jackson returned to the now empty desk. Before he could ring the bell, Linc returned with a piece of paper clutched in his hand. "Let's go."

"Go? Go where?"

Linc handed Jackson the paper. It was a grainy picture of an old man with shorts that went well past his knees and a t-shirt that appeared to have holes in it. His face had jowls and a double chin, and his dark hair looked dyed even though the picture was black and white. It was combed over to hide a bald spot. He was overweight by about sixty pounds, his belly hanging out from the bottom of his shirt.

"Who the fuck is this guy?" Jackson said to nobody in particular.

"I don't know, but we need to get back to the office and regroup. If that guy left the phone here, he is clearly not stupid enough to take Day here. Besides, the guy at the front desk said there's a guard at the back entrance because there are too many people who try to break in on the other side."

Jackson was silent the entire way back to the office

while Linc called Webster and told him to rally anybody nearby. It was an all hands on deck situation. They stopped to give Jimmy a copy of the perpetrator, and Jimmy said he'd put out an APB and have Day listed as a missing person. He said he'd also check if any of the footage from the hotel showed a vehicle coming or going from any side. Linc had already examined the footage, but Jackson nodded anyway.

By the time they made it back to the office, a dozen people stood in the conference room, but only half of them still worked for him. Wyatt and Charlie sat on the conference room table with actor Elijah Dunne and his former boyfriend, Robby Shaw. Their husbands, Jayne Shepherd and Calder Seton, stood against the wall along with Donnelly, another of Linc's men, and Webster as well as Jackson's second-in-command from the Miami office, Hurley.

The only people who were supposed to be there were Webster and Hurley, who'd flown in to take a meeting with a potential client. "What's everybody doing here? *How* is everybody here?"

"Day's our friend," Wyatt said.

"Yeah," Charlie seconded. "We want to help."

Jackson looked to Shepherd and Calder. "You guys don't work here anymore."

"We were in town for Charlie's birthday," Robby

infuriating

said, smiling at the brunette sitting cross-legged on the conference room table.

"You've stepped up for us, even when we no longer worked for you. Now, it's our turn," Shepherd said.

Elijah smiled at his husband before nodding his head towards Wyatt. "He says this boy, Day, means something to you. So, he means something to us. We're all here until we find him."

"You always show up for your family," Calder said. The others bobbed their heads in agreement.

Jackson swallowed the lump in his throat, looking at Donnelly. "Aren't you supposed to be in Australia on mandatory vacation?"

The burly former boxer shrugged. "Wyatt caught me at the airport. Figured this was as good a use of my vacation time as any."

"I appreciate you all coming, but I don't even know where to start. All we have is one grainy sketch and Day's cell phone."

Wyatt scrambled across the table. "Do you know his access code?"

Jackson frowned. "It wasn't locked."

Wyatt smiled. "Give it to me."

Jackson frowned harder but handed the phone over, grateful he didn't give it to Jimmy when he'd asked for it. They all watched while Wyatt went through

Day's phone, scrolling far faster than Jackson could have managed. "No pictures of the guy or the location. No phone calls. Hah," he cried. "Look, he tried to text you, Jackson. He never got a chance to hit send," he added, his voice not nearly as excited anymore.

"What's it say?" Shepherd asked.

"Ser." Wyatt now sounded deflated. Jackson didn't blame him. What the fuck was he supposed to do with S.E.R.?

"Is it a code of some kind?" Calder asked in his slow southern drawl.

"None that I understand," Wyatt said. "Only the first letter is capitalized. Could it be a name? A place?"

Jackson racked his brain to try to understand what Day might have been trying to spell and why he'd suddenly been interrupted. Was he still alive? Was he still breathing? "Fuck. I don't know. He had a friend. A girl. Sarah."

"Maybe she's his stalker?" Charlie asked.

"She's dead," Jackson said, voice dull. "She died when Day was seventeen."

The room went quiet, eyes downcast, nobody speaking. Jackson understood, though. There was nothing to say. They had no leads. No evidence but for a grainy photo of a man who meant nothing to any of them. Any of them except Day. Day who couldn't

infuriating

tell them anything because he was gone. Snatched right out from under Jackson's nose. Was he scared? Was he alive? Was he hurt? Was that fucking piece of shit hurting him even now while Jackson sat there, useless? Why hadn't he just taken Day back to the office first?

"We're gonna find him," Webster said.

There was a sharp exhalation of breath from Wyatt and a strange almost moan of dread that chilled Jackson to his core. "I think maybe he found us."

"What the fuck does that mean?" Jackson snapped.

This time, it was his own phone that Wyatt held up. He handed it to Jackson. "I subscribed to Day's OnlyFans account the day we met at the office. It just sent me a notification that he's planning on going live in an hour."

All eyes looked at Jackson, and all the stalker's taunts about Day staying untouched, about the stalker intending to take Day's virginity, came rushing back. Hands shaking, he handed Wyatt back his phone.

"What's that mean?" Robby asked. "What's OnlyFans?"

Robby was the most naive of the group, a preacher who rescued kids and animals on his little farm up north. Charlie leaned close enough to whisper in Robby's ear. The color drained from the boy's face.

Jackson was sure his complexion was ashen. He dropped down in the conference room chair. What did they do now?

Webster began typing on his laptop. "I'm going to try to find an IP address. The guy clearly seems to be unraveling. Maybe he'll make a mistake."

The man already made a mistake as far as Jackson was concerned, and as soon as Jackson found him, he wasn't going to put him in jail. He would put him under it.

twenty-five

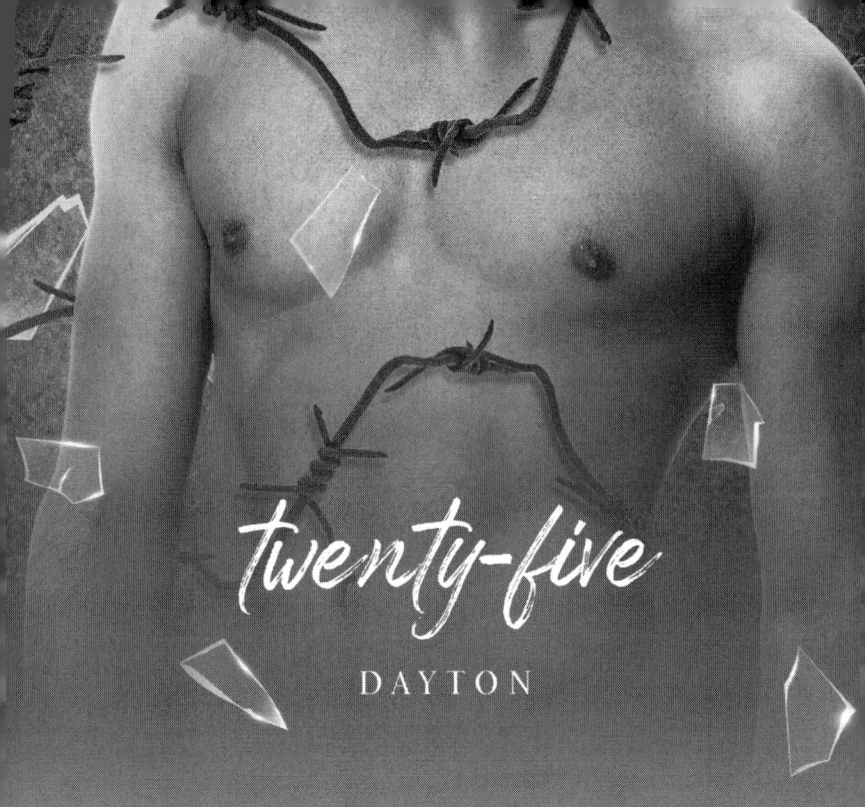

DAYTON

THE SCENT OF ROT PERMEATED DAY'S NOSE, CAUSING him to cringe away before his eyes were even open yet. He wanted to open his eyes, but it was almost like he couldn't. It couldn't be from the taser. His brain felt foggy, his tongue too big for his mouth. The rot stench got closer as Day realized he was on a mattress. Was that the smell? A finger with a jagged nail traced along Day's cheek and the scent of musty earth made Day recoil. He recognized the smell immediately, and he tried to keep the contents of his stomach down when chapped lips wormed over his.

Carl. Why? How could this be happening again?

Day laid there, eyes closed, hoping his former landlord wouldn't rape him while he believed Day to be unconscious. He tried to stay limp until Carl moved away, leaving a trail of saliva across Day's chin. "You don't have to pretend with me, Dayton. I can feel the way your breath increased when I kissed you. The drugs should have worn off by now. Open your eyes."

How long had it been since he'd last heard that nasally, gasping voice? Three years? Four? It still made his stomach clench and his whole body heavy with dread. Carl had always sounded half out of breath, even when he'd just been sitting there, petting Day's head while he blew him and telling Day he was worth every penny in that whiny, disgusting voice. Day didn't want to open his eyes. If he looked at Carl, then this was all real, it was all happening, and once again, Day's chance at a fairy tale was snatched away from him.

"Don't push me, Dayton. I've gone to a lot of trouble for you. The least you could do is show me the courtesy of looking me in the eye."

Day could do this. Day was good at this. He'd been faking this for as long as he could remember. He just needed to buy time. He'd never gotten to finish his text. He didn't even know if he was spelling it right, but he'd been too afraid to use his voice to text. Would Jackson figure it out? Would he find him in time? Day fought back the bile rising in his throat. He'd rather die than submit to whatever Carl had in mind for him. He just couldn't do it. Not again. But he could pretend… That was his goal. Pretend and fake interest to buy time until Jackson found him. *Fuck, Jackson. Please, find me. Please.*

Day forced his eyes open and gave a weak smile. "Sorry," he croaked before clearing his throat and trying again. "Whatever you gave me is making me groggy."

Carl hadn't aged well, though it was clear he'd tried to hide it. Despite being well into his late fifties, the man had dyed his thinning hair shoe polish black, his lips looked puffy like he'd had lip injections, and his unlined face seemed shiny, like it was pulled too tight. Like a mask. A grotesque mask.

"You look…different. Good," Day said, trying to ignore the stench coming off the man and his soiled, unwashed clothing.

Day forced himself into a sitting position, his head swimming and stomach sloshing when he saw the usually dim motel room was eerily bright from stage lighting, cameras surrounding the old mattress he'd once shared with Sarah. It was like being sucked back into a nightmare after he'd fought so hard to claw his way out. The walls, which were once a dingy white, were warped and dotted with brown water stains, and the dark carpet had a fine layer of fur that Day could only imagine was actual mold. The mold that had killed Sarah. Rage flared in his gut. Why the fuck would Carl bring him back there?

Carl ignored Day's compliment, sliding off the bed to busy himself making adjustments to the cameras surrounding the room. It was obvious Carl planned on getting what Day had dangled before his audience, with or without Day's consent.

"So, what is all this?" he asked, fighting to keep his voice casual, even pleasant.

Carl's gaze flicked to him from the camera directly in front of the bed. Behind him sat a laptop. Day recognized the dashboard for his OnlyFans account. Jesus. Was he planning on broadcasting this to Day's fans?

"Are we recording?"

"No, not yet. I thought you'd want to fix yourself up a bit before we go live. I know how important your appearance is to you. You've always been so fastidious with your clothes and hair and makeup, even when this was your home. But now that you're a big star, it's much worse. I watch you get ready for your videos almost every night." Day's stomach dropped, but he fought to keep his face neutral. "Or I did," Carl said, his voice quivering, "before you moved in with that… man." He scoffed, shaking his head. "If I'd have known you were going to throw yourself at the first cock you saw like some nympho whore, I would've just skipped killing that attorney and taken you that night. Luckily, the cops are stupid and still have no idea it was me."

Carl didn't even seem to be talking to Day anymore, but himself. Some kind of stream of consciousness rambling that Day suspected happened often. Day really thought he might be sick. How different it all could've been if Carl had simply kidnapped him that night. He would have never met Jackson, would have never felt his kiss, his touch, would have never known what it felt like to have him inside his body, his heart. Jackson had made Day losing his virginity a moment that had meant something to him, even when Day had sworn virginity was just some mindless, human construct created to police people's bodies. Jackson had made Day feel loved.

Day swallowed the lump in his throat. No matter what happened, Carl couldn't take any of that away from him. Even if Jackson never found him. The last few weeks with him would be enough to sustain Day, no matter what came next.

"The clock is ticking, Day. I put your things in the

bathroom. Mind the broken tile. There have been so many vandals and squatters since the motel shut down. You can't shower, I'm afraid. No running water anymore. But I put a light in the bathroom for you. I want you to look perfect for our special night. It is your final performance, after all."

The last comment froze Day's blood in his veins, but he slowly crawled from the bed, aware of the gun tucked into the waistband of Carl's filthy shorts. He recoiled at the spongy feel of the carpet beneath his bare feet. This had once been his home. He'd felt safe in this horror show of a room. He did his best to blink back the tears threatening to escape.

Once he entered the bathroom, he paused. There was a light on a tripod highlighting the gaping holes and graffiti on the crumbling walls. The mirror was cracked, tiny hairline fractures crawling along the glass like a spiderweb, as if somebody had punched the surface in a fit of rage. Was it Carl?

"Keep the door open," Carl said from behind him.

True to his word, a bag full of makeup sat on the counter. Not Day's makeup, but his favorite brands and products were in there. How long had Carl been watching him? His hands shook as he applied his makeup in the cracked mirror, doing his best to take his time without looking like he was deliberately

infuriating

dragging it out.

"That's enough. Here, I bought you something special, for your special night." Carl smiled, revealing a mouth full of chipped and broken teeth.

Day forced a smile onto his face as he took the zippered bag. "Thank you," he said, batting his false lashes.

Day started to force the door closed, but Carl slammed a hand against it, his watery blue eyes hardening, his lips flattening into a thin line. "I said, door open," he snapped.

Day's heart skipped at the barely contained rage in his trembling voice and the spittle glistening on the man's lips. He lowered his gaze. "Sorry, Daddy," Day said, his organs quaking as he felt the words leave his lips. *Sorry, Jackson.*

Carl's anger seemed to dissolve almost immediately. His rough hand with its filthy chewed nails cupped Day's cheek, and he did his best not to recoil. "Get dressed, baby. I want to show you off to your fans. I want them to see how a real man treats his boy."

The word 'baby' falling from Carl's lips was a punch to Day's heart, but he nodded and turned his back to lower the zipper on the bag. He recognized the lingerie immediately. It was designed by the same woman who did all his custom designs, but this one had been on a mannequin in the back. A custom order for a man online. A bridal set. *Jesus.* Carl was living out some kind of fucking wedding night fantasy with Day starring as the blushing bride.

How did this get so far out of hand? He withdrew the items, a lacy, deep-v camisole in snowy white and a matching set of lace panties that had a ruffle around the waistband and nothing to the back except two straps that hugged the bottom of each ass cheek. He wished there was more to it. Something complicated with lots of buckles, straps, and a thousand buttons, anything to slow the progression of what now seemed inevitable. But before he knew it, he was all finished. He turned and gave a shy smile. "How do I look?"

Carl's beady, insect eyes took him in, his tongue darting out of his mouth with obvious excitement. "Perfect. You look perfect. Just as I imagined."

How many times had Carl imagined their current scenario? How many times had Day been just a moment away from assault each time he'd met with Carl to 'pay' the rent? He didn't want to know. He didn't want to think about all those times he'd convinced himself that going to his knees for this foul creature was somehow the safer option than walking the streets. How had he not seen the obsession that must have been there all that time? He'd been so in

infuriating

denial. He'd been a coward. He should have fought. He should have tried harder, somehow. But he couldn't even imagine what that would have looked like. His shoulders sagged. It was useless to blame himself for something that had happened when he was barely fourteen.

When Carl leaned in like he was going to kiss Day, his hand shot out without thought, covering the old man's mouth. "Wait!"

Carl's hand shot out, fire trailing across Day's cheek, his head jerking from the blow. He cupped his cheek, eyes wide. Carl's expression became instantly apologetic. "Daddy doesn't like when you touch him without permission or when you refuse him."

Day gave a shuddery breath. "I-I wasn't refusing you. I just wanted to save it for the show. My audience expects a show. Don't you want to show them how good we are together?"

Carl's gaze narrowed, and he studied Day's face as if to see if he was tricking him somehow. "I suppose you're right. After seeing you with that…overly muscled freak in the mask, I suppose they deserve to see you with somebody who knows how to treat you."

Day's chin started to wobble, but he clenched his teeth to keep himself from bawling. He could do this. He had to do this. He just had to find little ways to keep stalling. He'd been through things far worse than this in his life. Jackson would find him. Day just needed to give him time. Jackson promised he'd always take care of Day. He'd promised.

Day walked to the bed, his knees quaking with each step. When he knelt on the mattress, Carl almost tripped over himself to follow. Day tried to think of anything to stall the man once again, but he knew his time was running out. Carl wouldn't keep letting Day put him off. It was clear he'd had this planned for so long.

Too long.

twenty-six

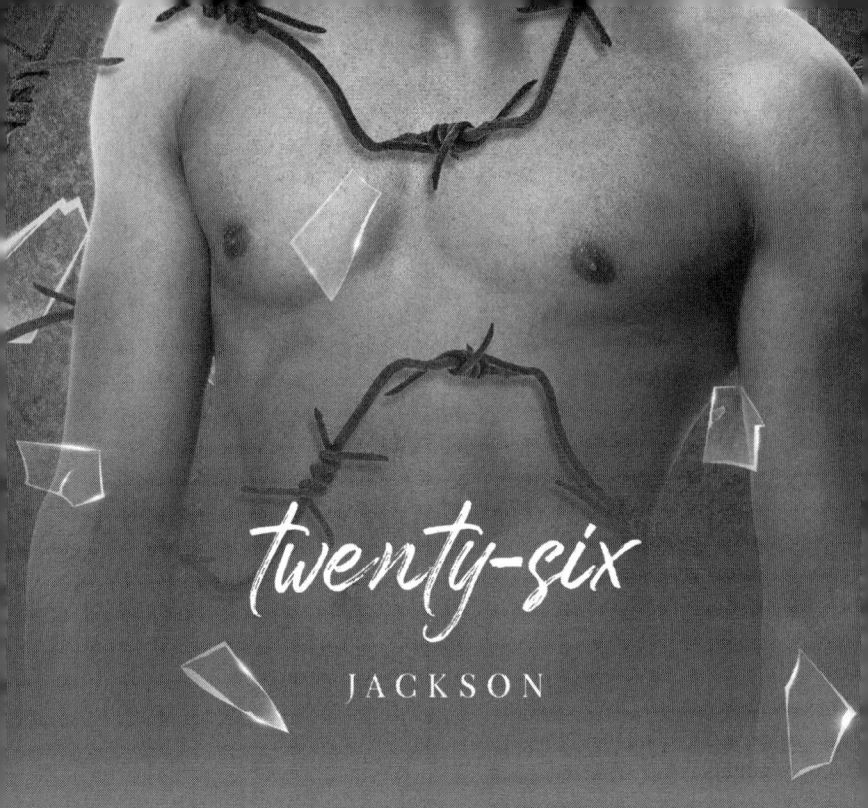

JACKSON

"TELL ME SOMETHING GOOD, WEBSTER."

Webster gave an apologetic look that sent Jackson's stomach plummeting to his feet. "Sorry, boss. This guy is bouncing his IP address off a dozen satellites. It's impossible to trace."

"I don't want to hear what you don't fucking have!" Jackson shouted at Webster, slamming his palm down on the table. "He's had Day for three fucking hours. Do you have any idea what he's probably doing to him right now?" Jackson's voice caught, and he turned away from the others, trying to get a grip on the terror clawing up his throat at the thought of whatever this anonymous maniac might be doing to Day right then.

"Give us the room, guys," Linc said.

Jackson listened to furniture move and scrape as people exited the conference room. When the door shut, Jackson turned and dropped into the chair at the head of the table, burying his face in his hands, bracing his elbows on his knees as he tried to pull himself together.

When he opened his eyes, Linc was leaning against the table beside him, his hands in the pockets of his jeans, expression pained.

Jackson gave him a stubborn look. "I'm not apologizing."

Linc shrugged his broad shoulders. "You don't have to apologize to me, brother. But we both know that what's happening right now is not the fault of anybody in this room and you exploding at them won't change a goddamn thing for Day. All you're doing is stressing them the fuck out more than they already are. We all want Day back. We're not going to stop until we find him. It's as simple as that."

Jackson looked up at Linc, his chest feeling like there was a gaping hole in it. "I promised him I'd keep him safe, man. I told him I wouldn't let anybody hurt him. He's had him for hours. We don't even know if he's still alive."

infuriating

Even saying the words gutted Jackson. If Day was dead, Jackson wasn't sure he could survive it. They were supposed to have more time, time enough for Jackson to convince Day they were soulmates, destiny. He shook his head, his brain rejecting the idea that this was the end for him and Day.

"We do know he's alive. Whoever has him set up that livestream. They have an agenda, and as fucking disgusting as it is, his stalker showed his hand with those messages he sent each time a video went up. He thinks Day is a virgin, and he's living out some warped fantasy where he is the winner of Day's virginity auction, and he wants us all to see his prize. He wants you to see it."

Jackson's gaze darted to Linc. He wasn't saying anything new but hearing the words uttered out loud set off a whole new chain of emotions for Jackson. How had he let it come to this? Day had spent his entire life being used and abused by adults who were supposed to love and protect him, and he'd put his trust in Jackson to finally be the one to take that burden away from him. This was all on Jackson. If some creepy fucking pervert hurt Day… "This is my fault. I should have waited for you or taken him to the office or never agreed to go on his channel. We pushed this freak into making a move early. If he hurts him—"

"Jesus, Jackson. Enough. The only person at fault is this fucking head case who has a hard-on for Day. It has nothing to do with fault or blame. It just is what it is. You aren't thinking with your head. We need you to be the fucking level-headed leader we all signed on to work for right now. You can fall apart later when Day is back home. No matter what happens with Day or to him, as long as he's breathing, he has a chance. Do you want to spend valuable time snapping at your team and letting your emotions get the best of you, or do you want to find the man you love?"

Jackson took a deep breath and let it out. Fuck, Linc was right. He wasn't helping anybody, least of all Day. He was spiraling. He needed to just breathe and think. Somebody in the other room held the solution to their dilemma. They needed to work together to figure out who had Day and why before it was too late.

"You're right. Thanks, man."

Linc clapped him on the shoulder before walking to the conference room and waving the others back in.

As soon as they were all gathered, Jackson said, "I'm sorry for the outburst."

"It's all good," Calder said. "We've all been there. I did have an idea, though."

"Me too," Wyatt said.

"Let's hear them."

infuriating

Calder spoke first. "Do a deep dive into Day's past. A detailed background check. Maybe something in his history will help us understand what S-e-r might have meant to him. It had to have been important if he was willing to spend his last minutes attempting to text you instead of just hitting 9-1-1."

Webster started typing. "On it."

Jackson looked to Wyatt. "What was your idea?"

Wyatt blew out a huge breath and looked at Linc and then Charlie before biting his lip. They both nodded at him. "Day had his information saved on his OnlyFans account. I can easily get in."

Jackson frowned at the hesitance in Wyatt's voice. "Why does that sound like a bad thing?"

"I don't know much about being a creator on OnlyFans. If I sign in, it might knock Day out of his account or alert his kidnapper in some way and spook him, which could make him do something desperate."

"So, why is it worth the risk?" Jackson asked, keeping his voice neutral so as not to, once again, scare off the people he considered his extended family.

"Because, if it doesn't boot him offline, I might be able to start his live feed from here, and we might be able to see where he's being held." Wyatt swallowed audibly. "We also don't know what we might see when we turn the camera on…what his kidnapper might be doing to him. I don't want to upset you."

Wyatt's words were like a knife through Jackson's heart. The idea of flipping on that camera to find Day being raped or abused or...worse...might be more than Jackson could bear, but what was the alternative? But if he turned on the camera and it alerted Day's attacker and spooked him... No. No. Linc was right. He needed to take Day out of the equation. If this was literally anybody else, any other client, Jackson would risk it. He had to risk it.

"Do it."

"Are you—" Wyatt started.

Jackson cut him off. "Yes, just do it before I change my mind." Wyatt nodded, picking up Day's Care Bear phone case and punching in a few keystrokes. "Wait!" Jackson barked. Wyatt froze. "Webster. Is there a way to hook Day's phone to the big screen? We're going to need all eyes on the room. I don't know how long we'll have before they figure out we can see them."

"Yeah, boss. Easy," Webster confirmed.

Wyatt hit two more buttons and then handed the phone to Webster, who pushed a few buttons, and then everybody turned to the screen as it went blank.

"Look for any identifiers. Anything with a name. If there's an open window, look for buildings with any kind of decorative detailing that might help us pinpoint his location. No matter how small."

Charlie sucked in a breath as Day's image came into focus. Robby and Elijah gathered close to her and Wyatt, like they could insulate them from the image before them.

Jackson was torn between relief and anguish as Day appeared on the big screen. He wore a lace lingerie set, something white and frilly. His face was made up heavier than usual, his lips overly lined, his lashes clearly fake, but the fear in his eyes seemed in direct conflict with the coquettish way he sat, feet tucked beneath him, leaning on his hand, staring at somebody just off camera.

"He looks so scared," Robby whispered.

"He looks like a survivor," Elijah countered. "He's playing a part. Look at his body language. He's trying to appease the man."

"The room's filthy," Robby said, louder this time. "Like, not just dirty… Look at the walls behind the bed. Those are water stains. There aren't any sheets on the bed, either. You can see the bare mattress under the blanket he's sitting on. Who lives like that?"

"That's not a house. That's a hotel room," Charlie said.

"She's right," Elijah agreed. "Look at the way the light attaches directly to the side table."

"If that's a hotel, it's abandoned."

Jackson's heartbeat galloped. "It's a motel. Day lived in a motel when he was a teenager. The guy there used to…" He swallowed. "He used to molest him as some kind of payment. Fuck. I should have known. How did I fucking miss that?"

"Oh, my God," Charlie gasped. "Poor Day."

"Webster, find that address. Now," Jackson growled.

Webster's fingers were flying over the keys. "I'm looking. I'm looking. Day doesn't seem to have even popped up on the grid until he was eighteen, and the only address I have is the one he fucking lives at now. I'm not giving up."

Day had said he had to work under a fake name until he turned eighteen because he wasn't old enough to cam. Why hadn't Jackson asked more questions? What had his name been? What was this Carl piece of shit's last name? What was the motel he'd lived in? God dammit. He'd never even asked Sarah's last name.

Sarah. Could she be who Day was trying to spell? Jackson's organs twisted at the thought of Day trying to type out a message, knowing how he struggled with reading and spelling, knowing that he used his precious minutes to try to get a message to Jackson and not the police. It had to be something important. A clue. Maybe it was a misspelling or maybe not. He had to try every possible lead. Even if it was just a hail Mary at this point.

"Calder, get online and look for any hotels or motels that start with Ser in sketchy neighborhoods. Webster, I need you to do something illegal."

"Shoot," Webster said without hesitation.

"I need you to find the records of a transplant patient who died in LA from an infection somewhere around 2016."

Webster gaped at him. "I'm gonna need more info than that."

"Her name was Sarah. She had a double lung transplant, and she died in an LA hospital due to a fungal infection caused by that fucking hotel room right there. If we can find her records, we can find that fucking hotel."

Webster looked to Linc and then Jackson. "Boss, I want to help, but I don't think even I can do that."

"You might not have to," Calder said. "There are only four hotels that start with Ser and only one of them is here in LA. The Serendipity Motor Lodge. It was closed by the county health inspector after a girl died from an infection caused by black mold."

"That has to be it," Shepherd said. "That's no fucking coincidence."

"Does it say anything about the owner?"

Calder swung the laptop around. "No, but it shows the manager. Carl Frankel."

Jackson's blood ignited as he stared at a picture of the man from the still footage of the hotel. That was him. The man who had Day. The man who'd abused Day for years. Jackson was going to make sure he didn't have the ability to so much as write his own name when he was done with him.

"Shepherd, you and Linc are with me. Calder, patch us into the conference room and turn the sound up so I can hear what's happening in real time. Webster, call Jimmy. Give him this guy's name and stats, and tell him to get as many units as he can to that motel, right now."

Jackson gave one last look at the screen and at Day's wide pool blue eyes. *Hang on, baby. I'm coming. Just hang on.*

twenty-seven

DAYTON

"CAN I ASK YOU A QUESTION?" DAY BLURTED AS CARL attempted to join him on the soiled mattress.

Carl didn't stop advancing; he simply knelt on the corner of the bed. He took the gun from his belt with a careful deliberateness that sent an icy finger of fear along Day's spine. The room was hot and damp, they were both sweating, and Day couldn't help but wonder about all the things he might be inhaling simply by breathing in the hot stagnant air of the abandoned motel room.

Carl placed the gun across his meaty thighs. "Sure. One question."

"Why? Why me?"

Carl gave an almost impish smile that caused goosebumps to erupt along Day's skin. "Are you asking if you were my first?" Day definitely wasn't asking that, but Carl didn't seem to care. He kept speaking as if Day had answered. "There have been other boys, younger boys. Sweet, innocent boys who stepped off that bus thinking they were different, better...but they weren't. They all came to me eventually, letting me do whatever I wanted to them just so they could have a place to sleep. You were all so weak. So helpless. The others eventually gave me all of them, and then they were useless to me. They lacked principles. They lacked the courage of their convictions. But not you. Never you, Day."

Carl seemed to be reliving some memory, his fingers fondling the gun in his lap as he spoke with fondness. "You drew a line in the sand, and you never let me cross it. I loved that about you. You were so special. You understood your worth. You told the world that if it wanted to touch you, it would have to pay top dollar. I was the only one you'd ever been with until then, but I wasn't mad. I was willing to pay for my prize." His smile turned into a sneer. "But then you had to go and let that man have you. I almost killed you both the night I broke into his apartment. Did you

infuriating

know that? I knew if I crept upstairs, I'd find you in his bed and then I'd have had to kill you."

The casual admission caused Day to shiver despite the heat, his gaze darting away and his mouth falling open as his gaze fell on something. The laptop. Day's laptop. How had he not noticed that before? The light beside the webcam was glowing, and people were already logging in. People were commenting, but Day was too far away to see what they were saying. There was no way Carl had started the livestream. He still believed that they were alone. Just the two of them.

"So, you would have killed me instead of claiming your prize?" Day asked, voice flirty. "That seems a lot like cutting off your nose to spite your face. I never let him have me…not like that. I do know my worth," he lied smoothly.

"Oh, I'd have taken my prize, whether you were dead or alive. But it's not as much fun when they just lie there staring up at the ceiling."

Jesus. Fucking. Christ. This man was a fucking lunatic. A serial murderer of children. Day had always seen him as gross. Maybe a little sad. He'd felt sorry for him once upon a time, the way children do when they don't know any better. But now, all he felt was revulsion. How many others had there been since Day?

"I can see you don't like the idea of me being with

others. I'll admit I'm flattered by your jealousy. But they weren't like you, I promise. Let me show you how much I care for you."

When he went to turn towards the laptop, Day panicked, jerking towards him, stopping short when Carl pointed the gun at him. Day held up both hands. "I-I just…" He took a deep breath. "I just thought, maybe, you know, the first time could be just us. Just the two of us. Without my entire subscriber list watching." Carl lowered the gun slightly but tilted his head, like he was considering it.

Day had to think of a way to tell Jackson where he was. Something more obvious than his convoluted text message.

"You know, I thought about you a lot over the years. I tell people all the time how you saved me, helped me figure out how to work around my disability, gave me a place to stay. Who knows where I might have ended up without you? I always wished I'd done more to thank you," Day said, running his top teeth along his bottom lip before dampening it with his tongue. "I thought I'd wasted my chance. I know it seems like I'm stalling, but it's just because I'm nervous. I've never done this before, and you're so much more experienced." Day's stomach churned at the way Carl's pupils dilated and he leaned in, hanging on

Day's every word. "Maybe this is fate. You and me, here, in this motel. Serendipity. Did you know that's what serendipity means? Like fate. Here we are at the Serendipity Motor Lodge."

The moment the words left his mouth, Day knew he'd gone too far. He couldn't stop himself from gazing over at the laptop, and Carl's gaze followed like a shadow, his face contorting as he realized they were live. Day's face exploded as the butt of Carl's gun clipped the side of his face, sending him sprawling backwards until he hung half off the bed. His mouth filled with blood, and he had this faint notion that maybe his eyeball was missing. He laughed at the thought as his head swam.

Fabric ripped as Carl yanked him back on the bed, but Day was no longer scared. He knew he was going to die there in the same disgusting piece of shit motel room where Sarah had caught the infection that killed her. There was some sort of kismet to that. Fate. Like Day had told Carl.

When Day laughed again, Carl hit him again, this time, definitely knocking out one or more of his teeth. He didn't feel the pain. That was probably a good thing and a bad thing. They say your body shuts down the pain when things are just too horrific to stomach. Maybe that was true.

"You were never going to be my first, you fucking demented piece of shit. Jackson was my first. He loved me. I loved him. It was perfect. He's perfect. You're just a sick fucking pedophile and a murderer, and now, everybody fucking knows it. I might be dead but you'll go to jail," Day promised, blood splattering Carl's furious face. "They love pedophiles like you in prison."

Carl screeched like some kind of feral animal, and Day's head exploded, making a sound like a piece of wood splintering into a thousand pieces. Then there were voices filling his head. Strangers' voices. Carl's weight disappeared, and he gazed up at new faces through a haze of red. Two men stared down at him. He recognized one of them. Linc.

"Let me see him. I need to see him. Day!"

Jackson. He tried to say his name but it sounded mushy. He tried again. Then Jackson was staring down at him.

"Oh, Jesus, baby. Why did you do that? Why did you taunt him like that? I was coming for you."

"How?" Day managed. "How d'you fin me? My wor's feel funny," he said, lids fluttering closed briefly.

"Your text."

"I shent it? I didn't think I shent it. I hoped. Jackshun, is my eyeball still there?" he asked, heart floating at the idea of Jackson solving his ridiculous clue.

infuriating

"Please, stop talking, baby. Yes, your eye is still there, but you're a mess. I need you to let these men help you, okay? I'm going to be right behind you, but right now, you need to stop talking."

"'Kay, but one more thing," he said, forcing the words out slowly despite the growing pain starting at his temples and spreading lower, like lava flowing from a volcano. "He didn' toush me. Okay? Just you."

"I'm glad he didn't hurt you like that, but it wouldn't matter. I love you. Jesus, you know that, right?"

Day whimpered as the pain started to overwhelm him, his head pounding and his whole mouth feeling like somebody was hammering slivers of metal into each socket. "I feel funny. Hurts," he managed, wetness spilling onto his cheeks. "Ow. Everything hurts, Daddy," he whispered.

Jackson's face contorted into a pained expression that Day thought his face might make if it wasn't the consistency of mashed potatoes. "Shh, baby. I know. They're going to give you something to make the pain go away. Okay? They're gonna take you to the hospital right now." When Jackson stood, Day reached for him. Jackson squeezed Day's hands. "Get them in here. Now."

Once more, strangers surrounded Day, and he was being lifted, a soft collar going around his neck as he was set on a hard board. His eyes fluttered once more as he heard fabric ripping and felt things being stuck to his body. He cried out at the feel of the wind on his face. Even the breeze hurt.

"Can't you give him something for the pain? Look at him."

"Sir," a woman's voice said. "Let us do our job. The sooner we get him looked over and in the bus, the faster he gets what he needs."

"Come on, Jackson. We need to figure out what you're gonna tell your detective friend about Carl's little accident."

twenty-eight
JACKSON

"AN ACCIDENT?" JIMMY SAID, HIS TONE IMPLYING HE didn't believe it for a second.

Jackson shrugged, glancing over the railing of the Serendipity Motor Lodge to the once empty pool below that now contained the bent and broken corpse of Carl whatever-his-name-was. "I mean, I suppose he could have jumped. It was all a bit of a blur once my guys got him outside. He was fighting to get away. They said it looked like he tripped."

"If my boy said it was an accident, then it was an accident, Jimmy."

Jackson's gaze jerked up to see his mom marching

towards him, dressed in a green dress and mustard yellow sweater, her hair pulled back off her face in a casual style that told Jackson she'd had no intention of leaving the house that day. Beverly Avery was always dressed to the nines when she left her house. She always quoted Coco Chanel, 'Dress like you might meet your worst enemy today.'

"Mama? What are you doing here?" he asked.

"That boy called me. The pretty one who's married to Lincoln. He said Day was in the hospital and you were here with the police, so I came straight over and sent your sisters to the hospital to watch over Day until we get there." She looked over the railing and sucked her teeth. "That him? That the one who hurt our Dayton?"

"Yeah, Mama. That's him."

She made a disgusted noise before turning on Jimmy. "You giving my boy a hard time, Jimmy?"

Jimmy shifted on his feet, looking contrite. "Of course not, Bev. You know you're family. We just need his account for the official record. That's all."

"And it couldn't wait? His boyfriend is in surgery and you're asking him foolish questions about how the man who put him in the hospital came to be lying in the bottom of a swimming pool? Seems to me he is exactly where he belongs."

infuriating

Jackson had never needed anybody to plead his case before, but he leaned against the railing and folded his arms across his chest, giving the man a hard look.

Jimmy's partner, a young, copper-skinned man with honey-brown eyes named Detective Graves, gazed over the railing with casual disinterest. "You say you got this guy on tape admitting to being a pedophile and a child killer?"

Jackson gave a single nod.

Graves shrugged, his boredom obvious. "Looks like an accident to me, Jimmy. Are you thinking anything different?" Graves asked.

Beverly crossed her arms just as Jackson had, her brow arching at Jimmy.

"No. No, of course not. We're good. You should get to the hospital and check on Dayton. Tell him we're all rooting for him at the station when he wakes up."

Jackson couldn't help the look of surprise he gave Jimmy. "Uh, yeah. Sure. Okay. I'll do that."

Jackson's mother waited until they were walking down the steps of the dilapidated building, far from earshot, when she asked softly, "You do that to him?"

Jackson knew she was asking if he'd put that man in the bottom of that pool. He had. He hadn't even felt bad about it. By the time Jackson had made it up to the motel room, Day's face had been almost unrecognizable. The swelling. The blood. And all Day had wanted was to explain to Jackson how he hadn't let Carl touch him. It shattered Jackson's heart into a million pieces. If there hadn't been an ambulance and three officers down below, he might have taken his time with Carl, made him feel everything Day had and then some, but he'd only had a small window of time to make a quick decision. He'd decided Day's mental health was more important than his vengeance. Day would only have peace with Carl dead.

Jackson believed in the justice system. It was more than possible that, after a long drawn out trial, a jury would have found Carl guilty of aggravated battery or something equally infuriating. It was likely that winning that verdict would mean Day being forced to relive every trauma this man had put him through starting when he was just fourteen years old. It was likely that a defense attorney would force Day to admit he was a sex worker. He would insinuate that, despite Day's age when Carl's abuse began, it was an arrangement and Day had not only wanted it but instigated it to negate getting a 'real job.'

If convicted, Carl might get a slap on the wrist, a few years in prison, but he wouldn't get the death penalty. Those other boys, whoever they'd been, wouldn't get justice, even with Carl's mediocre confession. No

infuriating

bodies, no crime, and Carl had no incentive to give up any names of the others.

In the end, tossing Carl over that railing had been as easy a decision as loving Day had been, and he'd never regret either. "Yes, Mama."

She nodded, patting Jackson on his shoulder. "Good boy. Good," she said again with another firm nod. "I'm driving."

Jackson looked at his five-foot-nothing mother with wonder. She was literally the strongest person he'd ever met. He thought about his sister and her request to finally tell their mother the truth so that Jimmy no longer had this hold over him. "Mama. Can I tell you something?" he asked once they were sitting in her SUV.

She gave him a look at the seriousness in his voice. "Is it that you're gay? I figured that out when you were twelve and I caught you out back with that Roger boy from down the block."

Jackson rolled his eyes. "No, Mama. I'm being serious. I need to tell you something. Something about Dad."

For the first time in as long as Jackson could remember, his mother looked wary. "If you're about to tell me your dad cheated on me or something, please don't. I don't want to know that. It's best things are left where they are."

Jackson frowned. "What? No. At least…I don't think so. No. It's about Dad and Jimmy. You know how Jimmy said Dad died from some unknown killer? It's not true. Dad…" Why was this so hard? "Dad killed himself."

She turned in the driver's seat to look at him. "Is that what's had you twisted in knots all these years? That you thought I didn't know your daddy took his own life? You think I didn't know the demons he wrestled with? That man was my everything. I knew how he struggled. I tried to get him to see a therapist, but that just wasn't done back then. He was afraid they'd kick him off the force. He was always a deeply thoughtful boy. It's why I loved him. He was too soft for the special investigations unit. Each case broke his heart. And there were too many people on the take." She paused, her gaze looking out the window. "I know the things they did weren't always on the up and up. Your daddy had to work ten times harder than everybody else just because of the color of his skin, and sometimes, he cut corners or turned a blind eye to the shit Jimmy and the others were doing. There's a blue wall that you just don't cross. It was self preservation, but he didn't see it that way. I don't know everything that happened, but I do know, in the end, it was too heavy a burden

infuriating

for him to carry alone and one he wasn't comfortable forcing me to shoulder. He left me a note. I never told anybody, especially after Jimmy and the boys went through so much trouble to make it look like a murder so we were protected. He just needed me to know why he was leaving us." She patted Jackson's cheek. "There. No more secrets. Let's go check on your man now."

She turned over the engine and started to back out. Jackson had no idea why he'd needed to unburden himself right at that moment. Maybe he'd been stalling. He wanted to be there for Day, but he didn't know if he could stomach seeing what that fucking monster had done to him.

As soon as they reached the hospital waiting room, his sisters ran to him, the three of them squeezing him tightly. The others from Elite were all there as well, taking up the majority of the waiting room. "How is he?" he asked Mariah, knowing she had privileges at the hospital, even though she was an OB/GYN, not a trauma surgeon.

Jackson's stomach rolled as his sister listed out Day's injuries with clinical efficiency. "He made it through surgery with flying colors. They're moving him to recovery now. They said they'll come get you as soon as he's stable and settled," Mariah said. "He had a fractured cheek and a fractured orbital socket they had to repair. They said a shard of bone was sitting near the optic nerve and that it might cause him to lose some vision in his right eye. He has a broken jaw, so they're wiring that shut. He lost a few teeth, but they say that's an easy cosmetic fix once his jaw heals. The doctor said a plastic surgeon would suture the lacerations to his face, but there was no way of knowing how he'd heal until the swelling went down. He's going to have a lot of pain for the first week or two but he was able to answer questions and they didn't find any swelling on his brain."

"It seemed the dickhead centered most of his blows directly to Day's face," Della fumed.

"Mr. Avery?"

"That's me," Jackson said.

"You can see your husband now if you follow me."

Jackson frowned at Mariah. She shrugged. "What? I told a little fib. Do you want them to think we're not his family?"

Jackson kissed her on the forehead. "Nope. This is his family."

Jackson followed the nurse down the hallway, who introduced himself as Brandon and said that he'd be taking care of Day for the evening and that, by happenstance, Day would be Brandon's only patient so to just use the call bell if they needed anything.

infuriating

Jackson nodded as the man walked out of the room and sat at a desk just outside Day's window where he could peer in anytime to see them.

It loosened something in Jackson's chest. Day would be safe from now on. Safe and cared for. He picked up the large reclining chair and sat it beside Day's bed, waving to Brandon, who looked up to see what Jackson was doing. He couldn't see much of Day's face. The right side was hidden by bandages, including his eye. The left side was swollen, covered in multiple black and blue contusions, his left eye swollen shut and his lips chapped and slightly parted.

"Jesus, baby." He picked up Day's hand, holding it gently, afraid to cause him any more pain. "I'm so sorry I left you alone. I'm so sorry. I never should have left you in that car."

"It's my fault," Day croaked through clamped teeth. "I left the car."

"Shh, don't talk. It is not your fault. None of this is your fault. Fuck, Day. I was so scared. I could hear him hitting you." Jackson's voice caught on a sob. "I could hear him hitting you, and we were so far away and you just kept taunting him. God, why, baby? Why did you do that?"

"I...I'd decided I was already dead. I wanted to go on my terms." Every word was forced and mumbled, only discernible when Jackson leaned in close, but they were music to his ears. Day was alive. Day was talking. Day remembered what had happened.

"Are you hurting? Do you need me to get the nurse?"

"Uh-uh. The drugs are nice."

Jackson smiled, lifting Day's hand to kiss the back of it. "Rest, baby. I'm right here. I'm not going anywhere. I promise."

"I do love you. Did you hear me tell him that?" he asked drowsily. "Did you hear me tell him how I loved you?"

"Yeah, baby. I heard everything. I love you, too. So fucking much."

"'Kay, good."

Jackson sat, watching Day sleep, afraid to look away for even a second. When Brandon entered, Jackson fixed him with a hard stare. "I'm not leaving this spot. I don't care what your visiting hours are."

Brandon smiled. "If that were my husband, I wouldn't leave either. But your friends and family were hoping for a quick update. I can sit with him while you let them know you talked to him. Like I said, he's my only patient so far tonight. I'll find you a pillow and some blankets so you can get comfortable when you get back."

infuriating

"Thanks. I appreciate it."

"No problem." Jackson was almost to the door when Brandon said, "Look, I'm not supposed to say this and I only know what little your sister said about who did that to him, but I really hope they got what they deserve."

Jackson gave a grave nod. "Believe me. They did."

twenty-nine

DAYTON

"YOU HEARD FROM OUR BOY YET?" MAMA BEV ASKED as she wiped her hands on her bright yellow kitchen towel.

Day looked up from the kitchen table and gave her a brief smile. "Yeah, he called when he was on his way from the airport, but you know LA traffic. He'll be here sometime between now and next Tuesday," Day said before stopping to massage his jaw.

Bev smiled, then frowned. "Still hurting? You need another pill?"

Day shook his head. "No, it's fine. I took some ibuprofen. It just aches sometimes. I think I'm going to rest until Jackson gets here."

She nodded, giving him an odd look. "Alright, sugar."

Sometimes, it felt like he was surrounded by a family of mind readers or body language experts. Ever since Day's assault four months ago, people seemed to try to interpret every word he said, like he was always moments away from snapping. Hell, maybe he was. It was hard to say. Sometimes, it felt like his life, like his face, wasn't his own anymore.

He'd shut down his camming accounts when they'd finally released him from the hospital. Not exactly a difficult decision when your face looked like ground sausage, but even if his face had been perfect, he could never see himself going back to it, not after everything Carl had done to him, *was* still doing to him in some ways. Little ways. But they added up over time.

Day hated to be alone now. Hence the reason he stayed with Jackson's mother every time Jackson was forced to go out of town for business. The plan was to eventually take Day with him back to Miami, but he didn't want to meet Jackson's Miami friends while looking like an escapee from a carnival. Wyatt and Charlie told him he was ridiculous and that he looked almost exactly the same, with the exception of a slight bump near his right eye. He didn't believe them, but he just didn't talk about it anymore.

Day had already had two reparative surgeries, one to correct the damage to his cheek and another to repair his broken teeth once the wire had been removed from his jaw. Through it all, Jackson was there, encouraging Day, going to therapy, rubbing his jaw, calling him beautiful. That was the one that ate at Day the most. Beautiful. It felt like Jackson was placating him. Day wasn't beautiful anymore, thanks to Carl. But that wasn't Jackson's fault. He'd been more than patient with Day. He never pushed him, never got angry. He was just always there, always steady. He was everything Day needed, and part of him hated how much he needed it.

Even after all this time, it felt like Carl was there, whispering in his ear, telling Day that Jackson hadn't touched him because he was ugly, he was damaged. Day's therapist told him he was projecting his own fears onto Jackson's behaviors as a self-defense mechanism. He knew she was right, but once a month, around the anniversary of his assault, the panic set in and that voice started all over again, forcing him to push Jackson away.

But not this time. Day might not look like himself, but for the first time in forever, he felt like himself. He didn't hurt. He wasn't swollen or sore or depressed.

infuriating

Jackson was coming home any minute, and for the first time in a long time, all Day wanted was for Jackson to touch him like he was more than a patient. Four months was a long time to be celibate, especially when he had a man as sexy as Jackson lying beside him every night.

It was weird to miss something and fear it at the same time. Part of him worried if they were intimate again, it would be obvious that Jackson was with him out of pity. Another part worried if his broken jaw would keep him from doing things Jackson liked, like oral sex. It was nice to be able to open his mouth to talk, but Day's jaw ached all the time.

His phone vibrated on the bedside table. A Snapchat from Wyatt and Charlie that showed an entire box of condoms spilled out over the bed next to an industrial sized bottle of lube. They'd scrawled 'good luck' across the bottom. They visited all the time.

In the beginning, it irritated Day that Jackson had spilled to the others that Day was afraid to be alone. As if a dozen people witnessing his assault in 1080p hadn't been embarrassing enough, but then Charlie and Wyatt had showed up and brought Robby who was a pastor and Elijah who was a fucking movie star, and they'd sat in a circle and shared their most intimate secrets with him. Robby's and Wyatt's abuse by their fathers, Elijah's acting coach raping him when he was a child, Wyatt retelling his times at conversion therapy. Charlie talking about a photographer who'd taken things too far.

It bonded the five of them, made Day feel less like a victim when they would all come and sit with him whenever Jackson left. It was stupid to need protection from a ghost, and Carl was a ghost if Charlie and Wyatt were to be believed. His sweet, peaceful, level-headed Jackson had tossed the old man into an empty swimming pool. But once a month, Carl felt as alive as he ever was, sitting on Day's shoulder and telling him the life he was growing to love was temporary. Day had told Linc about it the first time he'd sat beside him on Jackson's sofa and just watched old movies when it was his turn to babysit Day. Linc told Day about his PTSD. How the brain fights to protect itself in weird ways. How there was nothing wrong with therapy. He'd promised not to tell Jackson about Carl, and it seemed he never had.

There was a soft knock at the door, and then Jackson was peeking around the corner. Day's heart swooped at the sight of him. It always did. As always, Jackson dressed more for the runway than the boardroom, wearing dark jeans and a snow white sweater that made his dark skin radiant. Day didn't sit up, just held up his arms. He wasn't giving Jackson any reason to leave this bed.

Jackson flashed Day that panty-dropping grin before closing the door and crossing the room. He knelt on the floor beside him, wrapping his arms around Day, placing a gentle kiss on his cheek. "Hey, beautiful."

"Hi, Daddy," Day purred.

Jackson's brow arched, and his mouth curled upwards. "You haven't called me that in a while."

"We haven't been alone in a while," Day countered, sitting up enough to capture Jackson's lips with a moan.

Jackson deepened the kiss immediately, sending Day's pulse fluttering, his cock hardening as Jackson slipped his tongue inside to slide over Day's in a way that made him whimper. "Fuck, I've missed you," Jackson whispered against Day's lips.

"Me too. So much," Day promised, trying to pull Jackson up onto the bed beside him. "Fuck me?"

Jackson chuckled. "You know my mom is in the kitchen, right?"

"And I'm right here," Day whined. "We haven't had sex since the…since before. I finally feel good. I want you to make me feel better. Please?" Day pouted. He could see Jackson wavering. "Please, Daddy?"

"You're such a little tease," Jackson said. Day fist pumped in victory, but then Jackson was standing up and pulling Day to his feet. "Did you get your reading done today?"

Day groaned. His reading. His reading was molasses slow but with all the aids his neuropsychologist gave him, he was making progress. "Yes, Daddy."

Jackson swept his thumbs over Day's cheeks. "Did you take your pills?"

Day was on an antidepressant and a daily anti-anxiety medication. "Yes, Daddy."

"Did you have your appointment with your therapist yesterday?"

Day rolled his eyes. Jackson knew Day had gone to his therapy appointment. They'd talked about it last night. "Yes, Daddy."

"Okay, but I draw the line at boning in my mom's house. Let's go home."

"Fine, but you better rock my fucking world," he griped. "I'm already packed."

Jackson snagged Day when he was almost to the door, spinning him around and backing him up against the door, his mouth brushing over his. "Have I ever not rocked your world?" he rumbled in a way that made Day's knees weak.

"No, Daddy."

"That's what I thought. Stop pouting."

Jackson picked up Day's suitcase and opened the

infuriating

door for him. They said a quick goodbye to Mama Bev, and Day waited impatiently for Jackson to pop Day's suitcase in the trunk. Once Jackson was in the driver's seat, Day craned his head to lean into Jackson's space, teasing his tongue along the shell of his ear, his hand sliding along Jackson's broad chest. "Fuck, you look so hot today," Day whispered, biting Jackson's earlobe.

"I look hot every day," Jackson countered, his big hand sliding between Day's legs and palming his erect cock. "You're already getting hard. We've got a long drive ahead of us, baby."

"Whose fault is that?" Day said, arching to grind himself against Jackson's palm, his eyes rolling at the pressure. "You could have been buried inside me right now if you weren't so fucking proper," Day whined, rubbing himself against Jackson's hand. "Fuck, I'm so fucking horny. Do you know how long it's been since I've gotten off? Four months without so much as jerking off in the shower."

Jackson gave Day an appraising look. "Put your seat back."

Day looked at Jackson, startled. "What?"

Jackson gave Day a stern look, the one that liquified his insides and made him throb. "You want something improper? Put your seat back and let Daddy play with you."

Day was too turned on to even care about the whimper that fell from his lips at Jackson's words. He did what Jackson commanded before he let himself get too in his own head about it. Once he was reclined in his seat, Jackson didn't even untie Day's sweatpants, just plunged his hand inside and palmed his cock.

"No underwear? Dirty boy. You *are* horny."

Jackson's thumb teased along the thick vein at the bottom of Day's cock before squeezing him in his fist. "Oh, fuck." Day wailed, rocking himself up into Jackson's tightened hand.

"Feel good, baby?" Jackson asked, voice like gravel.

Day's eyes rolled at the sensation, not wanting it to stop. "So good. So good."

Jackson's thumb slid over the head of Day's cock. "Already leaking for me. Such a good boy."

"I want you so bad," Day said, words just spilling from his lips. "I want you inside me. I miss the feeling of your cock splitting me in two."

"Jesus, your mouth," Jackson muttered, squeezing Day's cock reflexively as the car swayed precariously.

"Jackson," Day moaned, eyes squeezed shut as he worked himself in and out of Jackson's fist, wondering if anybody could see what they were doing.

Day whined as Jackson's hand disappeared. "If you don't come 'til Daddy gets you home, I'll fuck you right here in the car. But only if you can hold off until we make it home in…" Jackson checked his phone. "Twenty-two minutes. Think you can keep from coming in Daddy's hand for that long?"

Day gave a sad sound but nodded. Leave it to Jackson to use this as a lesson in patience. When Jackson's hand returned, there was no more steady rhythm. Instead, Day writhed in his seat as Jackson played with him. His fingers jerked, teased and gently probed Day until he was an incoherent mumbling mess with his pants caught around his thighs and his hands rubbing his nipples under his shirt. "How much longer, Daddy? I don't think I can do this."

Jackson chuckled. "Five minutes, baby. You can hold on for five minutes. Don't you want to be good for me?"

Day didn't even bother to answer, just growled out his frustration. His balls were tight against his body, and every touch from Jackson sent shivers of electricity over him until he was sure a soft breeze would send him off like a rocket.

When Jackson's hand stopped moving, Day began to fuck up into Jackson's still tightened fist, needy little sounds spilling from his lips until he was sure he wasn't going to make it. "I'm sorry, Daddy," Day gasped, his orgasm slamming into him like a wave and sucking him under as his cum coated his stomach, his chest, even his lips and chin.

The car came to a stop and Jackson threw it into park, unbuckling his seatbelt, his tongue darting out to lick the cum off of Day's chin before kissing him long and deep. Jackson's hands shoved at Day's sweats until he was naked from the waist down and then he was opening the glove box. "Put your foot on the dashboard," Jackson growled.

Day had no idea what was happening, but he didn't even care. "Yes, Daddy."

Day yelped as Jackson's finger, cool with lube, pressed against his hole.

He looked up at Jackson with amusement. "You keep lube in the car?"

Jackson didn't smile back, just looked into Day's eyes and sank his slick finger inside to the third knuckle, pulling a gasp from Day. "With you, baby, I keep lube literally everywhere. I know how you get."

Day rocked himself on Jackson's finger, gripping the back of his neck just for something to hold on to. "How do I get, Daddy?"

"Needy," Jackson said, biting at the shell of Day's ear. "Desperate for Daddy to stuff your tight little hole whenever and wherever you want it," Jackson murmured. "Isn't that right, baby?" God, Day had missed this. Had missed feeling wanted. "Oh, fuck. Yes, Daddy. I need it so bad."

"Bad enough to ride Daddy right here in the car?" Jackson murmured, forcing a second finger in with the first and curving his fingers into Day's prostate, driving a guttural moan from him.

"Oh, fucking fuck. Yes, Daddy. Yes. Yes. Yes," Day chanted, long past caring about his spent cock or how oversensitive every nerve ending felt. He just wanted Jackson inside him.

The next couple of minutes were a comedy of errors and muttered apologies with seats moving too slow and Day's ass in the passenger window and even Jackson's zipper getting stuck and him ripping his jeans like the hulk, but as soon as Day straddled him and felt the thick head of Jackson's cock sliding home, all laughter stopped. Day swallowed the lump in his throat as he sank down onto Jackson, his body readjusting to Jackson's sensual invasion one inch at a time.

It hurt. Not like Day usually hurt those days, more a sharp sting, like his body fighting to remember. Day didn't care if it hurt. Having Jackson back inside him was everything. Having Jackson grip his hips and look at him like he was beautiful and wanted and normal felt like everything Day had missed these past four months.

"Fuck, you're so tight and warm. I missed this," Jackson told him, almost like he could read Day's mind. "I've missed you, baby."

It was an odd comment seeing as how they were almost always together, but Day let it go, kissing Jackson as he started thrusting up into Day with purpose, each thrust driving the breath from Day as he panted against Jackson's lips. Day didn't get hard again, just clung to Jackson. Day didn't care about getting off again. He just wanted Jackson's touch, his scent, the feel of his breaths and the way he moved inside him, like Day was the most important thing in his world.

Day could feel Jackson was close, his thrusts erratic as he started to drive up into Day while dragging his body down to meet him, again and again, until he gave one last hard thrust. He pulled Day down, their mouths colliding as Jackson gave a hoarse shout as his cock throbbed inside Day, spilling his release.

Day collapsed on top of Jackson with a satisfied sound. "That was just what I needed."

"Me too, baby. Me too."

Day stayed where he was, Jackson's softening cock still inside him. Jackson's fingertips traced patterns on Day's back while he hid his face in the crook of Jackson's neck.

"What did you mean earlier?"

infuriating

"What did I mean about what, baby?" Jackson asked groggily.

"You said you've missed me. We see each other all the time."

Jackson gave a heavy sigh that shook Day to his core. It was a sigh that spoke volumes. "Yeah, I know, beautiful. But once a month, like clockwork, you start to pull away from me again, and then I have to start over with you, scale your new reinforced slightly higher walls." Day didn't pick his head up. He couldn't. He didn't want Jackson to see his tears. "I know why you do it, and I don't even mind that I'm the only one you do it to, but when you get into those phases where you withdraw into yourself, it's lonely out here. Especially when I'm all alone. These last couple of weeks have been the longest you've shut me out."

Day did sit up when it became clear Jackson had said his piece. Day opened his mouth to deny the allegations, but, instead, his words just started spilling from his mouth and the tears started rolling down his cheeks unbidden, like Jackson had performed some spell. "I don't mean to do it, Jackson. I swear, I don't. I have these nightmares that I wake up one morning and I'm all alone and everything between us is gone and I'm just this disfigured freak, all alone in my hospital bed, and he's won because he took you away from me."

Day's stomach dropped when he saw Jackson's gaze soften, like he felt sorry for Day, but he couldn't stop talking. It was like somebody had opened the floodgates, and it just kept pouring out of him.

"You call me beautiful, but I don't even recognize my face. I know you all think I'm crazy, but I get scared that you're all just humoring me and you're only sticking around because you don't want to leave your crippled boyfriend, and that scares me, not only because I don't know how to live without you now, but because my friends and family were your friends and family first, and if I lose you…" Day sobbed. "If I lose you, I lose everybody."

Jackson stared at Day in stunned silence for a full minute as Day's insides shriveled. But then Jackson was cupping his face. "Jesus, Dayton. Why haven't you said anything? Why are you so afraid to talk to me? I need you to hear me. Are you listening?" Day gave a hesitant nod, tears still falling. "Good. I'm never leaving you, Day. Ever. And not because I feel sorry for you. You're not disfigured. I know you're going through a lot because you look different, but different doesn't mean bad. I call you beautiful, because you are beautiful, inside and out, but even if you weren't… even if that fucking piece of shit had mangled your face, I wouldn't fucking care. Your friends wouldn't

infuriating

care. Our family wouldn't care. You are more than your pretty face. Christ, Day. I love you. We all love you."

"I don't mean to be like this, I swear," Day sobbed.

Jackson dropped his forehead to Day's. "You can be crazy if that's what you need. But please, don't think I don't love you. Please, stop shutting me out. If you're feeling insecure and you need me to tell you all the things I love about you, then tell me and I will. I will tell you when you first wake up in the morning and I'll tell you when you fall asleep at night if that's what you need. I told you months ago, I'm all in."

"You didn't even know me then," Day whispered, then sniffled.

"Yeah, I did. I've known you my whole life. I just hadn't found you yet. My gut has never been wrong."

Day's heart stuttered off beat at Jackson's words, but Day just gave him a watery smile. "You really are so corny and romantic."

Jackson kissed Day's lips. "You love it. Admit it."

"I love you," Day promised.

"That's a start."

epilogue

DAYTON

DAYTON SAT IN HIS OFFICE WITH HIS FEET UP ON THE desk, his headphones in his ears and his microphone in front of his mouth. He didn't look at the screen, just listened to the English translation and repeated it in French as his computer transcribed it onto the document before him. He glanced at the clock on his desk. It was ten after seven and they should have been gone twenty minutes ago. Day smiled. Leave it to Jackson to make them late for their own company Christmas party.

When Day saw Jackson's office door open, he ended his document and saved it so he could start again on

infuriating

Monday. Jackson shook the other man's hand and headed towards Day's office. He looked so handsome in his navy blue Hugo Boss suit with his crisp white shirt and black tie. "Hey, Daddy," Day purred when Jackson reached the door.

Jackson grinned. "Hey, yourself, beautiful. You ready to go?"

Day stood, showing off his tailored black pants, white shirt, and gold brocade jacket, complete with black bow-tie. "*I* was ready an hour ago, when you told me to be here. So, I've been finishing up the Arsenault contract while I wait."

Jackson grabbed him by the lapels and tugged him closer, kissing him until Day's toes curled in his overpriced shoes. "Gold star for you. I promise it will reflect nicely in your annual review."

"As your boyfriend or as your corporate interpreter?" Day murmured, smile smug.

"Both," Jackson countered, slapping Day's ass.

Eighteen months had passed since Jackson and Day had crossed paths, but Jackson couldn't keep his hands off Day. He supposed the same could be said for him. Every day together was a new adventure. Some good, some bad. They had a lot of hurdles after Day's attack. His panic, his body dysmorphia, his constant feelings of inadequacy. Mama Bev having a mini-stroke,

Chloe's school trying to put her in special education classes. Ruth having another baby, an eleven pound bruiser named Joshua. Day struggling to learn to read. Jackson and Day making it through a year of couples therapy and coming out the other side more in love than ever. Like most things in life, the good and the bad ebbed and flowed.

When Jackson had first floated the idea of Day working for Elite as a corporate interpreter, he'd been furious. It sounded like a made up job somebody gave their boyfriend so they didn't feel like they were sponging off him. But it turned out corporate interpreters were not only a real thing, they were in demand and also something Jackson desperately needed in Miami where it was a melting pot of people who spoke Spanish, Haitian, Creole, and French, the languages Day just happened to speak. He was also becoming quite fluent in Japanese.

Once Day had figured out how to work around his dyslexia, it turned out that his slow reading didn't actually slow down him or anybody else. Nobody really cared how Day got his job done, as long as he did it. He'd even started accepting some clients on the side, including Jackson's gun-running friend, Angel, and his wife, Sylvia.

Jackson pulled the car up to the small boutique

hotel off of Lincoln Road, tossing the keys to the valet before opening Day's door and taking his arm. Day's head was on a swivel, taking in the beveled mirrors everywhere and the sleek black, white, and turquoise color scheme. "This place is neat, very art deco." Jackson pulled his phone from his pocket, and pressed a few buttons before returning it. Day leaned up against Jackson, voice flirty. "What do you say we skip the party that you already made us late for and get a hotel room, then I make sure you have the merriest of Merry Christmases?"

Jackson chuckled. "I already got us a room for tonight. The honeymoon suite. But we have to make an appearance at this party. We're throwing it."

Day stuck his tongue out at Jackson. "You're no fun."

Jackson tugged Day into a small dark alcove, kissing him deep, his hands gripping his ass as he whispered, "I'm a lot of fun. If you're a good boy, I'll fuck you out on the balcony and you can be as loud as you want. See if you can get us kicked out of yet another establishment."

"I still maintain that if they don't want people fucking in the middle of their club, they shouldn't put a bunch of beds everywhere," Day said haughtily.

"Pretty soon, we're not going to be allowed in a

single place in Miami," Jackson laughed, leading them into the restaurant.

"Good thing Florida is a big state," Day countered.

Jackson nodded to the hostess and pointed to the back to the closed double doors. Day frowned when two servers opened the doors, beckoning them inside. He only made it five feet inside when it happened.

"Happy Birthday!" the people inside roared in unison, blowing on horns and setting off party poppers.

Day stood there, shocked, not sure if he was making the appropriate facial expression or not. His eyes darted from person to person, relieved to see it was all people he knew. Charlie, Linc, and Wyatt. Angel and Sylvia, Shepherd and Elijah, Calder and Robby and their three kids, Daniel, Grace, and Faith. Jackson's mother and his sisters and their husbands and kids. Connelly and Webster.

"Surprise," Jackson whispered.

"I thought this was the company Christmas party," Day muttered, plastering a smile on his face.

"Nope, that's next week. At work. Come on. I didn't invite strangers. It's strictly inner circle. People who wanted to give you a proper birthday party for once in your life."

Day looked around at the gold accents and the ornate tables with lavish flower arrangements and a

infuriating

throne sitting in the middle of a small stage front and center. "I'm not sitting in that."

"You'll sit wherever I tell you, and you'll smile and be the sweet and gracious boy I know you can be or your birthday spankings will have a slightly heavier hand than last year. Got it?"

"Are you trying to talk me into being good or bad? I honestly can't tell," Day said without looking at him.

"Me either. Smile and wave. Say thank you. People are staring."

Day smiled. He waved. He said, "Thank you!"

After a few minutes of awkwardness, Day relaxed. Jackson was right, these were Day's people. His adopted family. Charlie plopped a gold crown on his head and dubbed him, "Queen of the Night. You know, like Whitney Houston."

They ate and talked and drank champagne. Day danced with Jackson's mom and his nieces. He did the Macarena and the Cupid Shuffle. After a dinner consisting of all the things Jackson had gotten Day the first time they'd gone grocery shopping together, the kitchen rolled out a stunning three-tiered gold cake with a twenty-four scrawled in black as the centerpiece. It was a decadent chocolate fudge cake with cherries inside.

Day frowned at Jackson. "You hate cherries."

Jackson grinned. "Yeah, but you love them, and I love you."

Day blushed, shoving him. "Still so corny."

"You ready for your presents?" Charlie asked the moment Day's plate was empty.

Day flushed, shaking his head. "Presents? No. Come on, this is already way too much."

"Oh, there's only one and it's from all of us. Come on." She dragged him from his seat to the big throne onstage.

Day covered his face until his crown went askew and he was forced to look up or risk it falling to the floor and shattering. With his luck, it was some vintage trinket worth millions. When he raised his head, Charlie had a mic in her hand. "Oh, God, who gave her a microphone?"

The crowd laughed, and Charlie curtsied, then she looked at Day with a warm smile that lit up his belly. "Day, you were the last to join Elite's merry band of misfits, and even though you kicked and screamed the whole way, we're so glad you're here. You're funny and glamorous and one of the smartest people I know. You pick up languages like I pick up dates and Wyatt and Linc pick up sex toys." The crowd snickered, and Linc groaned. Charlie continued. "You managed to live twenty-two years without a single person

infuriating

realizing you couldn't read. You survived a horrible attack and came out stronger for it. We're all kind of in awe of you, and we hope this is the beginning of a new tradition where we all get to recognize you for the perfectly magical unicorn you are."

Day's pulse hammered in his ears, and he blinked back tears, realizing she still wasn't done.

"We wanted to get you something to show how much we love you, but since you went and snagged the richest dude we all know..."

"Not richer than me," Angel cried, making the crowd titter once more.

"The second richest guy we all know," Charlie corrected. "We weren't exactly sure what to give you that Jackson hadn't already thought to lay at your feet." She cupped her hand over her mouth, whispering directly into the microphone, "Except maybe a ring. Hint. Hint." Day covered his face in his hands. "Anywho, after much consideration, we all chipped in and got you this, so that you can help others like you helped yourself."

Day took the envelope from her hand, opening it carefully. When he pulled the paper free, he froze. It was a letter...or maybe a receipt. It was a thank you from the Literacy Coalition thanking him for his recent donation of fifty thousand dollars. "I—" He cleared his throat and tried again. "I don't know what to say. Thank you, everybody. This… This is amazing." He flushed at his lame attempt to express how he felt. His ears burned.

"Jackson, it's your turn."

"Wait, what?" Day said, watching as Jackson stood and walked across the room to take the microphone. "Jackson Andrew Avery, if you hand me a check or a ring, I will divorce you before we are even married. I swear to God."

Everybody laughed, including Jackson, but Day was overwhelmed. "Relax, baby. I promise it's not a check…or a ring…yet."

Day rolled his eyes, but his shoulders sagged. He loved Jackson and he believed with everything he had that Jackson was it for him, but he needed a little more time to be sure he was it for Jackson.

"Despite what Charlie says, I've given Day very little, because, as soon as I turn my back, he's taken it back to the store and exchanged it for something for me. Day is the sweetest, most selfless person I know. He's also the prickliest and meanest person I know, especially when it comes to standing up for others. So, since you refuse to let me spoil you the way I want to, I took a page from the others and figured the best gift I could give you was a gift for the person who meant

infuriating

the most to you."

"You got you a gift for my birthday?" Day asked, suspicious. "I suppose that's one way to get around me returning it."

Charlie handed Jackson a tablet, which he promptly handed to Day. He couldn't stop the gasp that slipped free. It was a picture of hospital doors and above them read, *The Sarah Gunderson Cystic Fibrosis Center*.

Day ran his finger across Sarah's name. "What is this?" he whispered.

Jackson crouched down beside Day's chair. "It's a way for Sarah to live on and help others like her."

Day tried to wrap his head around what this must have cost Jackson to accomplish such a gift. "You can't... This must have cost you millions. It's too much."

"It's already done," Jackson told him softly. "You can't exchange it for twenty-million presents for me."

Without warning, Day started ugly crying in the middle of the room. "Why are you like this?" he wailed, while everybody else 'aww'd' around them.

"You don't like it?" Jackson asked, looking genuinely worried.

Day looked at him with his red eyes, wet cheeks, and snotty nose. "No, you idiot, I love it. I love you. Stop being so perfect."

Jackson chuckled, leaning in. "You want me to take you upstairs and rough you up a little bit?"

"Mic's still hot, sweetie," Charlie said.

Day groaned, but Jackson stood, this time, speaking directly into the mic. "Uh, we're heading upstairs for the night. This room is ours for another hour. Feel free to hang out and enjoy the cake and open bar. Or don't. Up to you."

Jackson tossed the mic to Charlie and snagged Day's hand. He started to put the crown down, but Jackson stopped him. "Uh-uh, birthday boy. Bring the crown."

LATER, AFTER JACKSON HAD DONE EXACTLY AS HE'D said he would, fucking Day silly on the balcony with nothing but his crown on, they lay curled up in the plush bed with Jackson playing little spoon for a change. "Thank you," Day said, kissing Jackson's bald head.

"For the orgasms? My pleasure. Seriously, anytime," Jackson said, looking back over his shoulder.

"No. Thank you for the party and for my presents. This was the nicest thing anyone's ever done for me."

"The nicest?" Jackson said. "Ever?"

"Yes, ever."

infuriating

"Then can I ask you for a favor?" Jackson asked.

Day frowned. "You could ask me for a favor either way." Jackson leaned forward and opened the top side table drawer. "Unless you're about to try to read me the bible," Day said, then snickered.

"Nope," Jackson said, then rolled over and opened a small ring box with a platinum band set with four small diamonds. "I'm going to ask you to marry me… someday."

Day smiled in spite of himself. "You're asking me to marry you…someday? I need clarification. Someday, you'll ask, or you want me to commit to marrying you eventually?"

"The latter," Jackson said. "I know you still think that I'm going to wake up one day and run, but I promise you, every day I wake up next to you is a great day, no matter what shitshow comes after that. I don't need you to say you'll marry me tomorrow or next week or even a year from now. Just say you'll marry me someday, even if it's when we're both side by side in the nursing home."

Day held out his left hand and waggled his ring finger. Jackson grinned, leaning up on his elbow to pull the ring free and slip it into place. Day snuggled up under Jackson's arm before rolling over and holding up his hand to look at how the ring sparkled. "So, it's a date then," Day said. "You and me, the chapel at our swank nursing home fifty years from now."

"Fifty?" Jackson choked. "I'm a lot older than you. I might not make it to my own wedding."

Day sighed dramatically. "Fine. Forty. Maybe. Unless I'm not aging well, and then maybe thirty-five."

"I'm not trying to be pushy here, but I'd like to enjoy our wedding night without fearing one of us will break a hip," Jackson joked.

"How about tomorrow?" Day countered.

"What?" Jackson asked.

"Let's go get married at the courthouse tomorrow. Let's make it official."

Jackson stared down at Day like he'd been replaced by a pod person. "I was only teasing, Day. We can do it whenever you're ready. I just like seeing that ring on your finger, knowing you're mine. Forever."

Day smiled. "I know. But tonight made me realize that I want to see a ring on your finger, too. I want everybody to know you belong to me just like I belong to you before somebody snatches you up."

"You don't need a ring for that, Day. You've had my heart since the day you walked through my office door."

Day rolled onto his belly and kissed Jackson's lips.

infuriating

"Yeah, I know," he said, tone cocky. "But now, I want your last name."

Jackson grinned. "Then it's yours."

THE END

DEAR READER,

THANK YOU SO MUCH for reading *Infuriating*, Book 4 in my Elite Protection Services Series. I hope you loved this book and the others in the series as much as I loved writing them. As always, here is my mea culpa regarding any liberties taken with how camming sites work and stretching their limitations to suit my fictional narrative.

Also, I truly hope nobody reads this book and thinks I'm in any way shaming sex workers. I have family members in the business, and I worked in the porn industry myself for years. I have nothing but respect for sex workers, truly. I even have a sex positive sex education comedy podcast called Deep in Thot coming soon anywhere you listen to podcasts.

In regards to Day's severe dyslexia and his inability to read, my goal was to show just how many children from indigent families get left behind when it comes to accessing the skills and techniques necessary to help them succeed.

I haven't completely said goodbye to the men of Elite. At some point, there will be a M/M/F book so that Charlie will get her happily ever after, and look for Webster's book, *Endangered Species*, to bridge Elite with a new series I'm working on. I love Elite too much to say a forever goodbye to them.

For teasers, mini-fics, updates, and extras, check out my website and sign up for my newsletter. I love to interact with you guys, so please hit me up on my social media or join my Facebook Group: ONLEY'S OUBLIETTE, where you can interact with other readers and have access to exclusive giveaways. If you really love my books and want to read them before anybody else as well as gain access to things like signed paperbacks, consider joining my PATREON.

If you did love this book (or even if you hated it), I would appreciate it if you took the time to review it. Reviews are like gold for authors.

Thank you again for reading.

ABOUT THE AUTHOR

ONLEY JAMES is the pen name of YA author, Martina McAtee, who lives in Central Florida with her children, her pitbull, her weiner dog, and an ever-growing collection of shady looking cats. She splits her time between writing YA LGBT paranormal romances and writing adult m/m romances.

When not at her desk, you can find her mainlining Starbucks refreshers, whining about how much she has to do, and avoiding the things she has to do by binge-watching unhealthy amounts of television in one sitting. She loves ghost stories, true crime documentaries, obsessively scrolling social media, and writing kinky, snarky books about men who fall in love with other men.

Find her online at:
WWW.ONLEYJAMES.COM

Printed in Great Britain
by Amazon